Her peripheral v
something just a
up, straining to i .....it was. All
she could make out was a dark, flying, bird-
like silhouette.

It flutter-flapped its wings, body bobbing with every flap. It hovered
briefly just above her head before it disappeared into the night.

Her long, ebony hair began whipping in the wind. She had to
occasionally spit long strands from her mouth and pick away the
strands that clung to her tear-soaked cheeks. Diluted mascara
mixed with foundation, looked like an iridescent oil spill as it
cascaded down her cheeks, creating facial-art that resembled dead,
spindly branches – or the thin jagged fingers of lightning … if
lightning were mostly black.

She thought of how nice it would be to never be cold again. She
was beginning to sober up a little, to feel not quite so sick, as she
remembered that she'd written a FUCK YOU note to the world
a couple of days ago. She'd been toting it around in her purse for
this very occasion. Just a note asking anyone who'd give a shit to
tell her sister, Sally, that she was sorry that she hadn't been strong
enough to have stayed with her at their Aunt Evelyn and Uncle
Roy's house after their mother's death. What Sally was too young
to understand at the time was that Uncle Roy was often a bit too
friendly with her big sister. Aunt Evelyn was either blind to that
fact or, more likely, simply found the solace she required to deal
with that knowledge from an endless supply of Valium prescribed
to her by her favorite pill-pushing doctor. Aunt Evelyn usually
chased her pills with frequent pulls from her twice-weekly-
purchased fifths of cheap vodka. All aboard the S.S. Reality
Escape. Now departing on its daily 3 p.m. voyage down the exotic
River Denial.

But mostly, she wanted the world to know that she hadn't always
been Lucy. That once, a lifetime ago it seemed, she'd been a
frightened, innocent little girl named Brenda.

She dropped her purse by her side, hoping that someone wouldn't just snatch it, vanishing her last words into oblivion.

One by one, she kicked off her shoes as she began hiking her near skin-tight, black leatherette skirt up to a point where her panties would have been well exposed if she'd been wearing any. She then began climbing over the guard-rail.

As she stood on the other side of the guard-rail, holding onto it with only her left hand, she closed her eyes and began to lean forward. She was ready to let go. Suddenly startled, she opened her eyes wide, instantaneously becoming aware of an unseen presence behind her. She stood wobbly-kneed. The heels of her bare feet were supported only by the thin plank that overhung slightly on the river-side of the strong, wooden guard railing.

In one deft motion, one that to even the sharpest of eyes would have appeared to have been no more than a blur, a hand reached around and covered her mouth, preventing any chance of her screaming.

Mere seconds later, absolute terror set in. It took a moment for her mind to catch up and begin comprehending what was happening. In that instant of realization, her olfactory sense was assaulted by the thickest, most putrid, noxious odor she'd ever smelled. What felt like warm drool began dripping onto her neck and shoulders, instantly causing goose pimples to well up and the tiny fine hairs on her neck to stand erect.

She didn't see anything other than the long, dirty fingernailed hand that held her in its powerful grasp. She felt her shoulders being kissed and caressed by corpse-cold lips as she felt herself being lifted up.

What came next was instantaneous, excruciating pain caused by what felt like razor-sharp daggers that penetrated the side of her neck in one great thrust. Then momentary euphoria overcame her. Then, there was ... nothing except the enduring, cold kiss of ultimate darkness.

Lucy died that night just moments before midnight. Just not as dead as she'd intended.

RED TIDE

VAMPIRES OF THE MORGUE

DAVID REUBEN ASLIN

To Nevin

David Reuben As[lin]

Dedicated to my beautiful wife, Denise.
My five fabulous boys: Dustin, Devan, Drew, Cody, and Moe.
Without their loving support, this work would not have been possible.

To Mom, love eternal ...

Edited by Monique Happy Editorial Services

Stories of the macabre, horror, and the unexpected.
For more books from author David Reuben Aslin, please visit
www.authordavidreubenaslin.com

> "Ask not for whom the bell tolls;
> it tolls for thee."
> ~ John Donne

Last Night:

She thought a lit match and a liquefied spoonful of Mexican brown sugar injected in the most delightful way would be her ticket to ride away from it all. One last comfortable slip-slide down the rabbit hole, tripping to any destination that wasn't here and now. She wasn't worried about going to Hell. She was already there. She'd contemplated for days that it would be the easiest, best way to assure the inexorable end to her abysmally bleak – at its best – darkly melancholy life.

She was ready to climb aboard and take that journey to the beyond right now. The problem was, she had no money and no junk left to facilitate the trip. She was tired. Too tired, and way too high, to try and go back to find someone that she could bob her head or spread her legs for.

She'd just left the waterfront club. She couldn't even remember the name of the place. All she knew is that she had to get the hell out of there before she got any sicker than she already was. Too much to drink – way too much. Too much oxy and the last two lines of coke that she'd been graciously given by some luckier-than-herself whore in the ladies room not five minutes ago, had added exponentially to her already chemically-induced, spiraling spin-out.

It was a tunnel-dark night, exceptionally dark even for this time of year. The nearly full moon held little sway over the dense cloud cover, one that presently offered little more than drizzle but threatened to open up and pour at any moment.

What little light there was came from a smattering of poorly-placed street and parking lot floodlights. But even with heavily-dilated pupils, somehow she managed to proceed with her intentions in spite of her present condition.

This was it. Her last night in this shitty crap-hole of a town. She'd moved to Astoria from Portland just one week previously under the advisement of, and with, two other of her prostitute semi-friends. The girls had sold her on what they said they'd heard; in Astoria, you didn't need any pimp for protection; the Johns that frequented this new Astoria waterfront Goth club, though a bit weird regarding their fetishes, for the most part were easy pickings, and they paid well.

She'd decided hours before all of the drugs and booze had rendered their toxic effect, further bending her already severely bent mind – that this night would be the end of the proverbial line. The end of her train wreck of a life, as she saw it.

Drunkenly, she staggered down the boardwalk, straining her alcohol- and dope-blurred eyes, trying desperately to keep herself upright and keep moving forward.

At this point, all she could think was that travel by way of taking the long swim was her last, best choice. Not her first choice of travel to her final destination, but one that would get her there just the same.

Her shoulder-strap purse swung clumsily as it bounced against her waist, swinging in countermotion to the broken rhythm of her shapely, twenty-two-year-old hips. She tried to be mindful of not getting her high heels caught between the boardwalk planks, whereby potentially impeding her from reaching her intended destination … at least without accumulating painful slivers. Her destination: the edge of the parking lot, then onward to the edge of the dock, and finally twenty feet below in the frigid waters of the Columbia River.

Almost hypnotically, the river's rhythmic tidal waters seemed to be pulling her forward, calling out for her, calling her home. She thought to herself that she wouldn't be the first person to plunge into the river with no intention of swimming for shore – nor the last. She mused, *This'll be the least of my sins to try an … explain. Lucy … you've got some splain-un' tah-do. That's if God even gives a shit. Maybe I'm gonna be interr… interror-grated – given shit by … Saint Peter … er, Jesus … er … fuckin' Mister Plumber.* She laughed the laugh of the seriously drunk and stoned. Lucy was her assumed name. Her hooker name. It had been so long since anyone had called her by her real name, Brenda, that she had almost forgotten it altogether. To her, Lucy fit who she was, who she'd become: an amalgamation of the words loose and easy. Loose and easy. Lucy. Just another homeless runaway … junkie … prostitute. One who in her view had grown too tired of all the bullshit associated with her life, such as it was, to desire any continuance.

Not long ago, she thought she'd gotten pregnant. That at least would have been some reason to go on, she'd reasoned at the time. That is, until she'd gone to the free clinic in Portland to be checked, driven there by the excessive vaginal bleeding that she'd experienced that morning, only to find out that she in fact had been pregnant but had miscarried. In addition to that little slice of hell, some pasty-faced, wanna-be nurse with all the bedside manner and compassion of a would-be Nazi seemed to have actually taken pleasure in informing her that she was HIV positive.

So here she was at last. Standing at the very edge of her existence. She leaned her chest against the guardrail and began gazing down at the water. After no more than thirty seconds, she almost lost consciousness for an instant due to her intoxicated condition as it mixed with the mesmerizing effect of the undulating water; it appeared to her to look like millions of amorphously-changing pieces of shattered, mirrored glass that sparkled like diamonds as they danced on the surface of the turbulent deep.

She could smell the faint essence of salt in the air and that train-track oily smell of the hundreds of uneven creosol-soaked planks that collectively comprised the boardwalk and waterfront parking lots.

Though her senses were somewhat dulled at the river's edge, that wharf smell that she so detested was strong. It wafted in the wind all around her, filling her nostrils with the reek of fish entrails. The primary source was the Hawthorn Cannery, located just two blocks further down the pier.

She could still hear and almost feel the waves as they pummeled the pylons thirty feet below the suspended docks. She recognized the low moan of a ship's horn and the faint clanging/chiming sounds caused by buoys hundreds of yards off-shore. The chiming brought back a memory that, try as she might to suppress, somehow always seemed to revisit her time and again like an evil specter waiting in the dark, waiting to snatch what little remaining soul she might still possess.

The chiming echoed and reverberated almost painfully in her brain, bringing back memories of the seemingly endless ringing of the bell that her morphine-addicted, advanced-stage lung-cancer-stricken mother would ring when wanting – demanding – more injections, more pills, to be fed, or to be changed out of her urine and feces-filled *Depends.*

They didn't have the money that a nursing home required, so it had been her job to take care of her mother since age twelve. By fourteen, she'd had all she could take of the relentless ringing of that damn bell.

That is until one night when she had changed the last adult diaper that she felt she could. When she had given the last morphine injection that she could stomach. She took a deep breath and once again cleaned her mother up after spoon-feeding her, kissed her on the cheek, and told her she loved her.

Her mother, now too weak to hardly move, let alone ease her own pain, just laid there gasping for each breath until she finally managed to point towards a pillow near the end of her bed. With a half-smile and a nod indicating that she appreciated everything that her daughter had done for her, but that she had endured much more suffering than she could endure any longer, she motioned for her daughter to pick up the pillow.

"I love you … and Sally. Please … help me this one last time," was all that her mother could manage to say in a soft, gurgle-throated, nearly breathless, desperately pleading voice.

She trembled almost beyond control as she placed the pillow over her mother's face. At first, she didn't think she could do it. But then something welled up inside her as though a force beyond herself began guiding her actions. Right or wrong, she began pressing the pillow down with a strength she didn't know she possessed. With both hands, she pressed the pillow to her mother's face, harder and harder. She began holding her own breath as she pressed the pillow down with all her might just to see how long anyone could last, until finally, the bell fell from her mother's quivering, shriveled hand.

Almost two minutes and a dozen kicks from her mother's legs passed before it was done, offering the first peaceful shank of an evening in over two years; once, that is, the police had left and the coroner had taken the body (which would later be cremated) —all satisfied that her mother, Helen, had died a natural death.

She thought about a quote that she'd heard a hundred times but one that had never held any significant meaning to her until this very moment. *Ask not for whom the bell tolls; it tolls for thee.*

Some people run away seeking adventure. Some run away from their past, though it always seems to catch up with them, starting their bell ringing all over again. Standing near the dock's edge, she could clearly make out, though blocks away, the sounds of cars and trucks that were rushing to and fro, heading to their pointless destinations. Her destination wasn't pointless. To her it was more to the point than any she'd ever known.

She could see the tiny, faint lights from some ship and a tugboat downriver. Just then, her peripheral vision caught a glimpse of something just above her head. She immediately looked up, straining to focus on what it was. All she could make out was a dark, flying, bird-like silhouette. Almost instantly, she surmised it to be a seagull. It flutter-flapped its wings, body bobbing with every flap. It hovered briefly just above her head before it disappeared into the night.

Her long, ebony hair began whipping in the wind. She had to occasionally spit long strands from her mouth and pick away the strands that clung to her tear-soaked cheeks. Diluted mascara mixed with foundation, looked like an iridescent oil spill as it cascaded down her cheeks, creating facial-art that resembled dead, spindly branches – or the thin jagged fingers of lightning … if lightning were mostly black.

She thought of how nice it would be to never be cold again. She was beginning to sober up a little, to feel not quite so sick, as she remembered that she'd written a FUCK YOU note to the world a couple of days ago. She'd been toting it around in her purse for this very occasion. Just a note asking anyone who'd give a shit to tell her sister, Sally, that she was sorry that she hadn't been strong enough to have stayed with her at their Aunt Evelyn and Uncle Roy's house after their mother's death. What Sally was too young to understand at the time was that Uncle Roy was often a bit too friendly with her big sister. Aunt Evelyn was either blind to that fact or, more likely, simply found the solace she required to deal with that knowledge from an endless supply of Valium prescribed to her by her favorite pill-pushing doctor. Aunt Evelyn usually chased her pills with frequent pulls from her twice-weekly-purchased fifths of cheap vodka. All aboard the S.S. Reality Escape. Now departing on its daily 3 p.m. voyage down the exotic River Denial.

But mostly, she wanted the world to know that she hadn't always been Lucy. That once, a lifetime ago it seemed, she'd been a frightened, innocent little girl named Brenda.

She dropped her purse by her side, hoping that someone wouldn't just snatch it, vanishing her last words into oblivion.

One by one, she kicked off her shoes as she began hiking her near skin-tight, black leatherette skirt up to a point where her panties would have been well exposed if she'd been wearing any. She then began climbing over the guard-rail.

As she stood on the other side of the guard-rail, holding onto it with only her left hand, she closed her eyes and began to lean forward. She was ready to let go. Suddenly startled, she opened her eyes wide, instantaneously becoming aware of an unseen presence behind her. She stood wobbly-kneed. The heels of her bare feet were supported only by the thin plank that overhung slightly on the river-side of the strong, wooden guard railing.

In one deft motion, one that to even the sharpest of eyes would have appeared to have been no more than a blur, a hand reached around and covered her mouth, preventing any chance of her screaming.

Mere seconds later, absolute terror set in. It took a moment for her mind to catch up and begin comprehending what was happening.

In that instant of realization, her olfactory sense was assaulted by the thickest, most putrid, noxious odor she'd ever smelled. What felt like warm drool began dripping onto her neck and shoulders, instantly causing goose pimples to well up and the tiny fine hairs on her neck to stand erect.

She didn't see anything other than the long, dirty fingernailed hand that held her in its powerful grasp. She felt her shoulders being kissed and caressed by corpse-cold lips as she felt herself being lifted up.

What came next was instantaneous, excruciating pain caused by what felt like razor-sharp daggers that penetrated the side of her neck in one great thrust. Then momentary euphoria overcame her. Then, there was ... nothing except the enduring, cold kiss of ultimate darkness.

Lucy died that night just moments before midnight. Just not as dead as she'd intended.

Yesterday:

Charlie … Ian … have either of you read today's Oregonian? There's a weird story on the second page. Seems Astoria, Oregon is dealing with some kind of vampire cult that's moved in and opened some kind of underground club. They call themselves sanguinarians. Sounds like they're under some suspicion regarding a number of unexplained deaths … likely murders. It says here that bodies have shown up totally drained of blood! Reminds me of what'd been going on around here.

Ian reminisced regarding what Jenny Hovermire had spoken about back at Harmony Falls. It had done more than merely intrigue him. It had motivated Ian to pay a visit to the small city located at the mouth of the mighty Columbia River. That was dealing with some big problems that at least at face value appeared to be right up his alley.

"Well, boy, looks like we've made it. Welcome to Astoria. I don't know about you, but I'll be glad to get out and stretch my legs. I'm getting a little hungry. You probably are too, huh boy? Say, since I've got a few coins in my pocket since Charlie squared me up, how 'bout I spring for some lunch at a restaurant? I know what you're thinking. I spend too much money eating out. Yeah, you're right about that. This will be the last time for a while. Say, maybe later this evening, we'll spot us a nice grocery store and stock up on some groceries. This is nice. It's been a long time since I've had anyone to talk to while on the road. You're not much of a conversationalist. But you sure are a good listener, aren't you, fella?"

Ian petted Scout's head. Scout wagged his tail and panted happily. They were bonding fast.

Ian and Scout were heading through downtown Astoria. "Look

boy, there's a nice-looking restaurant just up ahead. And by that I mean it looks nice enough for the likes of me. Not too expensive, if you know what I mean. But no dive either. Scout, it's called *Pigs-In-A-Blanket*. With a name like that, it's gotta be good, right? You know, just like that jelly. With a name like *Smucker's*, it's gotta be good! I always thought that was funny, like the word Smucker's sounds good." Ian laughed at his levity. Scout barked his approval at the humor.

"Okay then, boy. I'll tell you what. You're gonna stay here in the Jeep. I'll crack a window for ya. When I get back, I'll have a little surprise for you. Maybe some bacon or sausage. How's that sound, boy?" Scout barked once loudly as if he understood completely.

Ian pulled his Jeep and trailer into the far back of the restaurant parking lot so as not to block any traffic.

"All right then. You keep guard of all my worldly possessions. I won't be long. Hey, while I'm inside, maybe I'll get a good tip on a nearby campground or RV park. One that doesn't cost an arm and a leg. One that takes shaggy guests like yourself. Okay … there, the windows cracked just a little 'cause it looks like it could start raining any time. It's pretty windy and cold, so I know you won't get overheated. I do hate to leave you just when we've started getting to know one another. The worst part is you don't understand much, if any, of what I'm saying. Well, if somehow you can understand – just know I will try and be fast. You be a good boy while I'm gone."

Ian climbed out of his Jeep and locked its doors. He then walked across the parking lot and into the restaurant.

Once inside, Ian looked around until he spotted a sign that said, "Seat Yourself." He did just that and immediately picked up a menu and began looking it over.

Hmm … Breakfast served twenty-four hours a day. Nice. The "Pacific Coast Special" breakfast: Two farm fresh eggs, your choice of either three *slices of bacon or three sausage links, hash browns and toast: $8.99. Well now, that sounds perfect.*

Ian looked up over his menu and noticed his server was waiting with a smile on her face. "Can I get you some coffee or something to drink while you decide what you'll be having?"

Ian noticed the pretty young woman's name badge.

"Hello, Jennifer. I'll have a large tomato juice and the Pacific Coast Special breakfast … for lunch, that is."

Jennifer smiled. "Good choice … Sausage or bacon?"

Ian paused for a second. "Uh, bacon."

Jennifer continued, "What type of toast would you like?"

Ian thought about that one for a couple of seconds before he replied. "Sourdough."

Jennifer smiled and made her notes on her order pad. "Oh, and how would you like your eggs?"

Ian returned a smile to Jennifer. "Over hard would be great. Say, Jennifer, have you lived here in Astoria long?"

Jennifer looked at Ian with a slightly surprised look on her face as she replied, "No, sir. I've been staying … I've been house sitting for my aunt and uncle for a couple months while they were traveling. But they just got back this week. I was living before, and will be returning to, Seattle. I got this job about a month ago. You know, seasonal help. And actually, today's my last day. This job ending actually worked out perfect, timing wise. 'Cause I just got a letter of acceptance a few days ago to the nursing program at the University of Washington in Seattle. That's where my parents live. Anyway, I've been working here and there for the last couple of years saving what I can for school. Oh my gosh … I've practically told you my life story." Jennifer began to blush.

Ian held up his hand, gesturing that it was quite all right as he smiled. "No, no, it's good to hear your plans are working out for you.

Say, one more question. What do you know about a new nightclub in town? I've heard it's sort of a place where … I don't know … kind of attracts, what's the word? Goth people, and persons interested in the occult … or … uh … let's just say alternative lifestyles. I'm doing some research … some investigation you might say … and …"

Jennifer flashed Ian a sly grin as she half-rolled her eyes. "Yeah, you don't look the type that goes there. But you're talking about … you described the new club in town called The Morgue. That place is just a couple blocks from here. Down on the wharf … the waterfront. Pier Thirteen I think? I've never been there. I mean I've been by it. I've never been inside. But I've heard stories. It's a real creepy spot. The city's been trying to shut it down ever since it opened last June. But I hear the owner has deep pockets and has powerful lawyers and all that. Anyway, he's been able to keep the place going even with all the local church groups and negative press and the like. You're right. The place attracts lots of Goths and, you know, all those vampire poser types. Real freaks, some of them. I'm surprised there's enough people into that sort of thing in this little town to keep a place like that going. I mean, maybe in Portland or Seattle … but Astoria?"

"But I guess people come from all over to go there. Probably mostly weirdos from Portland."

Jennifer covered her mouth and blushed slightly as she glanced around, checking to see if she had offended any listening ears before continuing. "Well, I'm no one to judge. Different strokes and all that. But that place is not my thing if you know what I mean. Not at all."

Ian smiled and shook his head in agreement. "Yeah, I hear that. Not my cup of tea either. It's just … well … like I said, I'm doing a little research."

Jennifer smiled. "What are you, some kind of private investigator or undercover cop?"

Ian took a deep breath; then, with a Cheshire Cat-like sly expression on his face, winked at Jennifer as he replied, "Something like that. Say … do you know the name of the person who owns or runs the club?"

Jennifer giggled. "Yeah, but it's gonna cost you. In the form of a good tip, that is. Good information doesn't come cheap around these parts."

Ian laughed, "No, I don't suppose it does. If the food here turns out to be half as pleasant as the conversation, you'll be well compensated."

Jennifer laughed. "Good, 'cause a girl's got to pay for her schooling somehow, right? His name's – and you're gonna love this – I read in the paper that his name's Vladimir Drago Salizzar. Doesn't Drago mean dragon or something like that?"

Ian smiled and nodded a silent yes. Jennifer continued, "Molly said people just call him Salizzar. Now doesn't that sound just like out of a movie or something? I've never seen him myself. But the girl, Molly, who used to work here? She told me he's like out of this world good looking. Long, black hair that he keeps pulled back in a bushy pony tail, dark eyes, and a perfect, though really pale, complexion. She said he talks with some sort of European accent. She said he even … and get this …" Jennifer paused once again to look around to make sure no other ears were listening. None were. "He, like, wears eyeliner, red lip gloss, and clear nail polish. But Molly said he didn't seem gay. Maybe bisexual. How weird is that? I mean sure, in a big city, but around here in a town of mostly loggers and fishermen? The guy wears make-up. No wonder nobody ever sees him during the day. Looking like that in this town, he'd probably get beat up. But I guess somehow it works for him 'cause Molly said he's like totally hot. Anyway, I almost went with her once to check him … to check that club out.

But the whole thing sort of freaked me out. I backed out at the last minute. I never got a second chance to go with her 'cause soon after, she just never showed up for work anymore. That was a few weeks ago. She was like me. Not from around here. She probably got fed up with small town living and all the rain and moved back home or wherever. She was from somewhere back east. Chicago, I think?"

Ian interrupted, "Say Jennifer, do you know of any good campgrounds or RV parks close by?"

Jennifer suddenly got a very thoughtful expression on her face as she gently tapped her pen against her cheek. "Of course there's lots of camping near the beaches, but on this side of the river? Hmm … Warrenton I think would be the closest. Then there's Seaside and Canon Beach further away, but not very far. I'd guess around a twenty to thirty minute drive from here. Oh, and there's lots of places across the bridge over at Ilwaco and around Long Beach, which is really nice. They're probably about the same distance away. Maybe a bit closer, around a twenty minute drive I'd guess. But real close. Hmm … near to town here … I don't know. I don't think there's any."

Ian smiled and extended his right hand. "Jennifer, my name is Ian McDermott. It's been my pleasure to meet you. I want to thank you for all the information. Oh, and good luck with school." Jennifer responded likewise, and they shook hands cordially.

Jennifer smiled brightly, "Nice to meet you, Ian. My last name's Dowling."

Ian smiled as he asked, "Jennifer, do you ever go by Jenny?" Jennifer looked at him with a slightly surprised look on her face as she responded to his provocative question.

"Yeah, actually … my family and friends call me Jenny. Why do you ask?"

Ian grinned as he replied, "Oh, no reason. It's just you remind me a bit of a very nice gal who works for a friend of mine in a town I just came from. That, and Jenny just seems to fit you."

Jennifer smiled and left to turn Ian's order in to the kitchen. Ian's food came just a few minutes later. It was good – very good. Before leaving, Ian wrapped a couple pieces of bacon that he'd saved in a napkin and put them in his coat pocket. He then left a sizeable tip at the table for Jennifer, the aspiring nurse.

After exiting the restaurant, as Ian headed back to his near-vintage Jeep Wagoneer, Scout spotted Ian and started barking happily.

Ian unlocked the door of the Jeep and began petting Scout, who had been a very good boy. Nothing was chewed on or disturbed in any way.

Ian retrieved the napkin-wrapped bacon from his coat pocket and gave it to his very appreciative companion. He then put a leash on Scout and walked him to an abandoned lot just across the street from the restaurant parking lot. Scout did his business, then they returned to the Jeep.

"Okay boy, next order of business. Keep your eyes peeled for a print shop of some kind."

Ian and Scout drove out of the restaurant parking lot and proceeded up the road to the main street of Astoria.

Ian glanced for a second over at Scout. "There. Right over there. Scout, do you see it? It's just ahead on the right: a FedEx-Kinko's. They do good work, and fast. I'm gonna have them make up some business cards for us. How does Ian and Scout's Investigations sound?"

Scout let out a groan, then yawned.

"Oh, I suppose you'd prefer Scout and Ian's …?" Ian chuckled as he shook his head.

Scout, as if he understood every word Ian was saying, wagged his tail and barked three times.

Ian glanced at Scout once again. He looked into the bright eyes of his four-legged friend, and he couldn't help smiling. Then, trying to put his game face on, Ian took a deep breath and exhaled as he spoke, "All right, seriously Scout. What would sound good?"

After much contemplation, Ian began ascending from the depths of his thought. Then, with a grin on his face, he exclaimed out loud, "Scout, I've got it. I think we're gonna have to go with Ian McDermott, Ph.D., Paranormal Investigations."

CHAPTER 1
Oscar's on the Ocean

Present Day:

Upon raising his head from his pillow, Ian discovered a terrible knot that had set up camp overnight within the deep recesses of the back of his neck. It was coupled with gnawing muscle spasms. All the stretching he attempted just seemed to result in further inflaming the condition.

It's no wonder, Ian silently mused as he mustered a half-smirk, *with all that I endured hiking all over hill and dale back up around Mt. Saint Helen's and those damn Ape-Caves.*

Ian then shuddered, bowed, and shook his head at the thought of it all. He suddenly became very somber as he pondered his latest exploits. He couldn't help but get misty-eyed as he thought of all those lives lost or altered forever by the gruesome events back at Harmony Falls. Ian thought long and hard of the victims, their families and friends, the lives horrifically snuffed out or forever altered by the malicious course of events.

Ian himself had personally lost in that ordeal a person he greatly admired: Sheriff Bud O'Brien. But with that, along with the subsequent chain of events, he'd gained a close friend in Sheriff's Deputy Charlie Redtail. His bond with Charlie, Ian surmised, was the only thing good that came of it all. Well, that ... and ridding the world of a terrible "Monster." Ian actually laughed nervously at that very thought. Even as he thought about it, the whole thing seemed utterly outrageous and totally unbelievable. Ian actually had to remind himself that he wasn't crazy. That it was all true, every horrific moment. *I saw that thing with my own two eyes. And God help me, I helped kill him ... I mean ... it.*

Ian had to think of the thing as an it, not a him, or he didn't know if he could live with the guilt, regardless of what he knew to be all too true.

What he was suffering from, though he didn't recognize it, was post-traumatic stress, both mentally and physically. His body and mind were sending him messages loud and clear that it was time to relax and chill out.

As Ian lay staring up at the roof of his trailer, wiping the sleep from his eyes, he took a deep gasp of air and let out a sigh as he thought to himself, *Relax ... breathe. Wow ... I might be more stressed out than I thought. Maybe I should take some time off? Hmm, hopefully after I've finished checking out what I came here for. Relax ... If it were only that simple.*

Just then, while Ian was contemplating what his first move of the day would be, Scout bounded over to him and put his right paw up onto Ian's chest and then began licking Ian's cheek. Scout was exceedingly appreciative that his master had finally fully awakened from his restless tossing and turning, which had gone on most of the night.

Now sitting up, Ian pulled back the curtains of the picture window at the foot of the bed. It afforded a beautiful view of dune grass, scrub pines, and just a bit more than a sliver of a view of the ocean.

"Look out there, Scout," Ian pointed out the window to the ocean beyond. "You'd have to pay big bucks at a fancy motel to get a view like this, wouldn't ya, fella?" Ian stroked the top of his best friend's head.

"What the hell's the name of this place? It's something … Oscar. Oh yeah, Oscar's on the Ocean. The owner, Oscar, what a character. You should have heard him, boy. When I was checking us in, he went on and on about way back when he had his own fishing boat and commercially fished out of the Port of Ilwaco. What'd he say his last name was? Manly? No, that's not it. Mallory? Yeah, that's it. Oscar Mallory." He laughed just a little at the thought of the old sea-dog ex-fisherman and how he went on and on about the good ole days.

Ian continued talking to his furry friend, "Well anyway, boy, this place lives up to its name. Oscar's on the Ocean. If we were camped very much closer to the ocean, we'd just about be floating in the surf."

Scout inched his way in a slow climb up into bed and then lay alongside his human. Ian didn't mind one bit.

Ian began petting Scout as he spoke, "Well boy, what shall we do first? We've got to seize the day. Carpe diem. We need to cross back over the bridge to Astoria and try and get some work done. See what we can dig up on this Salizzar guy." Ian silently mused, *Dig up. That's a good one.*

Ian reached over to a small attached wall-desk, grabbing a small box and retrieving from it a few business cards. "These cards look great. See Scout, I told you that FedEx-Kinko's did good work. Maybe I should have included your name on the card? What do ya think, boy?" Scout wagged his tail and barked twice.

Ian also grabbed a map and some pamphlets and brochures of the Long Beach Peninsula that Oscar had as giveaways at the RV office.

Taking a cursory glance through some of the printed material of the area, Ian then began looking closely at the map, all the while pointing to various destinations as he read out loud to Scout.

"Okay, it says here on the front of this thing that the Long Beach Peninsula is an arm of land bordered on the west by the Pacific Ocean and to its south by the Columbia River. To its east is Willipa Bay, and to its northernmost tip is Leadbetter Point State Park and the Willipa National Wildlife Refuge. Cape Disappointment State Park is at the southernmost end. Just north of where we are now is the Pacific Pines State Park. Wow! This area sure has its share of state parks, huh, boy? Lighthouses, post-war forts, and museums, oh my. Anyway, it shows on the map that we're here. That puts us about half-way up the peninsula at ... Let's see, yeah ... We're at the Klipsan Beach area near the Cranberry Road beach access. Got that?" Ian's reading glasses nearly slipped off of his nose as he looked over the map and smiled at Scout.

"Hey boy ... looks like we're pretty close to a good fresh water fishing lake. Maybe we should take my pole over there and wet a line? Loomis Lake ... and go figure, there's another state park. Loomis Lake State Park. That's right across the street from the lake."

Momentarily satisfied with what he'd learned from his map and tourist pamphlets, Ian slowly climbed out of bed and began attempting to loosen his neck, with no success. After also stretching his arthritic back a couple of times, he then did two deep knee-bends, straightened himself, and proceeded to shuffle his way over to the trailer's semblance of a kitchen. Ian drew some water from the kitchen faucet, hoping to find it at least semi-potable. He filled his coffee mug of choice, the one with the picture of Big Foot on its front.

Ian scooped into his now two-thirds-filled mug of water his typical ration of too much out-of-date powdered grounds. He then placed his overfilled mug into his one fairly-new appliance: a shiny black Hamilton Beach microwave. In mere moments, he produced a steamy mug of instant sludge, which he generally referred affectionately to as a cup, or in this case mug, of "ole Joe."

Ian said aloud as he grimaced while trying to endure his first sip.

"Yeah boy. That's the stuff!" He took another sip and nearly choked. "Okay. This is no good." Ian laughed a small laugh then looked at Scout as he spoke while pouring the remainder of his mug down the sink. "It's definitely time to pick up some new coffee, boy."

Ian set his mug in the sink then proceeded to get dressed. Once dressed, he and Scout bounded out of the trailer.

He opened the driver side door of his Jeep. Without hesitation, Scout jumped in and moved over to the passenger seat where he set himself tall.

"So you've got your own seat, do you?" Ian couldn't help grinning ear-to-ear as he noted how happy Scout was to be in the Jeep, to be heading out on the road. Ian loved the alertness, intelligence, and confidence Scout exuded in all the seemingly little things that he did. The truth was, he felt more secure himself having Scout along with him. Even though Ian hadn't had Scout long, he loved everything about his dog.

Ian glanced over at Scout. "You must be on some kind of big-time growing spurt. You look to me like you've gained size and weight in just these last coupla days. You're a big, tough guy, aren't ya?" Scout barked loudly one time. He wagged his tail as he momentarily stood up on all fours before settling back down in a sitting position. He was beginning to wonder if his dog was some kind of a K-9 genius with the way Scout seemed to understand just about everything Ian said to him. Occasionally, it also seemed to Ian that all he needed to do was think about something, and Scout would act or react accordingly, as if there was some kind of psychic link between them.

Despite his restless night, Ian was becoming energized just anticipating the day ahead. He had disconnected his old Jeep Wagoneer from his even older Airstream trailer upon his arrival to Oscar's on the Ocean yesterday. He really wanted to get a quick start the next day.

As Ian and Scout began driving out of the RV park heading south, back towards the town of Long Beach, Ian glanced down for a second at a time at his unfolded map of the peninsula that he'd laid on his lap. He and Scout were driving on Highway 103, the peninsula's one main road – the one road that ran the entire twenty-six mile jaunt north to south, end to end. From the fishing town of Ilwaco, which was located on the extreme south-end of the peninsula at the mouth of the Columbia River, all the way north to the town of Ocean Park.

Ian noted that just above the town of Ocean Park was a housing community called Seaside Estates. It was the northernmost inhabitable area of the peninsula. He also made note that once they'd driven past downtown Long Beach, he could take a side road that would prevent them from having to drive into Ilwaco. As Ian plotted his course, he saw that he'd be going through a little town called Chinook. From Chinook, it looked like only another five or so miles east to the bridge that crossed over the Columbia River to Astoria, Oregon.

Ian pulled his Jeep over to the side of the road. He'd become enthralled with the map of the area and decided to take a good, long look at it. As Ian studied the map to better orient himself, he started taking mental stock of what he knew versus what he didn't.

He knew that the Pacific Ocean was less than a few football fields west from the highway they were on. He also knew that if they were to head east on most any connected road, it would lead to Willapa Bay. Ian thought to himself that he'd love to take the time soon to drive the entire peninsula just to see what could be seen. Last night while he was perusing through some information pamphlets regarding the places to see and things to do, he'd been especially intrigued by a small pioneer township formed in the 1800's. Oysterville was located on the northern Willapa Bay side of the peninsula. It was famous for its namesake: oysters. Ian prided himself on being a consummate consumer aficionado regarding devouring and subsequently evaluating a plate of fresh, lightly-battered and seasoned pan-fried oysters.

Ian put away his map and pulled out onto the road heading to the town of Long Beach. After less than ten minutes, he and Scout were driving through the main downtown area. As he drove, Ian admired the many different gift shops and clothing stores, restaurants, bakeries, candy shops and such that lined both sides of the main street for an area that spanned a couple of blocks.

Ian was somewhat startled as he noticed that many of the stores and shops were all decorated for Halloween as he mused, *I've got to start paying attention to what's going on in the world, beyond just my work.*

Ian was especially intrigued by a store on his right called *Marsh's Free Museum.*

"Scout, we've got to make time to check that place out. Looks strange from the outside. Imagine what might be inside." Ian chuckled at that thought.

Moments later, just about a mile south down the road, Ian noticed from another glance at his map that he'd soon be making a turn to the left. It would be easy finding his way to the bridge that crossed the Columbia over to Astoria from there. He also noted that to the right was a sub-area of Long Beach called Seaview.

"I tell you, Scout, for a relatively small area, this peninsula sure is chock full of little townships." Scout didn't bark but glanced momentarily over at Ian, his head bobbing a bit up and down as his body swayed from side to side, primarily due to the Jeep's worn-out shocks. It appeared to Ian as though Scout was nodding in agreement.

After leaving the Long Beach area and before reaching the little town of Chinook, Ian smiled as he spoke, "Look, boy. On your side, those red-colored swampy fields … Those are cranberry bogs. That's something you don't see every day. Well, unless you live here I guess.

Funny, I didn't notice them when we came through here yesterday."

Ian prided himself on his keen powers of observation, a necessary trait in what had been his line of work. It was absolutely essential in his new endeavor as a private investigator of sorts.

"Another thing I bet ya don't see often around here, especially this time of year anyway, is two straight days without rain." Ian glanced through his windshield up at the sky. It was completely cloud-covered, but it didn't look too ominous. The cloud cover was thick yet mostly light gray. There was very little wind, not much more than a breeze, but Ian noticed it was blowing from the south where there were some dark clouds beginning to form.

Ian guessed the darkening sky to be maybe thirty to fifty miles or so south of his position, across the Columbia over in Oregon. He glanced once again at the sky first through his windshield, then leaned to look further south out the passenger side window. His head nearly touched Scout's, who leaned towards Ian and lightly licked his right cheek.

"Ah, thanks boy. I like … I love you too." Ian glanced at his four-legged best friend and smiled. "Scout, this is what's commonly referred to as the calm before the storm, and you can bank on that." Ian nodded his head slightly up and down in agreement with himself. He meant what he said, both actually and metaphorically; he was familiar with coastal climate, having recently lived for a time in Winchester Bay on the Oregon coast. Ian was growing more nervous by the minute about what was coming next. His nervousness had little if anything to do with the weather.

CHAPTER 2
Introduction

As Ian and Scout drove through downtown Astoria, Ian decided that it would be best if he went to the Astoria Police Department. *Maybe if I speak directly to someone about the recent string of apparent totally exsanguinated victims, victims of obvious foul play, and ease into their thoughts a connection to that guy, Salizzar, and his club for weirdos ... If I can get any cooperation from the police at all, that would be a good place to start.* Ian figured it would be best for him to find out quickly if the police were going to take kindly or otherwise to his nosing around about it.

"Scout, I sure hope Charlie called ahead and spoke to the cops about me like he said he would." Scout paid little attention to Ian's last words. He was busy looking out the passenger-side window at all the strange curiosities that new sights and sounds offered.

"Well, there it is, Scout. We're here. The police station." Ian took a deep gasp of air in a near-futile attempt to help alleviate some of his apprehension. Then he pulled his Jeep over to the curb and parked on the opposite side of the street from the police station.

"You stay here and be a good boy. I shouldn't be long. I figure I'll find out soon enough if they're gonna roll out the red carpet for us or, more likely, try to run us out of town on a rail. Ha." Ian let out a half-laugh, a sudden outburst of nervous tension.

Ian crossed in the middle of the street. Any remote possibility of

9

getting ticketed for jay-walking right in front of the police department never crossed his mind.

As he stood at the front double-glass door of the station, Ian took another deep breath, then exhaled slowly as he proceeded through the doors. Once inside, he noticed immediately that the place appeared much larger and busier on the inside than it did from the outside. Ian thought to himself, *this community's really not all that small. And look. Halloween decorations.*

Within moments of standing just inside the entranceway, Ian was greeted by a female officer-receptionist. He was instructed to remove his keys, wallet, and belt, and stow them in a tray the officer handed him. Ian was then told that he could leave his shoes on and that the x-ray archway that had to be passed through wasn't set to be super-sensitive. Ian graciously complied, then, when instructed by the officer, stepped through the small x-ray arch. Once through, he was promptly handed back his personal belongings and quickly put them all back where they belonged.

Ian then stepped up to the information desk to another officer "Hi ... uh ..."

The female information officer cut him off. "Sir, please sign in here, then state your business." The officer flashed Ian a slight smirk as she tapped on the desk right next to the clipboard that was holding a sign-in sheet.

"Oh, yeah right." After Ian signed his name and the time on the sheet, the officer picked it up and glanced at it. Before Ian could say another word, she said, "So you're Mister McDermott? I'm going to need to see some identification, Mister McDermott." Ian quickly retrieved his driver's license and handed it to the officer. She glanced at it, smiled slightly, and handed it back to Ian as she said, "Thank you, sir. The chief's been expecting you."

Ian was surprised and relieved to hear that. Charlie had come through, as hoped.

The officer pointed to a bench across the hallway from her desk. "Take a seat over there. I'll let the chief know you're here."

Ian did just as he was instructed. He'd been waiting for about twenty minutes and had witnessed the beginnings of two separate bookings of arrestees before he heard another officer, this one male, walk towards him and call out louder than necessary, "Hey you, McDermott, come with me." The sound seemed to echo up and down the tiled halls.

Ian followed the officer down a short hallway. The officer stopped at a closed door near the end of the hall, then lightly knocked on the door that bore a bronze name-plate that read, "Chief William Mooney."

"Come in, come in." Someone within the office yelled out. Ian's escorting officer opened the door for him, then pointed for him to go on in. The officer then promptly went on his way back up the hallway.

Once inside the office of the police chief, Ian quickly handed Chief Mooney his business card. Police Chief Mooney didn't say a word; he glanced at it, then stared Ian up and down for a moment. Then the chief pointed to a chair across from his desk and motioned for Ian to sit down.

"So ... you're Doctor Ian McDermott. A Ph.D., are you?" Ian smiled and began to stand back up to shake hands. "No. No need to get up," Chief Mooney again motioned for Ian to stay put.

"I got a call from Harmony Falls' finest that you'd probably be paying us a visit." Chief Mooney then leaned way back in his chair and put both hands on his knees. He seemed to be less than thrilled about Ian being there.

"I tell ya, Mister McDermott, I generally don't take kindly to private investigators of the normal kind – or the paranormal. Poking their noses around in police business. And I'm not so sure what we got going on here fits into the realm of paranormal. But what's been going on sure as shit isn't normal, that's fer goddamn sure."

Ian started to reply but was cut off before he could get a word in edgewise. "No, now just bear with me while I complete my little speech. Anyway, like I said, under normal circumstances, I don't much like private investigators of any kind. Typically, my experience has been they're not worth whatever anyone pays them. More often than not, they tend to get in our way and often obstruct investigations that are much better left to professionals. That said … I said typically. But unfortunately, what's been going on here in my town lately has been anything but typical."

Ian shifted in his chair just a bit and almost spoke but then realized it was still not the time for him to say anything.

"Anyway, Mister McDermott … Like I said, I got a call about you from the newly-appointed Sheriff of Harmony Falls. One Mister Charlie Redtail. Now, I don't personally know Sheriff Redtail from Adam. But I do – or better said, I *did* know who he used to work for. Bud O'Brien. One of the finest lawmen … Well, just a damn fine man." Ian bowed his head just a little as he nodded in agreement to that.

"I met Bud at a law enforcement convention held in Portland a few years back. We got to jawin' and drinkin' one night and well … Hell, he was just a good man, and that's that. So when Sheriff Redtail told me of how you helped bring down Bud's killer; the same one that killed all those poor people … Well, that speaks volumes to me if you get my drift."

Suddenly, Chief Mooney stood up and extended his right hand. Ian nearly jumped up out of his chair in response to the gracious gesture. Both men shook hands and smiled at each other.

"I'm sure you can imagine we have to investigate murders now and again. Not too frequently, I'm glad to say. Mostly either domestic violence or a drug deal gone bad. A hooker gets done in, that sort of thing. Never any related string of murders like this. No serial killer types. Not here. Not ever before this anyway."

The chief looked Ian square in his eyes before continuing, "That said, I'm gonna do for you what I ain't never done for no private investigator before." Chief Mooney bowed his head just slightly for a second, then lifted it back up and stood tall. He looked Ian directly in the eyes. "I've been Chief of Police here in Astoria for over twelve years. Mostly all good ones … that is till lately. Ian, I'm gonna assign a liaison officer to assist you with limited – and I mean *limited* – access to the hard copy case files that we have regarding the strange and unusual deaths that we believe are murders, which have occurred over the last several weeks. I can't have anyone seeing you messing around with our computers or looking over the shoulder of anyone using one, or even hanging around the place. The fact you're here now is a little unsafe, so I intend to get you outta here fairly pronto. Now, most of the more gruesome details of the cases we've managed to keep out of the papers up till now. I expect that you will do me the courtesy of not speaking to any press person about any of this. And you will report anything that you might dig up directly to the liaison officer, who will then report directly to me. No one else. Understand? Have I made myself perfectly clear on this?"

Ian nodded and replied, "You bet. Perfectly! I understand." He paused for a second, then cleared his throat. Ian didn't know if what he was going to say next was going to be a huge mistake or not, but since the chief was being so openly cooperative, he too wanted all cards on the table.

"Um, Chief Mooney … one thing."

13

"Yeah, what's that?" the chief replied with a slight frown on his face.

"I … uh … I mean … I of course do private investigation, but I'm not actually officially licensed as such."

"Mister McDermott. Can I call you Ian?" Chief Mooney said, smiling.

"Certainly." Ian replied.

Chief Mooney continued, "I thought you were gonna start talking money. I don't give gull-squat about anyone who waves a private investigator's license around. Anyone can get one of them online for a couple hundred bucks or less. After I got that call from Sheriff Redtail, we did a little checking on you ourselves. You're the guy who found that fish everyone thought was extinct, right?" Ian nodded, though he wasn't sure where the chief was going with that little tidbit from his past. Ian was also growing very nervous regarding how he was going to demand, or rather ask, to be paid for his services. The chief was a large, intimidating man.

"Well, the way I see it, Ian, you know how to dig around to find clues. Ones that others might have overlooked. Maybe my department as well. I'm sure you got questions about what all's been going on, especially regarding that group of whackos who've set up camp in my town. I tell ya, Ian, that guy Salizzar … if he and his attorneys keep spreading money around as thick and deep as they've been, I'm afraid he's gonna have the mayor, and the entire city council for that matter, turning a blind eye on that shithole of his and the human refuse that's coming to our town because of it. I'm gonna get you hooked up with an officer I've got in mind who can help steer you on track. One that you can report any findings to. He's second in charge around here. You can ask him all the questions you got and are gonna have. I'll let him know if we can help you, we will. By golly, ya know, this just might work. You're not known in the area. It's a lot easier for an unknown to go undercover as it were. But if my suspicion of that guy and his freak show is right on any level, you best be careful. I know you've got a piece and a license to carry it."

Ian was stunned and unnerved at hearing that as he mused, *How the hell could he know about Ole Caretaker?* the name Ian had long ago given to his .32 Berretta. When he'd purchased it, it came with an ankle holster and was at this very moment stowed away under his driver's seat.

"Don't sweat it, Ian. Sheriff Redtail told me. Nothing illegal about the right of a private citizen to bear arms. Anyway, Sheriff Redtail told me how he temporarily deputized you, and your typical daily-weekly pay grade too for that matter. Anyway, he said how you helped him in a big way, bringing down that Gevaudan fella. So I trust you're responsible enough. Now mind you, I won't tolerate any sort of vigilante bullshit! You keep your head low and your weapon concealed and saddled. I don't want to end up having to arrest you."

Ian nodded. "Yes sir, I'm no hero, nor am I any sort of glory hound. Rest assured, I'll report anything that I might find that is even remotely related or relevant to this terrible string of ..." Chief Mooney abruptly held his hand up, palm forward, to stop Ian from saying anything more.

"Listen, McDermott. What you did for the people of Harmony Falls, again, speaks volumes. You, sir, are a hero. But I don't want you to end up a dead one. Let me cut to the chase. I've got access to a little fund that we keep in reserve for what we call 'black-ops', for lack of a better name. I know, that makes it sound pretty ominous. Really, it's just a relatively small cash reserve. A fund we keep for paying informants and other similar things, well, like this. Things that are better kept off the books, if you get my drift. So I'm gonna see to it that you're paid for your trouble, your customary wage. That is, should you, after you hear and see all the facts, still want to go through with investigating this. The victims were totally drained of blood. No easy task, naturally or otherwise. That's why I think the victims fell prey to some sort of Satanic cult or something. Murders committed by or directed by that guy Salizzar. I don't like anything about him or any of those freak-show clubbers that go to his place on a regular basis. I tell ya, Ian, it's like the goddamn Manson Family's moved into my town. Anyway, nobody, least of all me, is gonna blame ya if ya don't want to go through with any of this. 'Cause if you do choose to go forward, you'll have to go undercover and somewhat change your appearance. I don't know where you're staying. Better that nobody in the station does. But my strong advice is to stay somewhere off the beaten path. Not here in town. I can't do what the little town of Harmony Falls did. That is, make you any sort of official temporary lawman or anything. So you've got to play mostly by the rules of law … mostly. I'm sure you've already heard or read about Salizzar's nightclub down on the waterfront. It's called The Morgue, of all things. You're gonna need to get inside there and do some snooping. Problem is, you don't look much like … well forget about your age for a minute. There's no doubt plenty of middle-aged freaks. It's just, you don't look like what my teenage kids call Emo or Gothic or some such crap. You know the look. Like some deeply-disturbed heroin addict with jet-black hair and Johnny Cash clothes. And one of those long, black trench coats like you see in movies. That stereotype seems to hold more true than not with the freaks I've seen hanging around that place. When Salizzar first filed for all the required licenses to open his den of sin, church groups, the city council, and the mayor's office all initially did everything within the law to try and keep them out of our town. But I'll say this much for the freak; apparently, he's got pockets as deep as the ocean and big city attorneys in his corner to boot. He hides behind the Constitution like he was around when it was written. Or he buys whoever he feels is necessary to have on payroll, if you follow my meaning."

Ian shook his head back and forth, a small scowl on his face like he knew the type.

Chief Mooney continued, "The guy's gone so far as to purchase one of our oldest historic houses, a museum no less, from the local historical society for his personal use. His home. Oh, I'm told at first the historical society kept telling his attorney they wouldn't sell. But the son-of-a-bitch kept upping the ante till they would have been crazy to turn it down. That's pretty much how he bought that old waterfront warehouse that's now his nightclub too. That's how he does everything. He just keeps throwing money until someone catches it and puts it in their pocket. Before he even came to town, he donated a ton of dough to Mayor Marco's re-election campaign last year, and it at least helped Marco get re-elected. Don't get me wrong, Marco's a good man. It's just I don't like the idea of this element getting into anyone's pocket, least of all the mayor's."

Once again, Ian just sat there nodding in agreement with the chief as he thought to himself, *Unfortunately, money generally does more than talk. It screams.*

"Well, Ian, that's all I got. Let me connect you with my guy, who, once you two are away from the station, will give you some pay to get ya started." Ian was greatly relieved how the money issue took care of itself without him having to ask or even having to have said a word.

Chief Mooney dialed "9" for the front desk. After a couple of buzzes, the front desk officer answered. The chief spoke in a commanding voice, "Have Officer Ned Parker report to my office at once."

Immediately after arriving at Chief Mooney's office, Officer Parker was introduced to Ian. Moments later, Officer Parker and Ian left the office and stood, idly chatting for a few moments in the hallway just outside of the chief's office. But then Officer Parker's tone and mannerism suddenly changed. He became very serious. Ian noticed that Officer Parker also seemed to fidget just a bit and grow silent each time anyone, mainly police officers, walked by them. He then spoke in a rather stern tone, "Say, Ian, I don't know how much the chief told you about this recent series of deaths, primarily of young women; the fact is that at this time we only have our somewhat prejudicially-jaded suspicions regarding who the UNSUB or UNSUBs are." Ian knew that UNSUB was law enforcement's acronym for UNKNOWN SUBJECT, though to his understanding it was more frequently used by the FBI profilers than local law enforcement. Ian silently pondered to himself a moment on the thought of whether that meant something or not. *Perhaps the Feds are already involved?*

Officer Parker continued, "But if you really want to stick your nose in, you'll potentially be putting your neck out on this. And I mean from every direction. Especially with the kind of money this guy Salizzar's been spreading all around town, maybe inside these very walls. Neither the chief nor I am convinced that these walls don't have ears, 'cause the guy always seems to be at least three steps ahead of us. I hear Salizzar even recently donated a bunch of money to our local library, then turned around and donated even more money to our local cemetery and crematorium. And he did so in a way that was anything but anonymous. Strange fuck. Between you and me, if this shit continues, this town's either gonna lynch the guy or elect him for mayor."

Ian began panning his eyes up and down the hallway. He then looked directly into Officer Parker's eyes as he spoke. "I believe I understand the potential risks involved."

Officer Parker stared intensely at Ian for a long couple of seconds.

"Okay then. Don't say I didn't warn ya. Listen Ian, we need to talk away from here." Ian nodded, indicating that he understood and agreed.

Officer Parker continued, "Do you know where the Astoria Column is located? I'm sure you've seen it. It's visible from most parts of town and from the bridge for certain."

Ian smiled as he replied, "You mean that tall needle-style tower that you can see way up on the hillside above the town?"

Officer Parker grinned, "That'd be it. Anyway, to get up there's a piece of cake. Just follow about any road in town that heads up the hill. You'll see signs directing you once you've headed uphill a ways. It ain't far. Fact is, besides the Column, you should take a glance at where our suspect resides. Just follow the one-way road in front of the station here and take the second right. Follow that for about four blocks, and you can't miss it. Salizzar's house still has a sign out front that says the '*Flavel House Museum.*' It's been weeks since he moved in, and the son-of-a-bitch still hasn't taken down the sign. Between you and me, I think it's just another way he's sticking his middle finger out at this entire town."

Officer Parker walked with Ian towards the front entry of the station. "I'd show you out, but I don't want us to look too warm and fuzzy. You head up to the Column. Climb up to the top if you want. It's a hell of a nice view. I'll be up there in maybe an hour. I'll be in my own personal vehicle. It's a light gray Toyota Camry. I know what you drive. That Wagoneer." Ian was astonished by that declaration. What he heard next dispelled his astonishment. Officer Parker smiled and laughed, "No. I'm not psychic. And no, you haven't been under surveillance. I was near the front door when you got here. Just by coincidence, I saw you park your rig and cross the street. And jay-walk across the street, I might add."

CHAPTER 3
One Way Up. One Way Down.

At first, Ian figured that he probably had time to visit a liquor store to pick up a new bottle of liquid courage, but he changed his mind. "It's about time I start giving my liver a vacation." Ever since the vehicular tragedy that took from him the loves of his life, his wife and daughter – all Ian had cared about in the world besides his work – he hadn't thought there would ever be a time that he would muster the strength required to climb out of the bottle and stay out. He wasn't sure this was that time either. *One foot in front of the other. One step, and one day, at a time.* Ian thought about that phrase. It had seemed no more than a ridiculous twist on an old cliché to him at the time.

One foot in front of the other. One step, and one day, at a time, had been spoken time and again by a Catholic priest. One who counseled the twelve steps to a sobriety group that Ian had once sat begrudgingly through in a half-assed attempt at getting people, mostly relatives that he didn't even really know, off his back about his drinking. Back then, Ian wouldn't have taken advice from the Pope himself. What seemed to Ian to be fairly obvious, but nobody else seemed to grasp, was that it wasn't so much that he was addicted to alcohol, Jack Daniels old number "7" in particular, as he was addicted to his long-term depression. And especially back then, no amount of counseling or prescription antidepressants, all too often chased with booze, helped in any way beyond putting him momentarily in a state of comfortable numbness followed by passing into peaceful darkness that unfortunately sooner or later became painfully illuminated once again.

Then and now no treatment worked, other than what Ian himself very recently discovered: delving back into work was his only possible salvation. That in itself kept him too busy to sink back into his potentially suicidal depression. And now, even more important to Ian's reclamation than delving into the deep end of his newly reinvented work, was his new companion, Scout. Besides companionship, Scout gave Ian something that he hadn't even realized was missing in his life. Someone, or something, besides himself that he was responsible for taking care of every day, even when he might not care to take care of himself.

"Okay boy, I've got a good idea. Let's drive through that McDonald's that I spotted when we first drove through town. We can eat our grub on the way up to that tower." Scout, seeming to understand, stood up from his usual seated posture just for a moment, wagged his tail, and then settled back to his seated head-tall position in the passenger seat.

Ian pulled up to the menu and microphone. A pre-recorded message came blaring at him with a clearer tone than most order-board speakers. "Hi, welcome to McDonald's. Would you like to try our new limited-time, seasonal pumpkin McFlurry with your order today? Go ahead and order when you're ready!" Those pre-recorded messages ending with, "go ahead and order when you're ready," always threw Ian. He never felt like there was a human standing by actually ready to take his order.

"Uh … yeah, anyone there? Are you ready for my order?" Ian asked in a slow clear voice.

"Yes sir. Go ahead and order when you're ready." Ian heard clearly the polite voice of an obviously young, female order taker.

"Okay, hi … um … I'll have a number three quarter pounder with cheese value meal with a medium orange High-C for the drink. Oh, and give me an extra quarter pounder with my order. Thanks."

After paying for and receiving his order, then subsequently leaving the McDonald's parking lot, Ian reached into his bag of fast food and unwrapped a quarter pounder and handed it to Scout, who wolfed it down in about three seconds. "Wow, you were hungry, huh, boy." After having taken care of Scout, Ian began eating his meal while driving. He kept his eyes peeled, looking for a sign. "There it is, boy. *'To the Astoria Column.'* All right, here we go. Just like Officer Parker said. This is a piece of cake."

Upon arriving to the Astoria Column, that was located at the very top of the highest hill that overlooked all of Astoria. Ian instantly began marveling at the artwork that was etched and painted on the sides of the column. Which depicted aspects of the Lewis and Clark expedition.

"It ended up near here, boy. Lewis and Clark, they finally made it to the Pacific Ocean just beyond Astoria. Just a short distance from here; I believe they built Fort Clatsop near the mouth of the Columbia on this side of the river near where it dumps into the ocean. This entire area's riddled with the history of Lewis and Clark as well as World War I and II fortifications on each side of the mouth of the Columbia. Forts that housed enormous gun batteries built to protect the mouth of the Columbia against any enemy ships or submarines that might attempt to come up river and attack or even try and invade strategic deep water ports along the river like Astoria, Longview, and especially Portland. I think I read that the fort on the Washington side is Fort Columbia, and the one on the Oregon side of the river is Fort Stevens, which

22

also has right there on the beach the remains of an old shipwreck, the Peter Iredale, I think it's called. Nearby, there's the Battery Russell, a famous old gun emplacement. Just some fun facts. Do you like history as much as me, boy?"

Scout barked twice and began happily panting. Ian affectionately petted Scout from the top of his head, down his back with his right hand. There were only a few cars in the parking lot. None of them were gray Toyota Camrys. Ian decided to park his Jeep and take Officer Parker's suggestion to climb to the top of the column.

"Well, boy, now that you've had your history and geography lesson for the day, I think I'll climb that sucker and take a good look around."

Ian, being one who by nature paid attention to most every little detail, decided upon entering the tower to count how many steps it took to reach the top of the column.

Less than a month ago, if Ian had attempted the same climb, he would have been severely winded. But all the hill climbing and spelunking that he'd done recently back around Harmony Falls had him in pretty good cardiovascular condition. Even so, after Ian had been climbing for a few minutes, he began to get a little disoriented, almost motion sick, from the round and round, up and up you go, dimly lit, somewhat dank, massive spiral staircase that resounded with incessant reverberating echoes created from other climbers, whose chatting and clamoring feet on the metal staircase were only slightly less than thunderous to his ears. After another minute of climbing, Ian could see the top of the stairs. He was rapidly closing in on reaching the top of his climb.

One hundred sixty-two ... one hundred sixty-three ... one hundred sixty-four. "Piece of cake." Ian smiled and proudly proclaimed out loud as he opened the door and crossed the threshold to the outside world. He was a little out of breath but not too bad, and he was very glad to get out into the light and the fresh air.

"Fantastic!" Ian said in a feeble attempt to proclaim out loud the fabulous, panoramic view that the climb to the top of the Astoria Column afforded him. He then began walking around the tower's wrap-around viewing platform, taking in all that he could see, and he could see for miles.

From below in the parking lot looking up at the height of the column, he'd figured he'd get a good view from up above. But he never would have guessed that on such a cloudy day he would be able to see so very far in every direction. Ian especially noted that off to his left from where he stood was Saddle Mountain. He'd noted that it was a particular place of interest from his brochures and that it had a popular hiking trail that went from a parking lot below all the way up to its summit. Ian then gazed ahead towards the mouth of the Columbia and the ocean beyond.

After taking one more look all around, Ian glanced downward and noticed that a light gray Toyota Camry was pulling into a parking spot below, just two parking spots away from Ian's Jeep. Ian hurriedly began his descent down the column.

Officer Parker spotted Ian's egress from the column. He rolled his window down and held his arm out of the window up in the air.

Ian spotted Officer Parker's hand, and proceeded to walk briskly up to the driver's side of the car.

"Ian, go around and get in. I figure this is about as good a place to talk as any," Officer Parker said. Ian figured that the officer had chosen this particular area of the parking lot because he would be able to see all vehicles that were coming and going with ease.

Ian did as instructed. He walked around to the other side of the car, opened the door, and climbed in.

"What'd ya think of our little tower?" Officer Parker asked Ian with pride in his voice.

"It sure offers a fantastic view." Ian said earnestly.

Officer Parker smiled and nodded his head in agreement as he replied, "Yeah … the view is really something from up there all right. Ian, I see your Jeep comes with a security system." It took Ian almost one long second to get what Officer Parker meant by that.

"Oh, yeah that's my German Shepherd, Scout. He's a trained … He was a police dog that the former sheriff of Harmony Falls owned. Scout was given to me by the … new … sheriff there."

Officer Parker suddenly adopted a serious expression. "A large police-trained dog … Nice." Ian nodded his head in total agreement. He knew Officer Parker was wrapping up his chit-chat and was about to start talking shop. Ian, in prior quick study of the officer, had noticed the man could change topics and levels of seriousness on a dime.

"Okay, Ian. I can't stress to you enough how potentially dangerous undercover work can be for anyone, whether private investigator or law enforcement professional. What I can tell you is this. After you've taken a look at these pictures of the bodies, at least the victims we know of …" Officer Parker paused to catch his breath and a bit more composure. "Anyway, the bodies were fished out of the river with their throats, and or … various body parts … torn-apart, exsanguinated, and totally bled-out. Some organs were totally missing. We're suspecting possible organ harvesting. That said, suffice it to say, the pictures of them aren't pretty. And whoever is responsible is to say the least extremely disturbed and dangerous. Coroner says that it's possible the bodies were at least in part mutilated. Fed on by something like bull sharks that can live for extended periods in fresh water, which would account for some of the lacerations. That variety of shark has been known to come in from the ocean and travel quite a ways up rivers. But in each victim, it was determined that they were dead before they hit the water. Cause of death was not drowning." Officer Parker handed the photos to Ian. Ian instantly became wide-eyed as he grimaced and shuddered ever so slightly, hoping that Officer Parker wouldn't notice.

He did, and replied, "Ian, don't sweat it. You're not gonna impress me by trying to be a tough guy. When I first saw these pictures, I ain't ashamed to tell ya I nearly lost my lunch. And I'd even been present and seen some of the bodies fished out, seen 'em first hand." Ian looked up from the pictures directly at Officer Parker. He then slowly began shaking his head back and forth. With his mouth slack-jawed open, Ian began taking a series of deep breaths trying to gain composure.

Officer Parker reached down between the front seats and retrieved a large, unmarked manila file folder. He handed the folder to Ian. "In here's just about all the notes on the victims and summaries of statements of potential witnesses as well as various crime scene investigative reports. It may seem like a lot, but I assure you, with the number of deaths, it really ain't much to go on. Nothing we've got points directly at Salizzar or his nightclub. Not directly. What little information we have on the guy is mostly from public domain records like his business license application and such. He listed his full name as Vladimir Drago Salizzar. He's supposedly from Hungary, where he either came from big money or more likely made big money in drug trafficking and black marketing human organs. Maybe operates nightclubs for money-laundering set-ups and near perfect traps for attracting his victims. Salizzar listed on his liquor license application that he owned a few of those absinthe nightclub bars around Budapest. Ian, you heard of … You know about absinthe?" Ian nodded. He had heard about the stuff and wanted Officer Parker to know straight-up he was telling the truth about it.

Ian spoke, "Yeah, it's some kind of wormwood spirit. Very high alcohol content. It's popular in Eastern Europe. Well, all over Europe now. It's sort of becoming a fad here in the States as well. But besides the alcohol effect, absinthe is supposed to contain small traces of, if memory serves, a substance … well, a drug called Thujone from the wormwood. Wormwood extract ingested in any significant quantity is very toxic, like drinking turpentine. Thujone's hallucinogenic. But the amount allowed in absinthe, I've read, is very slight; its reputation for causing a hallucinogenic effect, beyond mere intoxication from its high alcohol content, is highly overstated to the point of near wives' tale. The 'buzz' one gets from drinking absinthe in moderate to heavy consumption, in common vernacular I believe, is colorfully referred to as, 'Chasing the Green Fairy'!"

By the raised eyebrows and the surprised expression on Officer Parker's face, Ian knew his knowledge on the subject required some explanation. "I spent some time years ago in Europe, mainly in Scotland, doing some zoological work around the Lochs."

Officer Parker was impressed nonetheless. "That's the stuff all right. He's peddling that green shit in his bar." Ian slowly shook his head and flashed Officer Parker a look of disgust, clearly intent on indicating to Officer Parker his sympathy to both the police department and the town's predicament.

Officer Parker paused for a few seconds to collect his thoughts, then continued. "Ian, just to keep the record straight, I know some things about you. For instance, I already knew that years ago you were in Scotland chasing after that Loch Ness Monster or some such crap. Doing your, at that time … job. I've been informed that people who go around looking for things like Big Foot and the Loch Ness Monster, and that … that *Moth Man* for that matter are sometimes referred to as cryptozoologists. Typically assumed to be pseudo-science. One that's generally thought to attract mainly hoaxsters and crazies.

"You didn't think we were gonna even consider entering into any type of cooperative arrangement with just anyone, did you? But I also know you're different. The exception to the rule. For instance, I know that over the years, you've investigated Big Foot throughout the Pacific Northwest, and in doing so have actually debunked a lot of hoaxes along the way. And you're the guy who once got a lot of press and were famous for a time for catching some thought-to-be-extinct fish off, I believe …"

Ian interrupted, "Madagascar. We found it in the waters off of Madagascar."

Officer Parker continued, "Yeah … right. Anyway, I know more about you than that. Like the terrible thing that happened to your wife and daughter. Very sorry for your loss, by the way."

Ian didn't reply or look in anyway surprised by all that Officer Parker knew about him. It was the police that he was dealing with, after all. He fully expected that his background would be checked into regardless of the recommendation from Sheriff Charlie Redtail.

Ian opened the file folder and started skimming some of its contents before he commented, "Well, this will help me get up to speed and maybe help with some direction."

Officer Parker smiled slightly and nodded just as slightly in agreement. "Okay, Ian. Since I've been calling you by your first name, I want you to return the favor. My name's Ned." Officer Ned Parker put out his right hand. The two men shook hands.

"Ian, I'm not here to tell you how to conduct your business." Officer Parker paused as if to collect his thoughts. Ian thought to himself how much he hated open-ended, trite, semi-reassuring platitudes.

Officer Parker continued, "It's your business. I mean you investigate this thing any way you see fit, as long as it doesn't break any of the laws that count. But my dime-store advice that's worth about a plug nickel's this. I'd start by coloring your hair dark. Black would be best. And maybe visit our Goodwill store downtown and pick up some clothes that don't make you look like a stockbroker on his day off or anything that'd make you look like a used car salesman, especially for when you visit the club. Remember, it's called The Morgue. Maybe for good reason. If you've got a laptop or smart phone, or a tablet, you can Google for the look of a Goth clubber easily enough."

Ian replied, "I … Right now, I don't have a computer, but I pretty much know the look you're talking about. I'll maybe go to an Internet café or a library and get online. I've been meaning to pick up another computer ever since mine completely crashed a while back. I just haven't got around to it yet."

Parker looked directly into Ian's eyes. "Well anyway, I'll bet that Chief Mooney referred to Salizzar and his club-goers as Satanists or some type of cult. From what I've been able to dig up on Salizzar and his club, the place is a nightclub for those underground Gothic types and for wanna-be vampire role players and generally fucked-up clubbers. You've no doubt heard of the types that hang out at those – usually in big cities – underground counterculture occult clubs. Club goers that cut a willing donor and drink small quantities of their blood to supposedly get some kind of physiological high. You know, all that master-slave sadomasochistic bullshit! Well, anyway, the very idea of it … ever since that article appeared just a couple days ago in the *Oregonian* – even just uttering the word vampire – and the chief goes nuts! He's made it plenty clear that any officer he hears using the "V" word, after being fired, would be lucky to get a job working security for Wal-Mart. I suspect it was that article in the *Oregonian* that brought you to us in the first place." Ian looked directly at Officer Parker as he half-grinned and gave a quarter nod, silently indicating that was a fact.

"So far, due to our office having some limited influence with our local paper, the *Daily Astorian*, they haven't gone so far as to label these as anything so fantastic, but due to the number and the nature of the killings, I fear it's just a matter of time."

Ian understood why Chief Mooney did not want the press spinning and printing anything for the public to read that would even remotely draw a connection to any possible vampire-cult murderous activities. The spread of any such rumor, even if it had a ringing of truth behind it, could cause massive panic and even the possibility of an angry mob looking to exact revenge outside of the law on Salizzar and his people.

Ian silently mulled over the concept of the murders being connected in any way to Satanists. That notion had been around so long that it had become its own pop-cultural stereotype, over-sensationalized in film to the extent that the public thought of it as somewhat Charles Manson-y passe. But vampiric slayings? That was another thing altogether.

"Well, Ian, that's about all I've got for now, except your Jeep … It stands out like a sore thumb. Be careful you're not being followed, especially whenever you leave the club. This is a pretty good place to meet. There's only one way up and one way down, and you can see everyone coming and going. So unless otherwise notified, let's use this place to rendezvous as needed." Officer Parker pointed to a file as he spoke. "Inside that file folder, you'll see my personal cell phone number. I've got yours from the business card that you gave the chief. Oh, and Ian, Chief Mooney told me you pack a piece. A little pea-shooter. A small Beretta. Undercover work can of course be very dangerous, and that could prove handy. Just make damn sure it doesn't get you into more trouble legal-wise than it's worth."

Ian shuddered ever so slightly as he silently reminisced on what he'd been forced to do with it back at Harmony Falls. *I never want to have to use "Ole Caretaker" again like that, silver bullets or otherwise.* Ian started to collect all of the material and put his hand on the inside car-door handle.

"Oh, one more thing." Parker opened his glove box and retrieved a fat, white business-sized envelope and handed it to Ian. "This is some seed money. That club, what with the cost of getting in and drinks and such, won't be cheap. Neither will picking up some new rags and whatever else that'll help you look the part. Also, Ian, just 'cause this guy Salizzar or one or more of his freak clubbers is our primary suspect, keep in mind it could be someone else entirely. Could be someone like maybe a religious nut-job who thinks he's doing God's work by getting rid of the trash in this town and is trying to make it look like Salizzar's behind it all. I mean, the fit's so obvious. Maybe too obvious! Sometimes I wonder if we're being overzealous regarding concentrating so hard just on Salizzar. But rest assured we aren't ruling out anyone who fits the profile, so to speak. We're actively looking into all the angles. We've already had plenty of the typical phone-ins and drop-ins at the station by whackos claiming they're our man or woman. Plus, tons of bullshit leads. None of them at all credible on any level, just the typical mental cases. But still, it's been my experience that where there's smoke, there's usually fire. I'm pretty confident the smart money's on Salizzar or one or more of his cronies. That or someone that frequents that club. There's where we're gonna solve this. All of the victims so far … they fit the assumable age demographic of clubbers. Most so far have been young, twenty-something women. A couple were runaways, prostitutes. All out-of-towners. Again, so far. The bodies have all been recovered within a mile of the club, usually so messed up we've had to rely on dental records to make positive identifications of the ones we could."

31

Ian replied, "Thanks, uh … Ned. And yeah, I agree. Though one thing seems especially strange."

Officer Parker interjected, "What's that?"

Ian cleared his throat and continued. "Why this town? I mean apparently, up till now, he's been a big city operator."

Parker shrugged at that but then replied, "Maybe it's 'cause of our deep-water port, which would give immediate access to ocean-going vessels perfect for smuggling drugs or, more likely, body parts and organs. There's that, and our small size, meaning limited police resources, yet our relatively close proximity to Portland and Seattle; it makes us a perfect distribution center for – and I say it again – drug trafficking and/or peddling human blood and organs on the black market. The club's probably just a front. You know, like a fishing lure, bait for a trap. Or, a money laundry. Hell, likely both. We may be just a bit lacking in certain aspects of law enforcement, but our strength around here's our near immediate access to the Coast Guard. And they've already been alerted to keep an extra eye on boats going to and from Salizzar's place. They're watching for scuba-divers that may attempt to rendezvous with ships dropping off or picking up cargo intentionally deposited into the river. The Coast Guard knows that Salizzar's club is a place of high interest to us regarding potential smuggling or worse. Who knows? They might even be in the white slavery market. I wouldn't rule it out, especially with his Eastern European connections. Anyway, we've had to invent every reason in the book to randomly pull over and check out various booze and food delivery trucks to the place. So far, we've been denied by the court to do any wire-tapping, but we're making progress on that. I think we're getting close. We've put undercover officers in the place a couple-few times, but male or female, I think they're made before they even entered the club. Like I said, with the kind of money Salizzar's been spreading around town, the walls of the station just might have ears."

Ian knew that the police's efforts and Officer Parker's theories all had merit. They made perfectly good, logical sense as very real possibilities to consider.

Officer Parker suddenly seemed to run out of verbal fuel. Ian could tell that for the time being, there was nothing further to say. Ian looked directly into Parker's eyes and slowly nodded, intent on letting him know that he understood the gravity and copious danger involved with proceeding with his private investigation of Salizzar and The Morgue nightclub. Ian maintained a good poker face, but the truth was he was starting to get an icy cold feeling in places other than his feet.

Without another word spoken by either man, Ian climbed out of Officer Parker's car and started walking back to his Jeep. Ian heard Parker start his car. He turned around briefly and watched for a moment as Parker backed his car out of its parking spot, then turned and began driving off, exiting the parking lot in the only direction there was to go. Ian thought to himself, *One way up … one way down.*

Scout had been waiting patiently for about twenty minutes. Ian reached into his denim work-style jacket pocket and retrieved the filled-to-obesity business-sized white envelope. Leaning up against the side of his Jeep, Ian looked with astonishment at the contents, all one hundred dollar bills. He then unlocked his Jeep, climbed into the driver's seat, and began counting his cash as he spoke out loud to Scout. "Holy cow-pie. How much did Charlie tell these guys is my going rate? There must be … twenty-eight … twenty-nine … thirty. There's three thousand bucks here. I tell ya boy, nowadays, it's not so much what you know, it's who you know. That, and whatever you've done lately. That's what makes or breaks ya." Ian looked upwards like he was talking to the heavens themselves and exclaimed, almost shouting, "THANK YOU, CHARLIE!"

CHAPTER 4
Once Bitten

Not five minutes had gone by since Officer Ned Parker's return to the station. He was just leaving the chief's office, having given Chief Mooney an update on his and Ian's intended future black-op investigatory activities, when all at once a heavy-set upper-middle-aged black woman came bursting into the front door of the police station. She was in near hysterics as she stood wildly wide-eyed just inside the threshold of the foyer, desperately attempting to catch her breath.

The woman was soaked and soiled from head to foot. To even the most amateur eyes, she looked to be a battle-torn casualty of some small war.

She was dressed in a tattered, dark purple, white polka-dotted semi-muumuu and once white, seamless, diabetic-approved stockings. No shoes. Her hair was as rain-soaked and dirty as her clothing. She looked completely disheveled, like she'd been a front row spectator of a hurricane. The woman had thick tears and mascara tracks running from the corners of her eyes down her cheeks. It appeared to everyone in the room, officers and citizens alike, that the woman was desperately trying to speak but nothing was coming out. After a few of what appeared to be painful attempts to speak, she feverishly began swallowing, gulping, and gasping as if attempting to swallow something the size of a jaw-breaker. A female plainclothes officer rapidly approached the woman and tried to grab and steady her since the woman looked like she might be having a seizure or perhaps some sort of cardiac event. But the woman pushed the officer away with all her might as she made one more painful effort to speak. This time, she managed to muster up an audible voice that, after a few seconds, manifested itself as a blood-curdling scream. "MA! MA! MURDER!!!"

Having heard all of the commotion, Officer Ned Parker ran into the front room of the police station. He then ran over to the woman, who was barely being held upright by the female officer. Ned Parker blurted out, "Okay, okay. Officer … Maggie … I've got her too." Ned wrapped his left arm around the large woman's underarm and back. "Maggie, let's get her over to that chair." Ned gave a slight nod of his chin and pointed with his eyes over at the nearest interrogation desk and chairs.

The large woman was shaking profusely as she stumbled, barely managing with the two officers' assistance to make it over to the chair. Once the officers had the woman seated, Ned nodded and winked at the female officer, indicating that, being the senior officer, he would take the lead. The female officer frowned but quickly acquiesced to Ned pulling rank on her.

Ned spoke slowly and clearly while looking directly into the woman's blank-looking, blood-shot eyes. "Uh, ma'am, are you having any sort of medical emergency?"

After a few seconds of silence, the woman looked up at Ned, still trembling, as she began murmuring "Murder" over and over but just barely loud enough for him to hear.

Ned looked over at the female officer. "Maggie. This lady's in some kind of traumatic shock. Go across the street and see if you can get that shrink. What's 'er name?"

Maggie replied, "You mean Doctor Tate? Doctor Selma Tate, I think's her name."

Ned fired back tersely, "Yeah, right. Good. Whatever. Get her over here if she's in. Tell her we've got a bit of a situation. Tell her … Ah hell, tell her whatever it takes to get her ass over here as soon as possible! Got it? Now … Go!" Maggie turned and in a near jog headed towards the front door of the police station.

Ned spoke in a kind, calm voice to the large woman. "I'm gonna leave you but only for a few seconds. You're safe here. Whatever's happened to you, you're safe now. I'm going to get you a blanket to help get you warmed up a bit. I'll get you a cup of hot coffee too if you'd like?" The woman managed to nod her head beyond its trembling, indicating that she understood Ned and that she'd like some coffee. True to his word, Ned was back in moments with a blanket and a cup of steaming hot coffee.

"Here ya go." Ned said as he wrapped the blanket around the nearly catatonically-in-shock woman. He then sat himself in a chair by the desk.

"Can you tell me your name?" Ned asked, speaking slowly and in a calm, soothing voice.

The lady, hands trembling badly, picked the cup of coffee up and with some difficulty managed to take a sip just before, to Ned's surprise, she spoke. "S… Sally's my … My name's … Sally."

After noticing for the first time that the woman had a large, marquise-cut solitaire diamond wedding ring on her finger Ned thought to himself, *Any mugger I've ever known would have snatched that ring, even if it meant whacking her finger off to get it.*

Ned continued, "Ma'am. Sally. What is it that you keep saying?"

Sally started trembling more violently and either would not or simply could not answer.

"Okay. Um … all right. Sally, darlin,' I know you're having a hard time finding your words right now. Uh, how 'bout you just nod or shake your head to answer my questions?"

That worked. Sally, though her entire body was shaking badly, managed to slowly nod.

"Sally, honey … Did you say, and I'm just guessing here, murder?" Ned asked softly. Sally nodded her head.

"Okay. All right, now we're getting somewhere. Sally, did you … Were you forced to … Sweetheart, did you see someone hurt or have to hurt someone?" Sally didn't respond. Ned paused to collect his thoughts, then continued his questioning.

"Sally, did you fear for your life and maybe had to hurt someone 'cause they were hurting you or were about to hurt you? Or did you witness someone hurt someone else?"

Still, Sally said nothing. Her eyes were glazed over, and she had a blank, far away expression on her face.

Normally, it wasn't in Ned's makeup to infantilize anyone he questioned. But his instincts told him this would be the only approach right now that might eventually bear fruit. Ned felt sweet talk was the best approach given her present state of near catatonia. His experience told him if she were lying down right now, she'd probably be rocking back and forth in a near fetal-like position.

After a few minutes of silence, Sally began slowly but very apparently intentionally shaking her tremor-bobbing head as she said, "No-suhr. I didn't kill nobody! But I seen … I seen …" Sally just couldn't bring herself to finish telling Ned what she'd witnessed.

But Ned felt he was on the verge of a communication breakthrough. "Okay. Honey … Sally … did you witness something bad?"

All at once, Sally's eyes opened wider than Ned had ever seen anyone's open … as she screamed out, "YES-'EM … I SEEN THE DEVIL-MONSTER … DONE KILL MY MAN!"

Ned was startled by Sally suddenly opening up, but before he had a chance to ask Sally any more questions, he spotted Maggie and the doctor from next door. He watched appreciatively as the attractive doctor of psychiatry sashayed her way across the station in her two-piece, perfectly figure-fitting, gray flannel skirted suit and white designer silk blouse.

Ned, though semi-happily married, enjoyed watching the fine-looking doctor come and go from her office across the street whenever timing permitted. His department had successfully used her services a few times over the last couple of years, mostly when dealing with runaways. Ned daydreamed for a brief moment as the lady doctor and Maggie were less than ten feet away from him and closing fast, *She's the perfecta-trifecta. Smart, beautiful, and blonde.*

Maggie made a point of mentioning all of the hats Ned had worn in their small department since he pulled rank on her earlier as she introduced him. "Um, Selma ... I mean, Doctor Tate, this is Special Liaison Officer and acting Deputy Chief Lieutenant Ned Parker."

Maggie continued, "And this is the woman that I spoke to you about."

Ned interjected to assert himself. "Doctor Tate, very nice that you could come over. I'd like to introduce you to Sally." Maggie lifted her eyebrows and nodded slightly as she flashed Ned a congratulatory smile that he'd gotten that much out of the woman. Maggie then turned and left Ned and the doctor.

Doctor Tate extended her right hand to Ned. "Ned. May I call you by your first name?"

Ned smiled as he replied, "Only if quid pro quo applies, Selma." They both smiled and laughed.

Selma continued, "Ned, we met around nine months ago I believe. Your department asked me to review the physiological health of a teen runaway. I've done some other work for your department but directed through case-workers, not yourself."

Ned spoke up. "That's right. You've a good memory. You've got a great reputation with our department."

After a long, extended handshake, Ned slowly retracted his right hand. "Good. Great! Uh, anyway, Doctor … I mean Selma. This here's Sally. She's … I mean I think maybe Sally here's been through something awful, and she'd like to tell us all about it. But she's having a tough time. Aren't you, Sally …?"

Ned quickly retrieved another chair for Selma, who smiled graciously, then sat down facing Sally.

"Sally. That is your name, correct?" Selma asked point-blank in a calm, collected voice. Sally looked up from the ground at Selma. Without much hesitation, she sheepishly answered, "Yes 'em."

Selma smiled and glanced over at Ned, who was now also seated near the desk that they were all huddled around.

Once again, Selma fired off a direct question in a perfectly base-line voice. "Sally. Are you hurt?"

Sally answered, "No … nut very bad. Juz my neck got pecked at some." Sally's arms were wrapped around herself with her hands tucked under her armpits. She began rocking back and forth in her chair.

Selma continued, "Sally, I see you're wearing a ring. Did your husband hurt you?"

That question seemed to bring Sally out of her near trancelike state before she answered, "No! No, ma'am. My man, he don't hurt me. He don't hurt nobody!"

To both Ned and Selma's surprise, Sally stopped rocking back and forth. She took a series of deep breaths and let the air out of her lungs slowly each time. It was apparent to both Ned and Selma that Sally was desperately trying to will herself, at least momentarily, to a functioning level of lucidity.

Sally took in then let out one more long breath of air before beginning to speak as clearly as she could muster, "My … my … husband … Loren … Loren Robinson … He was my beautiful man … My man for over twenty-three years, and now he dead. He da only one a us works. Now he dun got killed. What am I ta do? God'n heaven, what I ta do now?" Sally paused and took three more deep breaths. Her lips were quivering as she began to speak once again. "We been vacationin' here at da ocean. My man took me out fo' a fine dinner."

Selma glanced for a second over at Ned and gave him a subtle nod. She knew from experience that Sally was about to open up and tell her tale as best she could. Ned understood Selma's signal. He grabbed a notepad and pen and was all ears.

Selma then directed her attention back on Sally, then spoke directly, "Sally, who killed your husband? Sally, who killed Loren?"

Sally's eyes got wide as she blurted out, "Da Devil got 'em. I know it sound crazy, Mister … Ma'am … But believe me, be'n country don't mean be'n dumb! I know what I seen! Da Devil, he was like a man, but he ain't no human man. Da Devil, he a monster. Maybe some kind a ALIEN! All I know fo' sure is he done snatched up my big man and took 'em up in the sky. Da Devil, him first try ta get me 'cept my man, Loren, he a BIG powerful man! Him's was a pofesh-nel football player way back-n da day. Owe he beat dat devil-monster back and good fo' a bit. Not good'nuff fo' long, 'cause come find out he come back! No man can beat da Devil back too long 'cause dat devil-monster he done got up from a terrible beat'n by my man … an he done snatched my Loren up. He done snatched my beautiful man up and tooks 'em away!"

Ned couldn't help himself but fire off a question of his own. "Sally. What – what do you mean by some devil, or monster snatched up Loren?"

Sally looked all around the room as if it were spinning, then she glanced over at Ned before looking down at the ground as she spoke.

"We orig'nally fum Acadiana, outside New Iberia … Loosiana. Tell, affa Katrina done wiped us out! Den me and my man, we move ta Portland, far from da hur-canes! We juz come here to da beach fo few days. We was down at da docks laz-night look'n fo good place ta eat real late. We was walk'n in da moonlight once stopped rain'n. Den … from nowhere dahre he be. Da Devil himself. Da Devil, he got eyes dat's on fy-ehr. And him has da foulest breath! His teeth juz like da Bible say. Day were like dat of a dragon. Him had dragon's teeth!"

Ned replied, "Dragon's teeth? You mean like fangs?"

Sally replied, "Yes-suhr."

Ned fired off another couple of questions. "Sally, have you been just walking around since last night? I mean, where've you been since then? It's midmorning."

Sally rolled her eyes around as she spoke. "Been sleep'n da car … Don't know fo' how long. Woke'd up juz fo' sunrise cuz some damn bird I neva seen, but felt, had been peck'n at my neck mayhaps most all night! When I woke'd, I'z too sick ta drive. So's I'z walked … I'z walked he-ahr. Wazza-convertible car. Dat devil-monster done tore dat rag-top clean off and done took my man! Done tore'd dat roof clean off! My man ne-ahr five hunded pounds! Devil Monster flew way with my man … up in da air … Devil flew way with my man like him weigh no mo din a baby. Da Devil, him looks like a giant man-bat … and him can FLY! Him can fly. Him can …"

Sally's face went blank and she bowed her head down. It was then that both Ned and Selma both spotted for the first time the two puncture-like wounds on the side of her neck. Dried blood stained her neck all around the wounds that looked already significantly infected. Ned spoke as he looked over at Selma, "You see those nasty marks? Did she say something about being pecked at?" Selma raised her eyebrows as she nodded.

Selma spoke up, "Ned. I appreciate you needing answers. Way more answers than you've got here. But Sally … she needs to be seen by a medical doctor and possibly a psychiatrist for a full screening. Those wounds on her neck look bad, and well, you know, for other reasons. We're not going to get much more out of her that will make much sense until she's cleaned up and rested."

Ned nodded his head in agreement. "I'll have one of my men take her to the hospital straight away."

CHAPTER 5
Banana Books

It was getting to be late afternoon. Ian had stopped thinking about it a few hours ago, but just realized that his stiff neck had worked itself out and now felt fine. He was feeling good about how everything was progressing, especially how he was now "officially/non-officially" on a new case. He felt like he'd accomplished a great deal for his first day.

Ian decided it was time to head back to Long Beach. But first, he wanted to drive by the former Flavel House Museum.

Upon arriving, Ian pulled his Jeep over to the curb across the street and just sat staring at it. Ian was intrigued by the size and grandeur of the vintage Victorian mansion; it was surrounded by a seven-foot-high, spear-head tipped, black wrought-iron fence. The front gate was also grand. It boldly displayed an artfully-crafted, ornate black wrought-iron dragon with large, ruby-colored eyes. The beautiful gate hung from tall, brick-and-mortar columns, perched on the columns were large, black, concrete gargoyles.

What initially caught Ian off-guard were the security cameras mounted around the fence line and sides of the house, but he quickly realized that anything less would be contrary to Salizzar's role play persona.

Upon noting the camera's positioning, Ian realized there would be little chance of anyone getting inside the backyard, let alone inside the house without detection. Ian surmised that the cameras were also video recorders.

The most obvious anomaly were the windows of the grand house. They were all completely blackened. Ian presumed they'd been painted over, as the windows were darker than any type of window tinting that he'd ever seen or heard of. Upon closer examination, Ian noted two exceptions to the black, painted-over windows. There were two large windows, one located on each side of the house's front door. Those windows appeared to be covered by identical black curtains, possibly made of velvet.

At least from where Ian was parked, it was impossible to see into the house. No apparent light of any kind emitted from within. Ian thought intently, *Those totally blacked windows and all this security, that's gonna make any potential stake-out of this place useless and way too dangerous to keep my cover. I'm probably on candid camera right now. But whoever is monitoring them, they no doubt are used to lots of curious people parking and gawking at the place. It figures Salizzar would surround himself with all the stereotypical pseudo-vampiric lifestyle motif bullshit and all the related security that goes with being rich. I wonder how many people he employs to take care of the place. And how many bodyguards he's got? He's probably installed a secret passage behind the bookcase that leads down to the basement, down to the torture chamber, or down to where he keeps his coffin. Ha.*

Just then, Ian and Scout spotted two identical, large, black and tan Rottweilers patrolling the grounds. Scout went on instant alert. He began a low, deep growl, somewhat under his breath, and he was becoming more agitated by the second.

"Steady boy. Steady! Well, we came, we saw, let's get the hell out of here and head back to camp. We'll be checking out Salizzar's warehouse-

44

nightclub soon enough. That's, I'm sure, where the action is." Scout halted his low growling and barked once at Ian's declaration.

Twenty minutes later, Ian and Scout were driving through downtown Long Beach when Ian blurted out, "Look there! A bookstore. Banana Books; sounds like it could be an interesting place to peek around."

Ian pulled his Jeep over and wrangled his way into a parallel parking spot that was right across from the side street that the bookstore was on. "Wait here, boy. This shouldn't take long."

He walked briskly towards the bookstore, which appeared to him to be converted from a two-story house, possibly with living quarters upstairs. Ian thought the bookstore looked wonderfully quaint with a nice sun-deck out front.

As he approached, Ian noticed in the bookstore's front window a sign advertising espresso and all manner of flavored coffee. It meant little to him. When Ian drank coffee, which generally was only in the morning, it was of the simple, jet-black variety. Nothing fancy about it.

Ian opened the door to the bookstore and walked in. He was immediately greeted by a lovely woman who stood behind the counter, busily fixing a coffee for a customer. He vaguely noticed that there were paper cutout pumpkins and black and orange streamers hung throughout the store. But what immediately grabbed his attention was that nearly every inch of the relatively small store was utilized to its fullest. Ian was amazed by the sheer volume of books that were shelved from floor to ceiling.

Ian then noticed a man who was busily restocking shelves with books he was pulling from a large box.

After a few moments of looking all around the store, Ian walked up to the man doing the re-stocking. "Uh, excuse me. I was wondering

if you could point me in the direction of books on the subject of …
well, of vampires. Perhaps not so much horror novels per se as, uh, say
fact versus myth. Or well, that sort of thing if you've …" Ian instantly
became a little embarrassed as he realized how silly that might have
sounded.

The man stopped what he was doing and turned to Ian. He smiled
as he replied, "Well, we have lots of books about vampires, that's for
sure. A pretty fair representation of many of the popular titles." The
man pointed towards shelves just around the corner from where they
were standing. "We have some of the *Vampire Chronicles* by Anne Rice.
And I believe we have a couple copies of Steven King's *Salem's Lot*, all
still very popular." The man paused to collect his thoughts.

The man continued, "Hmm … Books more specifically on the
subject of legend versus fact, hmm?" The man put his right hand to his
chin and deliberated for a moment. "Ya know, now that I think about
it, I might just have what you're looking for. It's by a local writer who
coincidentally is going to be doing a book signing here tomorrow. Now,
the book is still a work of pure fiction. But I've been told – understand
I haven't actually read it myself – that there's quite a bit of material in
it that deals with the modern underground vampire counterculture.
People that hang out, or fang out, so to speak, at clubs for that sort of
thing." Ian laughed at the man's levity.

The man refocused and became more to the point. "Fact is, a club
like that opened across the river over in Astoria a few months back.
Has a lot of people over there up in arms about the sort of people they
claim it attracts." Ian nodded and raised his eyebrows, indicating he
could understand people being upset about it.

The man continued, "Anyway, about the book. I should have said
it deals with the once modern vampire counterculture. The book I'm
referring to isn't new. It was a pretty popular book around ten years

ago." The man pointed to a poster advertising the author, Clayton Collins, and his book, *Bloodlust Vampires 2.0*, which was mounted on the wall directly above a chair and small desk, which were positioned very visibly in a corner of the store, obviously made ready for tomorrow's book signing event.

The man went behind the counter and retrieved a copy of the book. He then handed the book to Ian as he continued, "The author, Clayton Collins? Nice guy. He's written several books on the subject of vampires. But his best seller, the one he's most known for, is this one: *Bloodlust Vampires 2.0.* "

Suddenly, with a big smile, the man extended his right hand. Ian quickly shifted the book from his right hand to his left, and extended his. "My name's Ed, and that's Mary over there." Ed nodded his head once in the direction of Mary who was hanging earrings on a display board.

Upon hearing her name and seeing Ed and Ian shaking hands, Mary smiled as she spoke, "Hello."

Ian returned the smile and gave a slight nod of his head as he replied, "Ed. Mary. It's nice to meet you."

Ian began flipping through some of the pages of the book Ed had handed him. Just then, two dogs came bounding up from behind the cash register area, where they had been previously laying quietly. First, they came over to Ed, then to Ian. One of the dogs a male, seemed very happy regarding a ball that he held pridefully in his mouth, Ian couldn't help but notice that his tail was wagging enthusiastically. Ian thought to himself, *I've got to get Scout a toy of some kind. Something for us to play fetch with.*

"What beautiful dogs." Ian said as he without hesitation stooped over and began petting the dog holding the ball.

Ian spoke while still petting the dog. "He's some variety of bull terrier, isn't he?"

Ed once again smiled with obvious pride as he spoke, "Why this here's Sobe. He's an American Staffordshire Terrier. He and Angel, well I guess you'd say they're sort of our unofficial mascots, if you know what I mean. They love people. Angel, she's a terrier mix." Ian was surprised to hear that Angel was a mixed breed because she looked very much like a slightly smaller, lighter-weight version of Sobe.

It was obvious to Ian without having to ask that Ed and Mary were the owners of the establishment. Their pride of ownership and love of what they did was written all over their faces.

After gazing through a few pages and having read the book's synopsis on the back cover, Ian was certain that this book would be about as helpful as any of its type. He thanked Ed for thinking of it for him. Ian then walked over to the counter that Mary was at. She was still hanging earrings onto a display board. Ian noticed that Mary was wearing earrings of much the same general style as the ones she was hanging. He then noticed the sign on the earring display board stating that the earrings were hand-crafted. He quickly put two-and-two together.

"Mary, do you make these beautiful earrings?" Ian believed he'd already deduced the answer to his question.

"Yes, these are some of my creations. Do you like them?" Mary asked enthusiastically.

Ian replied, "Oh, yes. Very much! My late wife … She loved artisan jewelry like this."

Mary placed her right hand to her chest. "Oh, I'm so sorry."

Ian interrupted Mary from saying anything more. "No, no. Nothing to apologize about. My wife Janet, and my daughter Sue Ann … They've been … They passed away a couple years ago. They were in a car accident." The words welled up and nearly stuck in Ian's throat. Time hadn't healed his wounds, not by a long shot. But what had up until very recently been no better than a light scabbing-over regarding his ability to deal with his gaping mental wounds was perhaps finally beginning to transcend itself into that of tenuously thin scar tissue.

Ian rapidly regained his composure. Later, he'd silently conclude that his recently-acquired ability to not get too shaken up, at least for very long anyway, was probably due in large to all that he'd endured back at Harmony Falls.

"Well, I meant it. Your earrings and jewelry are just beautiful!" Ian said with absolute conviction.

Mary smiled big as she replied, "Why thank you. I really appreciate your saying so. I enjoy making them."

Ian set the book down onto the cash register counter and picked up a business card and began reading it to himself. *Banana Books - Owners Ed Grey and Mary Johnson - 114 SW 3rd Street, Long Beach, WA.* Ian immediately deduced that Ed and Mary were much more than merely partners in this bookstore, they were partners in life. And that sentiment made Ian smile.

As Mary began ringing up the sale of the book, Ed spoke up from across the store. "Ian, if you can make it, you should come by tomorrow and meet the author. Bring your book, and have him sign it."

"That's a great idea. I'll try and make it." Ian said with sincerity as he thought to himself, *If given a chance to talk to the guy, he might have some insights that could prove useful.*

CHAPTER 6
Going Bananas (I)

Ian climbed into the driver's seat of his Jeep. He immediately began petting Scout for being so patient.

"Sorry, boy. That took a little longer than I expected. But look here. I've got me some new light reading." Ian's eyes rolled as he showed Scout his new book, which was just over four hundred pages long.

Ian started up his Jeep, pulled away from the curb, and once again was heading north on Long Beach's main street directly through the heart of the small town. Ian noticed there were many more cars and people walking around than he'd seen in town up to this point. It wasn't yet the weekend, so he wondered why the town seemed to be getting so busy.

When Ian got back to Oscar's on the Ocean, he was amazed to see that the place was almost completely full. When he'd checked in the day before, and this morning when he left the place, it was ninety percent vacant.

As Ian drove into the RV park, he spotted Oscar driving around in a covered golf-cart. Ian waved to him as he pulled up alongside him and rolled his window down. "Hey, Oscar, looks like business is good."

Oscar smiled as he replied, "Yep. Supposed ta be a honey of a minus-tide in the morning. State gave the green-light fer the dig 'bout a week ago. 'Bout time they lifted the ban. Them damn fish-n-wildlife tree-hugger types and their damn red tides!" He scowled.

Ian looked at Oscar with a blank expression. Oscar removed his soiled and tattered John Deere green and yellow ball-cap that sat atop what remained of his thin, wiry, white hair which adorned his bald spot like a snow-covered wreath. Oscar's head was of momentary fascination to Ian. All the random dark spots on the top of Oscar's head looked like a Rorschach inkblot test. And the indention ring formed by the rim of the cap appeared quite possibly to be permanently indented around Oscar's head from years of wearing it always fixed in exactly the same position, defying any amount of strong wind to remove it.

Oscar began rubbing the top of his head as he began looking all around his park. "Clam dig'n. Ain't that what you're here fer? Like most these other folks?"

Ian noticed for the first time, as he panned his eyes around the park, that leaning up against many of the trailers, fifth-wheels motor-homes, and vehicles were all manner of clamming paraphernalia, including but not limited to hip boots, waders, clam shovels, and guns.

"Clam digging … RIGHT!" Ian said, trying not to sound totally ignorant. "No … I'm not here to do any digging around of that sort." Ian chuckled silently to himself over that one. "No, I'm just here visiting the area, taking it easy. You know, seeing the sights and such."

Oscar put his cap back on. "Yep. Well, ya picked a good place to take-er easy. Less them damn tree-huggers keep shut'en down the diggin. No diggin, no business. Might have to sell the place an move to Arizona. Die in the damn desert."

Ian interjected, "Well, let's hope it doesn't come to that." Both men smiled.

51

"You take care of yourself," Ian said as he waved goodbye and continued into the park, heading to his trailer.

Oscar cheekily fired back, "Got to. Ain't nobody else gonna."

Ian had the best spot in the park in his opinion. Located at the very end, with nothing between him and the Pacific Ocean but a few hundred yards of dune grass, scrub pines, and sand. The trail that led from the park to the beach was only feet away from where his trailer sat.

Pulling into his spot directly in front of his trailer, Ian looked over at Scout. "You've got to be getting hungry, huh boy? First I'll feed ya, then take you for a walk to get rid of that cheeseburger." Scout barked twice. Ian and Scout quickly exited the Jeep and climbed into the trailer.

After grabbing the bag of kibble, Ian filled Scout's bowl to the brim and set it down onto the floor in the trailer's would-be kitchen area. Without hesitation, Scout went to work on it. Ian then poured some water into Scout's water dish and set it down beside the food bowl. "Okay, that's got you taken care of for now. Hmm, what should I do about some chow?"

Ian's stomach growled a couple of times while he thought about what to do for dinner. *There was a nice looking restaurant downtown pretty close to that bookstore. Probably as good a place to eat as any,* he thought to himself.

Once Scout finished his food, Ian put a lightweight jacket on and fastened Scout's leash to his collar for no reason other than it was the RV park's rules. He walked Scout over to a designated place in the park for doggie-walking. He was impressed; there was a station set up and stocked with a few old clam shovels, plastic baggies that dispensed from a pole-mounted dispenser, and a designated bag-lined trashcan all specifically for picking up and disposing of dog waste.

After successfully completing his mission, Ian and Scout continued their walk through the park, heading back towards Ian's trailer.

"Hey boy, there's not much wind right now, and it's not raining. Let's walk the trail down to the beach. Maybe catch a glimpse of the sunset through the clouds." Scout barked once, which Ian took to mean, *That's a capital idea.*

As they continued on their walk, the sky grew darker by the minute, and not just because of the time. Ominous, dense gray clouds were rapidly replacing what had been mostly thin, scattered clouds not a half-hour before.

"I don't know if this was such a good idea, boy," Ian said to Scout as he gazed up at the sky.

Ian and Scout had just reached the beach when it came. It began with flashes of lightning miles out at sea. Seconds later came the thunder. Then all at once, the heavens opened up. Strong gusts of wind seemed to come from nowhere as torrents of sideways wind-blown sheets of rain began pounding and soaking them.

"Come on, boy. Let's high-tail it back to the trailer," Ian said to Scout as he looked out at the ocean one last time, marveling at the crashing waves.

The surf's certainly up, Ian thought as he turned his back to the sea and wiped the rain from his brow. He and Scout began heading towards the dune path at a pace just south of a full jog.

Once back at the trailer, they were both wet from head to tail. Ian toweled Scout off, and changed into some dry clothes.

"Well, boy, I'm gonna leave you here for a while and go get something to eat. With the pay I got from Charlie back at Harmony Falls, and now with the additional front money to get started on this job, well, I think a nice dinner's in order."

Ian took one hundred dollars from the white envelope that Officer

Parker had given him and put it in his wallet. He placed the envelope inside a hardcover copy of *War and Peace* that he'd hollowed the center out of years ago, alongside the money that Charlie had paid him.

Ian placed the book inside an area of cabinetry that served as a book case, which housed in addition to his newly-acquired vampire novel around twenty assorted books in both hard and soft bindings along with various magazines, maps, atlases, and the like. The money was safe enough. He figured it was pretty well hidden, and his trailer had a top-notch security system: Scout.

The rain and wind had gotten even worse; it was now pounding hard in waves onto the top and sides of Ian's trailer. He put on a fleece-lined, heavy denim coat and an old Oakland Raiders ball-cap to help cover his slightly thinning, slightly graying head of hair. He picked up his keys and stuffed his wallet into the front left pocket of his jeans, a habit that he'd picked up from years of overseas travel doing research and participating in expeditions. He'd spent that time searching for any tangible evidence that might support the existence of animals like the Chupacabra, the Yeti, the Loch Ness Monster, and other celebrated and less commonly spoken of cryptid creatures whose existence all too often fell under what Ian himself would refer to as, "highly speculative at best." That is, until very recent events opened his eyes to the realm of extreme possibility or rather perceived impossibility.

"You be a good boy while I'm gone. I shouldn't be too long. Just gonna get something to eat and maybe a drink." Ian thought for a second that Scout gave him a scolding look about his comment of maybe having a drink. Ian silently mused, *Ah ... come on, boy. Not you too.*

The torrential rain was pouring down as Ian nearly ran to his Jeep. Once inside it, he inserted his key and started it right up and turned his wipers on full. The front windshield was fogged over from the humidity, so he cranked his heater on high and moved the heat directional lever to defrost to help clear it up. But it wasn't clearing fast enough, so Ian used his coat sleeve to wipe the windshield best he could.

Once he'd cleared his windshield enough to proceed, Ian drove his Jeep out of Oscar's RV park and headed south on the peninsula's main road towards Long Beach. He was deep in thought regarding what his next day's moves should be. *First, I'll go to that bookstore, and if I can, have a talk with that author. Probably won't amount to a hill of beans, but maybe he's got some insight on the subject of vampire wanna-bes. Authors often do a lot of research on the subject they're writing about.*

After less than ten minutes of driving, Ian was passing through the center of Long Beach's main street when he spotted what he'd been looking for. On the right side of the road was a restaurant located on the corner of the block he was on. It was the one Ian had seen earlier just around the corner from the bookstore.

"There it is, The Beached Whale." he proclaimed quietly. *The food's gotta be good with a name like that.* he mused.

Ian pulled his Jeep over to a parking spot on the main street just three spots down from the restaurant's front door. Even though the town's pace had picked up due to clam digging, there didn't appear to be much of an evening dinner crowd, especially in this weather. Ian could see inside the place, which had a mostly glass front door and large picture windows on either side of it. He was too hungry to further deliberate on whether this was a good choice for dinner or not. He turned off his engine, grabbed his keys and climbed out of his Jeep, then proceeded towards the restaurant's front door, getting rain-soaked by the second. The moment Ian entered the restaurant, he noticed that it was as much a bar as an eatery.

A young twenty-something female bartender greeted Ian and

flashed him a warm smile as soon as he breached the threshold of the place. "Hi there. Just one, for drinks or dinner?"

The more people Ian met on this small peninsula and surrounding area, the more he liked their apparent genuineness, their non-pretentious ways. It reminded him of his friends back in Harmony Falls.

Ian returned her smile as he replied, "Hello yourself. And uh, yeah. Just me. For dinner, I mean. And maybe a beer or two." Ian said beer, but what he thought to himself was, *I'd love a double Jack-n-Coke ... Hold the Coke.*

The waitress picked up a menu from behind the bar. "Sit anywhere you like. You can see we aren't busy. We had a bit of a rush a couple hours ago, but the town's pretty dead tonight."

Ian sat himself in a corner table near the front door. Even as quiet as the town had become, he still liked staring out at the occasional weather-defying, brave pedestrians to see where they might be headed. He noticed there were still a few stores open, the bakery across the street being one of them. They appeared to be getting the lion's share of what little business there was to be had on this cold, windy, and very wet evening.

With menu in hand, the waitress approached Ian. She handed him the menu as she spoke. "What-a-ya be having to warm ya up on such a night? You said beer. We've got a fair selection on tap as you can see on the back of the menu. Even more by the bottle."

Ian glanced over the beers listed on the back of the menu. "Say, do you have any local microbrews from Portland, or ..."

The waitress eagerly interrupted Ian. "We've got Fort Columbia Pale Ale on tap. It's by a brewery in Astoria. I'm not much of a beer drinker, but I've heard it's really good."

Ian smiled, "Perfect! I'll bet I don't even have to look at your menu.

I'm guessing you've got pan-fried Willapa Bay oysters, am I right?"

The waitress smiled, "You bet that we've got fresh, not frozen. The best in town. A half-dozen of them comes with your choice of salad or coleslaw and baked potato or fries. To go with, I'll bring you some of our house horseradish seafood sauce and our chef's own family recipe tartar sauce."

Ian smiled widely, "Again, perfect! I'll have the coleslaw and a baked potato with everything on it."

The waitress strolled away, and Ian relaxed and gazed out the window. When his dinner arrived, he enjoyed it immensely. He equally enjoyed the couple of beers he drank to wash his meal down with.

After having had his fill of food and beer, Ian left the restaurant. Without any further loafing about town, he drove straight back to his RV campsite.

Scout was very excited to see his master. Both Ian and Scout went to sleep shortly after laying their heads down for the night. Ian slept straight through, something he rarely did, and didn't wake until his cell phone alarm went off at 7:30 a.m.

Directly after getting up and dressed for the day, Ian took Scout to the doggie-walk area. After Scout had finished his business, they returned to the trailer, and Ian retrieved his travel kit, which housed his depleting inventory of personal necessities, including a careworn toothbrush that he kept within the confines of a small, aging, zip-lock baggie; a nearly empty tube of mint-flavored Crest toothpaste; and two sealed, motel-room confiscated miniature bottles of shampoo, mere remnants of what once was a very sizeable collection of motel-acquired sundries. The two surviving shampoo bottles were generically marked and could have come from any one of dozens of motels he'd stayed in over the last few years. There was a nearly new miniature bar of soap that had also been confiscated, which once boldly proclaimed on its neatly-wrapped, sealed covering: "Super 8". But its remains were now not so neatly preserved in a small, semi-rectangular-shaped wrapping of severely crumpled aluminum foil. There was one nearly-full, travel-sized dispenser of Gillette shaving cream and three disposable razors. Each were significantly less sharp and less attractively stubble-free than they had once been.

Ian briskly walked to the shower house to get himself cleaned up for what he hoped would be a prosperous day of information prospecting regarding Salizzar and his nightclub.

While still in the shower house, Ian stood in front of the sink and mirror as he applied a conservative amount of shaving cream and began to press shaver to neck. But he suddenly halted that idea before the first swipe of his blade as he thought to himself, *Maybe shaving's not such a good idea? Maybe somewhat of a scruffy look would better fit into that nightclub's scene? But then again, maybe a clean-shaven look is what is typical?* Ian chuckled nervously as he mused to himself, *I wish I knew what the average, self-respecting, middle-aged vampire clubber looks like and wears nowadays. Cape and fangs? Good Christ, what have I gotten myself into this time?*

Back at his trailer, Ian checked his cell phone for the time, which was 9:42 a.m. It was later than he'd thought. He retrieved the book he'd purchased the day before and read the title to himself: *Bloodlust - Vampires 2.0.* He chuckled ever so slightly as he briefly shook his head, once again wondering what he was getting himself into.

With book in hand, Ian looked over at his four-legged buddy. "Scout, we'd better get a move on. That author's gonna be signing autographs at that bookstore this morning starting at 10:00 a.m. I think they said he was only going to be there for a couple-few hours. There could be a big lineup of people to meet him, so ..." Scout barked three times, indicating he too was ready for them to get a move on.

CHAPTER 7
Going Bananas (II)

Ian pulled his vehicle over to the curb and parked just across the street from Banana Books.

"Okay, Scout, you be a good boy and wait here. This shouldn't take very long."

The sky was completely gray but not dark, and the cloud cover didn't appear very ominous. Ian didn't think it was going to do much more than a light drizzle, at least anytime soon, so he cracked open a couple of windows, then switched off his ignition. With car keys in one hand and his book in the other, Ian left Scout in the Jeep and began crossing the street to the bookstore.

The moment Ian opened the door to the bookstore, he was greeted by name. "Hi Ian, so glad you came. Help yourself to coffee and muffins." Mary said as she pointed to a card table covered with a red-and-white checkered, country-style tablecloth, one she had set up for the event. The table sported a beautiful silver serving tray full of cranberry muffins, and a vintage, restaurant-style glass, chrome-topped sugar dispenser, disposable cups, napkins, and a couple of varieties of coffee creamer bottles, all neatly positioned aside a press-pump coffee dispenser.

Gathered at the opposite side of the room, a half-dozen people with more coming through the door were forming themselves into a semblance of a line. Many of them were struggling with managing their coffees, muffins, and books that they wanted signed by the local semi-celebrity author seated at the table before them.

Ian immediately noticed a stack of books obviously written by the author. The books were stacked one on top of the other on the front counter. Ian picked up a copy and cursorily read the inside pages and back of the novel. He then set the book back on top of the pile of its clones as he mused to himself, *Hmm, Graveyard Shift. The title about sums it up.*

Ian began moving further into the bookstore. He decided to pass on the muffins, not because they didn't look good; they looked delicious. But after witnessing some of the people's juggling acts, he didn't want to try and negotiate too many things at once. Ian did pour himself a cup of black coffee before he migrated across the room to take his place at the back of the line. It was then that he noticed a poster that was held by a painter-style easel. The poster was basically the artwork that appeared on the cover of *Bloodlust - Vampires 2.0*. He was pleased that he'd purchased the book that the author was advertising.

One by one, the author's mostly female fans had their moments of praise and chit-chat with the author. The author, though seated, appeared to Ian to be slightly overweight. His hair had advanced past the fifty-yard line in the game one fights and eventually loses against time. In this case, the game fought between team black versus gray. Ian placed his age somewhere around the mid-fifties. The author wore sunglasses, though it wasn't particularly bright outside or inside for that matter. Nothing much about the author was at a glance remarkable. But Ian was impressed by how he seemed very willing to take his time with each one of his admirers, answering their questions. Questions that to Ian seemed to be repetitively reconfigured by one person after the other like a worn-out recording of the same tune. Finally, after nearly a forty-five minute wait, Ian's turn arrived.

"Hi, I'm Clayton Collins …" Clayton remained seated as he extended his right hand. Ian had finished his coffee and had thrown away his cup just a few minutes before. He quickly extended his right hand. The two men smiled at each other as they shook hands.

"Um, yeah. Hi yourself. I'm … my name's Ian. Ian McDermott. Very pleased to meet you."

Clayton glanced at the book that Ian held in his left hand. "I see you've got one of my more popular titles. But I must say, I'm not sure I would have matched you with this particular type of story."

Ian smiled. "You're very perceptive. It's true. Normally, this probably wouldn't be my first choice in reading. No offense intended. I'm sure it's a very good, well-written book."

Clayton smiled as he held up his hand, indicating to Ian that no further explanation was necessary.

"Well now, Ian. Would you like me to sign your book?"

Ian smiled as he replied, "Yes. That would be great! But to be honest, I purchased it at this store just yesterday, as a matter of fact, for a little research project I'm working on. And well, I heard you, its author, were going to be here today, and well, I was hoping that you might be gracious enough to meet with me away from here."

Clayton didn't reply as Ian paused to catch his breath and collect his thoughts before continuing.

"That is, I was hoping you'd perhaps be able to lend some insight into what I'm … well … here … Just a second. Perhaps this might help." Ian quickly retrieved from his wallet one of his business cards, which he handed to the author.

Clayton stared intensely for a moment at Ian's card before speaking. "So you're an investigator of the paranormal." Ian unabashedly nodded his head.

Clayton once again extended his right hand. Ian responded in kind. The men once again shook hands. "Certainly, Ian. I'd be glad to meet with you, away from here of course, and answer any questions you might have on the subject of vampires, I presume?"

Clayton paused as he laughed a small laugh, "It's not like I've got more pressing matters to attend to these days. Probably better not to meet at any of the local eateries. The grapevine in this town would astonish you. Tell you the truth, Ian, I was expecting to meet you here today and not by hearing of you from Ed or Mary."

Ian, having just spent some time in the tiny burg of Harmony Falls, was very aware how fast news can spread in a small town. Regardless, that bit of information made him suddenly a bit nervous as he began to ponder the idea that his cover might possibly already have been blown. *How is it I've stuck out and become the topic of anyone's conversation? Especially in a tourist town where out-of-towners are coming and going daily? I sure hope this town's grapevine doesn't extend across the river.*

Ian interjected, "I really appreciate you agreeing to meet with me. When and where would you suggest we meet? I don't mean to be pushy, but is sometime later today a possibility?"

Clayton glanced once again at the business card. He then panned his eyes up and down Ian as if he was sizing up the validity of the man who stood before him.

"I'll tell you what, Ian. Normally, I don't make it a practice to invite anyone that I've just met to my house. But you seem like a decent enough fellow, and it's not like I'm any sort of A-list celebrity author these days, worthy of any nut-case stalker." Ian quickly shook his head. Both men smiled and laughed slightly at that notion.

Clayton removed from his wool-tweed sport coat's inner breast pocket a small, spiral-bound notepad. He then jotted down his address and phone number and tore the sheet of paper loose. He paused just for a second, then handed the paper to Ian.

Noting Clayton's only slight hesitation in handing him the paper, Ian thought to himself, *Wow, this guy's sure the trusting type. Gotta love small towns.*

"Okay Ian, how 'bout you meet me this afternoon at my place, say around 2:30? That should give us both time to have grabbed a bite to eat. That way we can get right to the real nitty-gritty of what you want to talk to me about."

Ian thought to himself, *If this guy ever gets tired of writing vampire rubbish, he'd make a hell of an investigative reporter.* "Yeah, Clayton. 2:30 will be perfect!"

Ian then handed Clayton his book. Clayton smiled as he glanced up over his black, horn-rimmed, Ray-Ban sunglasses that had slipped down onto the middle of his nose as he signed his name to Ian's book. As Ian retrieved his book from Clayton and both men said their goodbyes to one another, more customers began entering into the bookstore, several with books in hand.

Ian stopped near the front door to briefly speak to Mary. "I haven't seen Ed," he said just loud enough to be heard as he took hold of and began twisting the front door's doorknob.

Mary looked up at Ian with a smile on her face. "He's in Seattle at a book auction. He's always looking for titles we don't have or ones we need more of."

Ian smiled at Mary. "Gotcha! Well, this was really nice. I'm glad I came. Thank you, and please thank Ed for me for me as well."

Mary smiled brightly. "I will, Ian. Come back and see us soon."

"That I will." Ian replied quickly. He didn't want to take up anymore of Mary's time. She was busy finishing ringing up a customer who had purchased several books, including one that Ian recognized at a glance: *Graveyard Shift*, the most recently published work by none other than Clayton Collins.

Most recently published, in this case, being a relative phrase. *Graveyard Shift* had been completed and published over four years before as a prequel to *Bloodlust - Vampires 2.0*. Ian would find out later that due to *Graveyard Shift's* lackluster sales (except to his "die-hard" or "undying" cult-like fans of his previous works), Clayton's publishing house – the one that had not a decade before told him repeatedly that they were going to make him a household name – subsequently dropped him like a bad habit in lieu of writers of less traditionally horrific, more sexy pseudo-vampire character types.

CHAPTER 8
Alliance (I)

"Battle not with monsters, lest ye become a monster,
and if you gaze into the abyss,
the abyss gazes also into you."
~ Friedrich Nietzsche

Shortly after picking up a couple of burgers and fries for himself and Scout from McDonald's, Ian drove the two of them back through town and towards the main beach approach. The approach sported a giant, white-wash painted concrete archway that proclaimed that he was about to drive onto the World's Longest Beach. Ian was already aware that this was one of the last, if not *the* last, beaches in the Pacific Northwest that you were allowed to drive on. Ian knew the proclamation was questionable, but he knew from seeing pictures of it in its entirety that it was truly a very long, unobstructed, beautiful beach, one that could be driven on for over twenty miles.

Before driving forward from the end of the approach out onto the hard-packed sand near the surf, Ian pulled over and climbed out of his Jeep Wagoneer. He turned-in the hubs of his front wheels, then climbed back into his Jeep and shifted into high-range 4-wheel drive.

Ian proceeded to drive about a half-mile up the beach before he parked near the dunes facing the ocean. It was there that he and Scout enjoyed their lunches.

After growing full from their meal, Ian decided a short nap to kill some time was in order. He set the alarm on his cell phone to go off in thirty minutes. Ian calculated that would give him about the perfect amount of time to take Scout back to his trailer, then head further up the peninsula to meet with Clayton.

Ian shut his eyes, and as Scout laid his head across his lap, Ian began slowly petting him. Between the soothing action of petting Scout and the hypnotic sounds of the ocean waves crashing the shoreline, in little time, Ian was fast asleep.

Buzz, buzz, buzz, buzz. Ian was suddenly startled awake by his cell phone's alarm. He was momentarily disoriented as he cleared his eyes, trying desperately to regain focus. Ian was amazed how deeply he'd fallen asleep.

Sometime during Ian's nap, Scout had moved to the back seats and for some time had been patiently waiting for his master to wake up.

Ian glanced towards the back of the Jeep. "Hey, boy. Wow, I must have been really out of it. We best get a move on. Let's get you back to the trailer so I can go and have a chat with Mister Clayton Collins." Scout barked once. He began wagging his tail as he moved back to the front passenger seat.

Once back at the point where the beach met with the approach, Ian got out of his Jeep and turned-out the hubs of his front wheels back to free rolling position. He then climbed back into his rig and shifted out of 4-wheel drive back to the standard 2-wheel running.

Ian drove back to the town's main street, where he then made a left, heading north back to their RV trailer site. Back at the trailer, Ian put out a pan of cold water for Scout. "Okay boy, you be good and hold down the fort. I don't think I'll be gone more than a couple of hours."

Ian stroked Scout a few times, then patted him gently on his head. Without further hesitation, he exited the trailer without his faithful companion. As Ian headed towards his Jeep, he retrieved the small piece of paper he'd previously tucked into his wallet. Ian glanced at the paper as he silently read 1128 J-Place, Surfside Estates. After climbing into and firing up his rig, Ian drove out of the RV resort and turned left, proceeding once again north.

After arriving at Clayton's home, which from the street looked to be a nice but somewhat modest ranch-style house, albeit one that had been built on prime real-estate alongside other spectacular homes, Ian quickly noted that all of the homes on J-Place were custom-built. They all sat like majestic soldiers perched on the elevated hillside.

Even though Clayton's house was nowhere near as large as many of the homes up and down the street, it represented itself well in this neighborhood. His home sat on what had to be the most desired piece of land on the block: an oversized lot that could honestly boast that it offered the best view of any of them. Even from Ian's vantage point as he remained for the moment sitting in his Jeep in Clayton's driveway, he could tell Clayton's view from his front windows and deck had to be at least a one-hundred-eighty degree panoramic view of the Pacific and its expansive light-gray, sandy coastline, all of which were not even a mile off in the horizon.

Ian took a deep breath and attempted to gather his composure. He was not even certain what questions he might be asking Clayton as he silently surmised, *Sometimes, it's best to just wing these things. Don't overthink it.*

Ian checked his cell phone; it was 2:27 p.m., and he was right on time. He exited his Jeep and walked directly up to the street-side front door. He noticed a medium-sized pumpkin, neatly carved into a Jack-o-lantern, seated on the porch just to the right of the front door. Ian cleared his throat twice as he rang the doorbell.

The front door opened. Clayton immediately smiled and shook Ian's hand. "Ah, Ian. Right on time. Please, come on in."

For the first time, Ian witnessed that Clayton had a pronounced limp. He walked with a cane held in his left hand. Ian also noted Clayton was still wearing his sunglasses.

Clayton gave Ian a quick little tour around his home. He then suggested that they both take a seat in his living room, which offered the best view of the ocean from inside the home. Once they both were seated, Clayton, without asking, poured Ian a glass of red wine from an ornate crystal carafe that exactly matched two equally ornate crystal glasses, all of which were perched on the coffee table before them. Clayton's glass was already filled.

Clayton then turned slightly in his swivel-rocker chair and stared momentarily directly at Ian, who was seated on the couch alongside Clayton's chair.

"Ian, please excuse the dark glasses. I have an eye condition. I'm supposed to refrain from exposure to bright light. Anyway, it's been said of me ... well ... that I'm a very assuming person. Occasionally too assuming, of that I'm certain. I hope you're a person who enjoys a glass of wine now and then. In this case a fine Chianti."

Ian smiled as he took a sip and replied, "As a matter of fact, I am. And this is delicious. Thank you."

Clayton smiled back as he continued. "Excellent! That said, I feel compelled to say ... well ... Ian, obviously you're a highly-educated man. I noted from your business card that you have a Ph.D. I can only assume in some biological discipline." Ian didn't speak but nodded his head slightly.

Clayton continued, "Still, you seem … How shall I put it? Not unlike one of the local good-ole-boys, so to speak."

Ian smiled and let out a small sigh. After a second's pause, he gave a slight up and down nod, indicating that at least that too wasn't far off the mark, as he silently mused, *He's certainly observant. A useful trait in both our fields.*

"To tell you the truth, Clayton, from where I sit, much the same could be said about you. I read in the back of your book that you received your Masters in English Literature from Emory University. Anyway, there was a time, not long ago, that I probably was pretty full of myself. But things and times change. For instance, I recently had the pleasure to work with and get to know a couple of the most down-to-earth people to be found anywhere. Smart guys. Very smart, competent law enforcement professionals. Something I've actually been experiencing to be the norm, well, regarding smaller communities, anyway. The two guys that I'm talking about … Neither had more than high-school diplomas that I'm aware of. But as far as I'm concerned, the notion of higher education making a man somehow better or smarter … Well, it doesn't. It just opens certain doors, ones that would otherwise remain shut, and makes pursuing various opportunities more plausible or at least a bit easier. Suffice it to say, I've been hanging around the northwest a while now. I guess the local vernacular and maybe my previously California-cated attitudes, especially pertaining towards people that I once would have referred to as hicks or rednecks, has changed somewhat for the better I hope."

Clayton smiled and lifted his glass of wine in salute to that. "Okay, Ian. Correct me if I'm wrong, but I'd bet my Aunt Gladys's Sunday bonnet – well, that is if I had an Aunt Gladys and she wore a bonnet – that you're looking into what's been going on regarding the recent unsavory happenings in Astoria, principally pertaining to the scuttle-butt one hears that there's one or more crazed lunatic serial killers of, shall we say, the nocturnal variety hanging about." Clayton smirked slightly.

Ian noticed for the first time that Clayton's glass of wine seemed, in the dim light of the room, to be just a bit darker than his own. He quickly surmised the effect was only an optical illusion and dismissed it from his mind.

Clayton took another slow sip from his wine glass and continued. "Perhaps, as it has been more than suggested, it can be linked in part, or entirely, to the owner or frequenters of that Astoria nightclub aptly named The Morgue. It's a club that principally attracts, besides just the curious, canine-dentured, undead role players and various persons turned onto the occult. I hear tell that the club's owner, Salizzar, is an Eastern European fellow. I tell you all this, all the while knowing with relative certainty that you already knew at least that much. But of this I am equally certain; you would have no way of knowing that Salizzar not long ago granted me a brief audience much like the one we are having now. It was at his home, at night. He, as you also no doubt already know, lives in Astoria at the once aptly-named Flavel House Museum. I asked him during said interview if I could perhaps stylize a character based loosely on him – and perhaps his club as well. Salizzar seemed genuinely flattered and agreed with certain conditions and limitations. At that time, I was allowed no further into the house than the front sitting room, though I've been promised a tour of the home sometime in the near future. I came away from the short interview, I believe, a little wiser for the visit. In my humble opinion, Salizzar, in the nomenclature of my profession, at the very least assumes quite convincingly the role of a charmingly suave though egocentrically narcissistic, nocturnal by necessity, possibly nefarious, self-proclaimed *nosferatu*. A term I'm confident you're quite familiar with, being a paranormal investigator." Ian nodded his head twice.

Ian enjoyed how Clayton spoke. It was pretty much how he assumed he would, being an author, whose words were the tools of his trade. Ian was slightly surprised at Clayton's presumption that he would have already known much of what Clayton had to say to him so far. Though so far, he was spot on!

Ian was also a very quick study of people. Had already made a couple of presumptions pertaining to Clayton, one being that authors often must be pseudo-investigators when it came to researching their topics. Ian had already come to the conclusion that the man who sat beside him possessed great instinct and powers of observation, much like himself.

Clayton briefly became silent as he momentarily stared out his living room window towards the surf. He then slapped his knee with the palm of his left hand, wineglass still held in his right. "Okay, Ian. Let's cut to the chase. How can a simple author of fiction, a novelist of vampire stories, further educate you? Assuming I'm correct that you're here to perhaps learn a thing or two on the subject, beyond the realm of what one can mistakenly presume to learn by watching humorous 80's genre films like *Fright Night* and *The Lost Boys* and so forth. Make no mistake, those films, among many others, I happen to enjoy a great deal. In those days, selling vampire stories that often ended up as movies was as easy as eating popcorn. Anyway, I suspect that you, being an investigator of the paranormal, may have on occasion seen for yourself at one time or another the line become blurred or erased altogether between the perceived normal and paranormal. I don't believe I need to tell you nor try to convince you, of all people, that there perhaps is truth to what Friedrich Nietzsche once so eloquently stated, 'Battle not with monsters, lest ye become a monster, and if you gaze into the abyss, the abyss gazes also into you.' Pointedly poignant, wouldn't you agree?"

After all that Ian had gone through over the last few weeks back at Harmony Falls, he had to nearly bite his tongue as he mused to himself, *When it comes to supposed fiction turning out to be fact … Clayton, you have no idea what I know to be true.*

After listening to Clayton talk for nearly the last half-hour, Ian's willingness to discuss the topic of vampires, and his investigation, with the man he was with had grown exponentially.

"Clayton, you are correct on every point. Understand, I am counting on your absolute discretion regarding what I'm about to reveal to you. I'm not even certain why I'm going to tell you other than I need some help. And you just might be a very valuable source of information, but I doubt you would be very informative if you don't know at least some of my reasons for asking the questions I'm going to be asking. So here goes. I am conducting a private investigation very loosely in conjunction with the Astoria Police Department. All strictly on the down low. I would be instantly disavowed by them and left dangling in the wind if my name was even associated as such. At this point, my investigation is principally targeted at Salizzar and his nightclub. No surprise there. But please understand, what I'm about to ask or tell you must remain strictly confidential if I'm to have any success. And perhaps remain healthy, if you get my meaning."

Clayton smiled. "Yes. Well, Ian, You can rest assured that I will not discuss your activities with anyone. That is, with one possible exception. But let me hear your questions before I decide if that might be a good idea or not. I will, if I can, assist you with what I understand on the subject."

Ian had to suppress his instant curiosity to ask Clayton whom he was referring to. But he decided for the time being to remain silent about it.

"Clayton, I have heard that there are supposedly different types of vampires. Looking past for the moment the presumption that it's all fiction, that is, other than role players and crazies."

Clayton took a sip from his wine glass then replied, "Yes, well, there are ..." Clayton cleared his throat then continued. "Basically, in my opinion, they can all be pretty much placed into four categories." Obviously having anticipated this question, Clayton reached into the pocket of his golf-style cardigan sweater. He retrieved a sheet of paper that had a list typed on it. Without saying another word, Clayton handed the sheet of paper to Ian and gave him sufficient time to read its contents.

1) Vampire – Psychic ... (rubbish).

2) Vampire – Role-players ... (real).

3) Vampire - Renfield's syndrome/Porphyria - mental/physical illness ... (extremely rare, though real).

4) Vampire – Sanquinarians ... (?)

Before Ian could comment on the list he'd just read, Clayton commenced speaking again. "Ian, as you know, vampires in lore as well as in reality in one form or another exist throughout the world."

Ian interjected, "You're speaking of creatures like vampire bats and insects like mosquitos and fleas and such, I presume?"

Clayton grinned impishly. "Quite right. But of course, in essence we're talking about something much different when we make the quantum leap to any sort of humanoid vampire."

Ian paused, then began his questions, paper in hand. "What's meant by a Psychic Vampire?"

Clayton sat back deep into his chair. "A Psychic Vampire is a person who believes they have the power to psychically, parasitically, draw from a human target, or donor, their energy. Their life force. This of course, like I wrote on that list you're holding, in my opinion is utter rubbish."

Ian nodded his head in agreement. "Okay. I'd say the role players ... Well, that pretty much is self-explanatory. I assume some do it just for fun and some take it more seriously. Some get into that self-mutilation bit by cutting their wrists and arms with razor-blades and drink a bit of blood from a donor. Stuff like that?"

Clayton nodded slowly. Ian continued, "Then that takes us to the mentally ill. That I get. I've read of things like Renfield Syndrome, taken of course from the character Renfield from Bram Stoker's novel *Dracula*. It refers to someone who, due to some form of schizophrenia, believes whole-heartedly that he or she is a vampire. But you have here physically ill listed as well?"

Clayton interjected, "Ian, have you ever heard of a disease called Porphyria?"

"No," Ian replied without hesitation.

Clayton let out a small sigh before continuing. "Well, without delving into a medical explanation beyond my depth, Porphyria is, in essence, a disease that can cause many of the symptoms which have been classically associated with vampirism. Blood lust. Aversion to sunlight. Some physical changes as well, like increased hair and fingernail growth. Even an aversion to strong scents from flora like, say, garlic. I subscribe to the theory shared by many scientists regarding a very plausible link in this disease to some vampiric conditions both mentally and physically. Some blood and flesh-coveting mass murderers have been diagnosed as suffering from Porphyria."

Ian didn't question that further. It sounded perfectly plausible – and explained some very serious human-vampiric phenomena. He took a deep breath. "Okay, then that takes us to number four, where I see you wrote a question mark. My guess is that the prior three types of vampires pale by comparison. No pun intended." Both men laughed.

"Is that where you place Salizzar? In the number four question

74

mark category?" Ian asked with nervous anticipation.

Clayton scooted forward in his chair. He looked Ian square in the eyes, then all at once, he became as serious as a heart attack when he answered, "Yes."

Ian once again took a deep breath before continuing, "If that's true on any level, then I'm going to need some help."

"Ian, based on years of research on the topic of vampires, werewolves, and all manner of things that go bump in the night, so to speak, I believe in some rare instances there may be a more demonic explanation far beyond anything modern science is willing to accept. Possibly tracing its roots all the way back to the Garden of Eden, if you believe your Bible stories. I've come to somewhat subscribe to the notion mentioned in Jewish mythology that Adam had a wife named Lilith, who preceded his wife of mention in the Bible, Eve. Lilith was cursed by God because she thought herself Adam's equal, refusing to be subservient to him. She further rebelled and defied God's law by procreating with the archangel Samael. Satan. And later, having been cast aside by Satan, she procreated with Carnivean, a much lesser demon. Whereby creating two related yet distinctly separate species of immortal nephilim, the spawn of devils, resulting in her being condemned by God and transformed from human into the first female demon. Lilith is revered by her followers as The Unholy Mother, the antithesis to the Holy Mother Mary to Christians. Her procreations created a sub-species of human-demon hybrids, if you will. Vampiric blood-lusting, soul-gathering, demon spawn of Satan, and lycanthropic, cannibalistically-carnivorous, demon spawns of Carnivean. Whose supernatural gifts, or curses, depending on your point of view, vary. But they share one commonality; their powers all tend to grow stronger, and in some cases more diverse, the longer they live, which for some could amount to be a very long time indeed. But that's all topic for discussion another time. Oh, but one more thing, dear Ian. Never invite or accept an invitation to enter any room from such a creature. It has been said, and I speak of course of Carpathian and European gypsy folklore, that should you invite such an entity into your domicile or willfully accept such an invitation to enter theirs, that that would enhance their influence over you, leaving you potentially powerless against them. Or at the very least, you would be more vulnerable than you would be otherwise to their bloodlust-driven cravings!"

Ian had a hard time not telling Clayton right then and there what he had personally encountered. That he knew too well of the existence and truth to at least one such supposed myth regarding demonically-contrived, shape-shifting creatures of the night. But rather than talk about that now, if ever, Ian decided to change the subject.

"Clayton. You mentioned earlier that there might be someone you'd discuss this with. To whom were you referring, and why?"

Clayton glanced out the window for an instant, then looked back at Ian. "Ian, I did some checking on the computer about you. I was genuinely sorry to read of your wife and daughter's tragic passing."

Ian smiled slightly as he nodded his appreciation for the sentiment. *So much for establishing any level of anonymity or cover. Maybe I should have given Clayton an alias when I first met him? Of course it makes sense that he would have checked me out, especially after inviting me to his home and all. Well, too late now. I guess I've got to trust someone besides Officer Ned Parker.*

Clayton continued, "You've probably noticed by looking around my home that it's sadly lacking any female touch. My ex-wife left me a few years back when the money-train in the form of royalty checks stopped arriving to this station. But I do still have one family member who lives on the peninsula here. My deceased brother's adopted daughter, Zoey. She lives with her friend, Todd, in downtown Long

Beach. They own a small hairstyling salon and live in a two-bedroom apartment upstairs. I made the point to say two bedroom so you'd understand that Todd … is … well, other than them being just friends, women aren't his cup of tea, so to speak. Anyway, Zoey … She just might be very resourceful, especially regarding helping you to not look so … How should I put it? Provincially conventional."

Ian silently agreed with Clayton's idea. *A hairstylist would be perfect for helping me effect the visual-demeanor of a Goth clubber.*

Ian had in fact noticed that Clayton's house was furnished more like that of a man-cave than a place shared by a woman. Lots of nautical furnishings. Items like a beautiful ship's wheel above the fireplace. Dark brown leather couch with matching loveseat, and Lazy-boy rocker-recliner. Some beautiful antique sea-chests. It was true, the home was obviously lacking anything even remotely feminine on the walls, tabletops, or anywhere about the place.

Clayton continued, "Though she's young, twenty-seven, she's as smart as they come. But well, let's just say she's been around the block and back a few times if you know what I mean. She speaks her mind, I can tell you that. A real no-holds-barred free spirit, that one. Regardless, if willing, I think she could be of some real help to you. Anyway, she's got the look. Like I said, she's a hairstylist. Well that, and she's a massage therapist as well. You know the look. Nearly anorexic with arms covered with Asian-stylized tattoos. Multiple piercings. Short, jet-black, cropped, red-streaked hair. Say, Ian, while I'm thinking of it, you should probably stop using your real name. Being a writer, might I suggest you stay with your first name and only change your last? How about Ian McBride? Most of the time, people only mention first names. You won't be apt to screw that up. And the last name McBride is also believable. It keeps with your ancestral roots and facial bone structure."

Ian smiled and nodded his head in agreement, then replied, "You of course have my permission to contact your niece on my behalf. And the name ... McBride ... I like it. Tell her that's my name. Tell her ... Tell her that I'm an ex-cop turned private investigator or something like that, and that I was hired by the family of one of the missing persons regarding what's been going on over in Astoria. I'm sure she's heard about it. Go ahead if you want and tell her I'm interested in checking out Salizzar and his nightclub. That too should come as little surprise. That's all close enough to the truth. I appreciate you being so helpful and informative."

"Ian, I am happy to help you all that I can, but understand I do this not totally unselfishly. I suspect this is not your first rodeo when it comes to this sort of thing. I also expect there is a great book in all this. I'm hopeful that you will graciously allow me to write it. Of course, names and locations will be changed to protect the living." Ian noticed a sly, impish grin on Clayton's face. Ian then grinned himself as he nodded his agreement.

Ian's head was swimming as he tried to digest all that Clayton had told him. But for the moment, all that he could think of without further deliberation had been said, asked, and answered. This had been a very successful first meeting. Ian stood up, leaned over slightly, and shook hands with his host. "Clayton, I can't thank you enough for all your insights. And I'd be honored for you to use ... to base some of your works on my exploits, for lack of a better word, as catalysts for your tales of fiction." Ian found it even more noticeable than before that Clayton had an unusually cold, clammy grip.

Clayton remained seated. He began to stare blankly out the front window, off towards the horizon and the surf beyond.

"Well, Clayton, you've got my business card with my cell phone number. You or your niece Zoey can call or text me any time. The sooner the better. Um, well, I'll just see myself out. Thanks again."

As Ian began to leave, Clayton continued staring out the window, not saying anything further. But just before Ian opened the front door, Clayton blurted out, "Take great caution, Ian, of whom you accept invitation to enter of your own free will."

CHAPTER 9
Alliance (II)

Ian drove straight back to Oscar's on the Ocean. When he opened the door to his trailer, Scout was as glad to see him as he was to see Scout. "Hiya boy, miss me?" Scout's tail was wagging wildly as he barked three times.

Ian kicked off his shoes as he glanced over at his travel clock on the shelf. It was 4:37 p.m. He sat down in his small, swivel recliner chair that was bolted to the floor. It was one of the few aftermarket additions he'd purchased and had installed around a year ago from an RV dealership in Coos Bay, Oregon. Ian put his feet up onto the small, built-in dining table. He then slipped on his reading glasses, opened his recently-autographed book, and began to read the prologue.

Not ten minutes into his reading, Ian's cell phone began chiming. He retrieved his phone from his shirt pocket. "Hello. Yes, I recognize your voice. Mention no names, no specifics. Okay. Right, I understand. Yeah, I've been doing some groundwork. Yeah, it's progressing." Ian paused to catch his breath and to hear more before replying, "Yeah, okay. Right, tomorrow at 10:00 a.m. will work. See you th—" Ned had already hung up his phone before Ian could finish his sentence.

Ian wondered for a moment why Ned needed to see him again so soon. But he quickly let it go and began once again reading his book.

After twenty pages, Ian began to get bleary-eyed. Moments later, he was snoring.

It was 5:45 p.m. and very dark out when Ian's cell phone began chiming once again, waking him from deep sleep.

Ian answered his phone. "Yeah, this is Ian. Um, hi, Clayton." He was fighting back yawning and desperately trying to clear his head as he listened.

"Ian, I hate to ask you to drive all the way back here, but my niece is gonna be here in a little over an hour. She gets off work at 6:00 p.m. I'd like to have a little more face-time with you before she arrives. I haven't told her anything other than I'm going to order pizza. She's coming for dinner. Ian, what kind of pizza do you like? Assuming you like pizza."

Ian replied, "Uh, yeah . Pizza sounds good!"

"What kind to you prefer?"

Ian, still a little groggy, cleared his head before answering. "Um, what kind? I pretty much like any kind. But since you asked, how about something with sausage and mushrooms and some olives and pepperoni?"

Clayton fired back, "Perfect! 'The Combination'. That's our favorite. I'll order a couple of them. I invite her over to visit in the evening now and again. I'm not much of a cook, so usually we either go out for dinner or order pizza or Chinese take-out to be delivered. I think she takes me up on it mainly because she appreciates a free meal more than my company." Clayton laughed just a little.

Ian interjected, "Clayton, I'll get cleaned up a bit and come over as soon as … I can be there in around a half hour. Thanks." After the call was concluded, Ian set his phone down on the table that had previously held his feet.

Ian looked over at Scout, "How about that, boy? Things are

beginning to move fast now. Hopefully not too fast."

Still feeling a tiny bit hazy from his interrupted nap, Ian left Scout in the trailer and walked over to the shower house. The park was more than adequately lit by a handful of well–positioned, pole-mounted flood lights, eliminating the need to carry a flashlight. As Ian stood at the sink washing his hands, he began to splash a little water on his face. As he looked up from the sink, Ian began staring into the mirror, which somehow sparked an unconscious mental metaphor, triggering his mind into reflection. He began running back over what he'd discussed just hours ago with Clayton, closely examining point by point the details of their conversation, trying to concisely formulate what questions he still might have for Clayton and which ones he'd already asked, but felt were not fully expounded upon.

Now somewhat refreshed and certainly more awake, Ian walked briskly back to his trailer.

"Scout, I've got a feeling you're not gonna like this, but I've got to leave you here one more time. I'm going back to see Clayton and to meet his niece. She might be able to help with …" Ian began laughing at himself. He just noticed that he talked to Scout as if he were more human than dog. Ian further mused to himself on the subject as he gazed affectionately into the eyes of his best friend. *You do understand, don't ya, fella?* At that very instant, Scout barked once and began wagging his tail.

Suddenly surprised by the timing of Scout's barks, Ian thought to himself, *Jesus. Bark once for yes and twice for no, won't ya? Ha.*

Ian changed into a nearly clean pair of jeans and an equally almost clean blue flannel shirt. The fresh socks and underwear he'd put on were the last ones he had.

"Scout, we're gonna have to seek out a Laundromat, and I mean soon."

Ian then put on his fleece-lined denim jacket and grabbed his wallet and car keys. Before exiting the trailer, he checked to see that Scout still had plenty of dog food and water.

Just as Ian was getting into his Jeep, his phone began buzzing. Not the sound of an incoming call but that of an incoming text message. Ian looked at his phone and scrolled to new messages.

CAUTION!!! *Regardless of bodies in river eaten by sharks or no – F.B.I. suspects black market ring – blood products/organ trafficking (drugs 2 likely). Bodies exsanguinated + missing organs: heart, liver, kidneys = sophisticated organization.*

After reading Ned's text, Ian thought to himself, *Holy shit. I'm so in over my head. I wish Charlie was here. I'm gonna need help.*

Ian made the drive north up the peninsula in good time, but arrived a little later than he'd planned. Clayton was standing on the front porch with his cane in his left hand and a lit cigarette in his right as Ian pulled his Jeep into the driveway and turned his ignition and headlights off. Ian climbed out of his Jeep and walked up to Clayton, who flicked the remains of his cigarette into a small, sand-filled bucket adjacent to his front door. Both men smiled at each other and cordially shook hands.

"Ian, so good of you to return on such short notice. I just decided to step outside for a smoke. I deplore the smell in my house. All information points to the seemingly undeniable fact that those things will eventually kill me. I keep asking myself ... when?" Clayton and Ian both laughed.

Clayton continued, "The young man who delivers for the pizza parlor said he'd be here, well, by now." He glanced at his watch and frowned slightly as he spoke. "I thought I'd meet that delivery boy out here on the porch on his terms rather than invite him in on mine. Good delivery boys are so hard to replace nowadays." Clayton suddenly laughed as though what he'd just said was very funny. Ian also laughed in response but thought to himself, *I don't get it.*

It was a particularly chilly evening, and it had begun to rain a little. "Well, let's go inside Ian, before you catch your … death." Clayton said as he glanced up at the sky. Without further hesitation, he headed towards his front door as he exclaimed, "That pizza boy's not going to receive much of a gratuity if he doesn't happen along shortly."

Once seated inside the house, Clayton in his usual chair and Ian back on the couch, Clayton took a deep breath then let out the air from his lungs with equal enthusiasm before he spoke. "Ian, I did a little more Googling regarding your background. Seems you are somewhat re-defining your previous vocation of cryptozoologist." Ian smiled and nodded his head once.

Clayton slapped, then rubbed his knees once with his hands as he spoke, "That's good. A man needs to change with the times. I've tried changing many times. I hear that now more than perhaps ever in the last century, a man needs to reinvent himself, evolve as it were … often time and again, lest we lose our edge, our very relevance. I often fear that my commitment to not sell-out, some would say, is fruitlessly stubborn. And by some, I mean my literary agent and numerous publishing houses. Anyway, my quite possibly self-destructive commitment to preserve the darker side of horror fiction could ultimately make me as obsolete as the video cassette recorder that was left in the wake of always-evolving video technologies."

Ian smiled as he nodded slowly in total understanding. He had often worried about much the same thing. He understood too well the dreaded fear of becoming hopelessly irrelevant, inconsequential, obsolete.

"Well, Ian, that's a worry you need not share with the likes of me. And perhaps mine is not founded either? That is, beyond the current, hopefully short-lived literary fad of sparkly-vampire fodder. The world may think it wants to read about sexy pseudo-monsters, ones we need not fear much more than perhaps catching a cold or a venereal disease. The truth is, I believe that most humans have an inherent need to have the hell scared right out of them. A nice thought, anyway. Such basic fear of the unknown lets many, I understand, feel truly alive. That they're not just going through the motions of living out their bleak, tasteless existence. It's a good thing humans have an inherent fear of the dark, Ian. It's good to fear what may be lurking in the closet or under one's bed, for darkness abides when the lights go out."

Clayton took a deep breath, then continued, "Parents are wrong, Ian. When they tell their children there's no reason to fear the dark. It's that basic, instinctual fear that keeps most humans alive. There is much darkness in the world, Ian. Great and terrible darkness. Dark forces more cunning and malevolent than all of the depraved lunatics akin to the likes of Ted Bundy, Jeffrey Dahmer, or Charles Manson combined. Darkness far beyond the scope of any fiction writer's feeble attempts to depict ... including myself of course."

Ian was beginning to get a little uncomfortable. Clayton was starting to get a bit …way out there.

"Ian, your recent vocational paradigm shift, so to speak, couldn't be more necessary or timely. Given the obvious constraints of traditional law enforcement, the world will always need its Van Helsings. Its monster hunters." Clayton said with a sly grin on his face.

Ian decided to change the subject to hopefully reel Clayton back in to the topic at hand. "Clayton, if you don't mind, I have some more questions I'd like to ask before your niece gets here."

Ian wondered for a brief moment if he should go on. But he decided to throw caution to the wind. "Clayton, not long ago, I personally experienced something … something that, to the best of my understanding, could only be explained by what you described this afternoon as being caused, or created, by some form of demonic phenomena. I'm not at liberty to discuss what I'm referring to any further at this time. But suffice it to say that I'm predisposed to accept much more than most at face value unless proven otherwise." Clayton gave Ian a look that Ian regarded as one of genuine intrigue.

"Clayton, unless I grossly misread you, you really believe what you were telling me earlier today. I mean, you really believe beyond it being just the genre that you write about in your stories." Clayton raised his eyebrows but didn't say a word. Ian continued, "Well, again, unless I'm way off the mark. Under that assumption, in your opinion, what are the typical characteristics, or 'powers', for lack of a better term, that they – your vampire type fours – possess? I mean, aside from what we've all seen in movies or read in books." Clayton once again lifted his eyebrows and started to speak, but he was instantly interrupted by Ian. "And besides powers and such, exactly what in your opinion would it take to destroy such a creature, supposing for a moment that they actually exist?"

A huge smile suddenly engulfed Clayton's face. Ian immediately surmised that Clayton was about to open up and speak of things that most people would automatically discount as utterly ridiculous. And that he was deeply pleased by the opportunity –perhaps due to a conscious or unconscious need to really open up without the threat of men in white jackets showing up at his doorstep wanting to fit him with a straight jacket and feed him applesauce from a tiny white Dixie cup, clandestinely containing a double dose of Thorazine.

"Like minds sharing the same madness. Folie à deux, Ian. Folie à deux."

Upon hearing Clayton speak that phrase, Ian immediately experienced an intense episode of déjà vu. He couldn't remember who'd spoken that phrase the last time he'd heard it, as it referred to a shared psychosis or delusion. It might have been Charlie Redtail, or it could have even been uttered by himself as a descriptive phrase regarding the situation he and Charlie had found themselves in. An attempt to colorfully reference the large French population that lived in and around Harmony Falls. Either way, Ian knew this much for certain. If that was where he'd last heard that phrase, it just showed how crazy he and Charlie had been to attempt to understand and ultimately deal with exactly who, or rather what, Jean-Chastel Gevaudan was.

"Okay, Ian. I'm going to tell you something I probably wouldn't tell another living soul, but I think you of all people just might believe, at least in part. I say 'part' because much of what I'm going to tell you is based on research, interviews, and a lot of my own conjecture, connecting the dots as it were, which can be very subjective. Subject to each person's interpretations of what are pseudo-facts at best."

Clayton was right about Ian. When it came to any sermon regarding the supposed supernatural, Clayton was preaching to an experienced choir boy.

"Ian, we probably don't have much time before Zoey gets here. So I'm going to cut right to the chase. When it comes to the very small percentage of what I've called class or type four vampires, the real deal as you so aptly put it, this is what I've surmised from many years of study on the subject."

Clayton adjusted himself in his chair. He leaned forward just a bit as he took a deep breath in preparation for his forthcoming verbal dissertation. To just about anyone other than Ian, it would prove itself as a thesis more than adequately deserving of achieving an advanced degree from the likes of the prestigious New York Institution commonly known as Bellevue.

"Ian, most of my research and subsequent fiction writing has been centered around villainous vampires. That much you know. I have dabbled with lycanthropic creature characters in some of my stories as well. But for now, let's stay on the topic of blood suckers of the fourth kind." Ian smiled and nodded in agreement. He was ready to hear that up is down and black is white.

"Okay, Ian. Here goes. I believe, and again, I'm not talking about the thousands of Gothic life-style or vampiric role players. I believe that there is a relatively small sub-culture of true sanguinarians that comprise various covens around the world. Most don't look like you'd expect them to. Not like Salizzar and his followers, who dress very stereotypically. Many real vampires, ancients anyway, are captains of industry, CEOs of major corporations, and so forth. You would never guess them to be vampires. They keep that aspect a very closely-guarded secret. They can of course live for a very long time. And in doing so, many have amassed vast fortunes. Salizzar is the rare exception. He chooses to live flamboyantly as a stereotypical gothic vampire club owner. Nobody would ever believe that he actually is what he wants everyone to think he is merely portraying. So he effectively hides in plain sight and rubs our collective noses in it."

Clayton paused to catch his breath and collect his thoughts. Ian pondered over what Clayton had just said. *Salizzar hides in plain sight. Why not? Clayton's right. Nobody would ever be the wiser. Well, almost nobody.*

"Ian, you asked, or at least inferred to me, the question: what separates Hollywood from reality when it comes to type fours? What their powers are and how they can be destroyed. This is what I've come up with. Now granted, my suppositions on the subject are based, of course, on much stereotypical folklore, but they are also riddled with theories of my own." Ian was all ears, hanging on Clayton's every word.

"I've come up with a phrase that I'm using in the book that I'm currently working on that I've titled *Red Tide*. One that describes some of their beyond natural abilities. The Unholy Power of Three."

Clayton once again paused. This time mainly to see if Ian was following him. Ian motioned for him to continue.

"The Unholy Power of Three. I've derived that phrase from the antithesis of the Holy Trinity. I've come to believe that a vampire of some seasoning has about the strength of three men. They can move, run, jump, and so on around three times greater than that of any top athlete. All of their senses are enhanced to a factor of three above any human being. They also emit some kind of strong pheromones that help make them nearly hypnotically attractive beyond their natural appearance, which is usually already attractive. You see, generally speaking, vampires, if choosing to turn a human into one of their own, often target attractive people. I'm sure you can imagine attractive males and females naturally tend to make very successful hunters, so to speak."

Ian nodded. Clayton paused for a brief moment to re-adjust himself in his chair before he continued. "Supernatural attraction, along with a ravenous lust for human blood, added with a demonic desire to destroy souls, makes them extremely effective as predators of the human race. I believe their life-span, left unaffected by intervention, could be as much as or even greater than three times three … times three … centuries. Rounded up … Ian, that's knocking on the door of three thousand years, or thereabouts. Of course, most are nowhere near that ancient. I'd guess that most are several hundred years old. Or in the case of the relatively recent, newly turned, not very old at all … their gifts, or powers, would be much more limited."

Ian let out a sigh and began slowly shaking his head side to side, an unconscious reaction to the possibility of any or all of it.

Clayton acknowledged Ian's astonishment. "I know. It bends my mind too just thinking about it. But freak accidents and over the last few centuries the likes of witch hunters, exorcists, and even vampire hunters have reduced their numbers."

Somehow, hearing about some vampires being caught and exterminated by witch hunters was almost comforting to Ian. If it was true, it helped dispel his understanding of the history of places like Salem, Massachusetts, that all of the witch-trials never accomplished anything other than torturing and murdering the innocent.

Clayton continued, "They have always desired that their numbers be relatively few by comparison to humans. This helps protect their anonymity as well as protect over-grazing their food supply."

Clayton paused to see if Ian was staying with him. Not only was Ian keeping up, his intrigue was nearly becoming fever pitched. Ian couldn't help himself from interjecting a quick question that had been burning in his mind ever since Clayton had begun speaking on the present topic. "Clayton, are they … type fours … really literally nosferatu, the undead?"

"Now that's an excellent question, Ian … and nice word usage, 'nosferatu'. No. Not really. Not literally, anyway. They are alive just assuredly as I am. But as you can imagine of a species that can live for hundreds if not thousands of years, their metabolism is much slower than that of humans, creating the illusion of no breath, no heartbeat, and no pulse. As you know, they feast by drinking blood, and of course in doing so, one must assume eventually they must urinate and defecate, albeit not frequently by human measure. I believe when they feast, they gorge. But if necessary, they can go a long time without sustenance much like the serpent."

Ian looked Clayton directly in his eyes, and with a tone to his voice that undoubtedly let Clayton know in no uncertain terms that he was dead serious, he fired off another question.

"All right, Clayton. Under the assumption that you are even half-right on your theories, how would a person …"

Clayton interrupted, "How would a person dispatch such a formidable demonic creature?"

Ian replied without hesitation, "Yes."

Clayton cleared his throat. "Of this much I'm confident. Total incineration – fire – cleanses and purifies just about anything. Decapitation is also a sure bet. And there's always the old standby though overplayed by Hollywood, but in this case, it holds true: total destruction of the heart as in the plunging of a stake directly through it, or some other instantaneous obliteration of the creature's heart."

At hearing that, Ian had to ask, "Does it need to be a wooden stake like in the movies?"

Clayton answered quickly, "It may be devised of any strong substance: Wood, metal, or plastic for that matter. Just as long as it's sufficiently driven through the heart to instantly and utterly destroy it. Or in the case of life in the twenty-first century, I should imagine that any sufficiently large caliber bullet, especially if fired repeatedly directly into the heart, should affect the same result. But Ian, mind you, you heard me say words like instantly and utterly. I use these words not lightly because another thing that I am convinced of is that true vampires are tough buggers to eliminate. If an absolutely vital organ is not totally, instantly destroyed, they will regenerate in their sleep in …"

Ian interrupted Clayton. "Don't tell me. Three days just like Jesus regarding the holy resurrection."

Clayton smiled. "That's right, Ian. Now, you're getting it. That would be the time it takes for total regeneration of a near-fatal wound. Less than near fatal wounds heal at a much, much faster rate depending on the severity of the wound inflicted. Simple flesh wounds and bruises may heal nearly instantaneously depending upon the age and power of the particular vampire, which works backwards to normal nature. The older the vampire, the faster it heals and the more difficult to kill. But my research does point to the suggestion that certain physical laws or universal constants apply even when dealing with the demonic supernatural of even the most powerful persuasion. As an example, they can't just defy gravity and simply up and fly away. That is, unless they could in fact shape-shift into a creature of flight like, say, a bat or a swarm of locusts. And I suspect ancient vampires of millennia ago may have had such abilities, giving birth to legends of dragons and the like. As you know, myths and legends generally have some foundation based in fact. But if there is any truth to the extreme ancients having the power of shape-shifting, it probably keeps that they could only change into the foulest of creatures. It is unlikely in the extreme that any such beings could have survived to the present."

Ian pondered to himself, *Oh ... shape-shifters exist.* He'd been painfully educated on that subject back at Harmony Falls. But at least for now, he was keeping that knowledge to himself.

Due to Clayton unselfishly sharing information and his theories, Ian was becoming bolder with his questions. "Clayton, what about sunlight? Will that destroy them?"

Clayton smiled slightly as he shook his head. "No, Ian. Not likely. But just as I listed as associated with type threes, type fours also suffer severe allergic reactions to direct sunlight and any form of ultraviolet light for that matter. But severely sunburned skin or burnt retinas will not kill them. Well, unless I suppose they were out on a sunny day in July from say sun-up till sun-down. Suffice it to say, unlike what you've no doubt seen in movies, that would not be a practical way to attempt to dispatch one. The ultraviolet exposure would have to be a very intense, protracted exposure to be potentially life-threatening to them. Anyway, no. They will not blow up or spontaneously burst into flames. Nor will sunlight cause their skin to sparkle like diamonds, whereby exposing them to the world for what they are, as one of my more romantically-inclined literary contemporaries depicted in her sickeningly-sweet series of teen and female-targeted novels."

Ian decided before Clayton's last rant headed them off course that he'd fire a short burst of more questions. "How about crosses? Uh, you know, crucifixes. And holy water? What about mirrors and having to rest in coffins or boxes filled with their native soil, garlic and … or a … Oh yeah, and silver and wolfsbane. Or was that just for werewolves?"

Clayton cracked a grin as he quickly interjected, "Know something of werewolves, do you?" Ian didn't answer.

Clayton gazed for a moment out the window at the ocean. But within mere moments, he returned his focus to Ian and began replying to Ian's questions with composure and congeniality.

"Being they are at least blood-connected to descendants of demonic copulations, I should think that vampires do have an inherent aversion to all things of Judeo-Christian symbolism. Likely to relics and artifacts from other religions that speak of one God as well. But I am certain that they can, if need be, tolerate them. One would not simply turn away and run at the sight of a crucifix, and a vampire I'm also certain will only be made wet if doused with holy water. The vampire may not like such things, but if you find yourself its target of revenge or potential food, I wouldn't place my faith in such trinkets and blessings. As for silver, werewolves, from all the information I've collected, are severely allergic to it, but we are talking about vampires. Silver and things such as mere plants like garlic and wolfsbane used successfully to repel or destroy a vampire are utter, folkloric nonsense. I should think that due to their own vanity, vampires would like mirrors and even silver. Anything that offers a reflective surface that allows them to gaze upon their ageless selves." Ian nodded once in acknowledgment that Clayton's theories at least seemed to follow a semblance of logic.

Clayton continued. "Now, the answer to your next question is a resounding yes. If I've guessed correctly to where your next follow-up question would have led. Of course, they will cast a reflection in a mirror or any reflective surface. Now, to address if vampires must sleep in any form of a coffin or box or seek out dark, dank surroundings that, say, mimic that of a grave or graveyard or must rest upon terra firma of their homeland. Stuff and nonsense, rubbish that is, unless they have a particular proclivity to maintain themselves as a damp, musty, severely-soiled, claustrophobic vampire. A room sufficiently void of sunlight is all they need. Well that ... and a comfortable mattress is generally desirable ... one would assume."

Ian and Clayton both smiled. Ian chuckled just a bit as he shook his head back and forth at Clayton's levity. He was beginning to run out of questions, but then primarily due to his recent experience back at Harmony Falls, Ian blurted out, "What about shape-shifting into bats or wolves or into mist? You know, like ..."

Clayton nodded his head. "Like Dracula? Well, Ian, I thought I covered that, but ... and here is where I'm probably going to lose you ... because I believe in the possibility of all of those powers. Like I mentioned before, shape-shifting and perhaps even more powers than we've discussed were possibly true at one time with the ancient, pure-blood, nephilim vampires. But thankfully, I believe that all or at least most of those types of powers have been lost over time due to blood-line dissemination. As an example, say two thousand years ago a vampire might have been a quarter or maybe even a half-blood demon spawn. But after hundreds of years of countless copulations by his decedents, well, you see where I'm going with this theory. Most vampires for the last few hundred years, and especially those created in or near present time, are only fractionally of demonic bloodline and therefore have lost many of the more spectacular abilities. And yet at least one aspect of vampirism remains as it has always been in literature, film, and in fact: the blood is the life."

Ian interjected, "Clayton, you said earlier something about them limiting their numbers. How is that possible if by being bitten, a person transforms into …" Clayton held up his right hand, signaling to Ian that he needn't go further down that path.

"Humans are food to them. As such, if bitten by a vampire, one does not just change into one of them. If that were the case, humans over a few centuries would have all become vampires, causing the extinction of both the human race as well as vampires. No, you have to be chosen by a vampire and specifically turned. No surprise. It takes being bitten and not sucked dry three times. Again, the power of three. This must occur over a span not to exceed three consecutive, or maybe I should have said 'con-suck-utive', days." Clayton grinned impishly as he delivered that last line. Ian chuckled as he slowly shook his head.

"Ian, this is important to remember. Vampires do typically sleep during the day, but they can go about their business, so to speak, during the day if they so choose. They tend to only feed at night though they can be equally deadly day or night. Again, they can sleep in any dark place. Though some, like Salizzar, I would expect do sleep in coffins mainly out of theatrics."

"Oh yeah … right." Ian said, feeling almost silly.

"Ian, based on my research, this is my theory about humans being turned into vampires or being put under their control. The first and second bites affect certain mental and physical changes to the victim or volunteer. The degree of the stages of change differ somewhat with each

95

individual infected. And the initial depth of effects from the infection can vary depending upon how ancient the vampire was that initiated the biting. Typically, a person's will remains mainly their own post-first bite. But after being bitten a second time, the lust for blood begins to become more uncontrollable. There can even become a psychic connection or link that develops between vampire and their familiar. Ian, I'm confident in your field you've heard of the term 'familiar' as used in the context that I just did?" Ian nodded.

Clayton continued, "Besides being somewhat hypnotized at the time of the attacks, it still is an incredibly painful process each time one is bitten. What occurs after being bitten thrice as best I can describe to my understanding, is like an amalgamation of the perfect infection with aspects of demonic possession. At face value, it can be very seductive. It seems more blessing than curse with the offering of perfect health and near immortality. But besides turning you into a charming (when desired), overtly attractive, homicidal monster, one that has an insatiable lust for human blood, it also unfortunately carries the terrible price of losing one's soul. Of that much, I'm certain."

Ian started thinking about Clayton's wine earlier, how it appeared to him to be too viscous, as he mused over a little theory he was beginning to develop of his own, Ian mused. *Gives new meaning to, "Once bitten, twice shy," and "Three's a charm."* Ian's concentration was suddenly interrupted by the doorbell.

Clayton got up from his chair and picked up his cane. He walked to the front door. It was the young pizza delivery man. He was nearly out of breath and blurted out, "I'm real sorry about being late with your delivery, Mister Collins. I had a flat tire on the way and had to change it to the little doughnut spare." The young man pointed to his car in the driveway.

Clayton smiled and replied, "No harm, no foul, Tim. Nothing

that a microwave can't reheat if need be. Glad you weren't injured." Clayton thanked him for getting there as soon as he could given the circumstances. Clayton paid for the two pizzas plus a tip sizeable enough to generate a smile on the young man's face.

Tim replied, "Sweet. Thanks, Mister Collins. See ya next time."

Clayton turned and went back into the house, pizzas in hand, and set them down on the dining room table. "Ian, if you don't mind, let us wait a few more minutes. I'm sure that niece of mine will be along shortly. She's typically a bit more than fashionably late."

Ian smiled. "Certainly. No problem!"

Clayton went back over to his favorite chair and sat down. "Say, Ian, there's one thing you haven't yet asked me about type fours that surprises me."

"Yeah? What's that?" Ian said with a puzzled look on his face. He thought they'd pretty much covered everything.

"You never asked me about fangs!" Clayton said very matter-of-factly.

Ian lifted his eyebrows as he slowly nodded.

Clayton continued, "When they feed, one of the seven seals, the seven faces of Samael – Satan – is unveiled. Demonic, with fangs and all."

Ian couldn't hold back his sixty-four-dollar question any further. "Clayton, it seems pretty clear that you've got more than just cursory research knowledge about all of this. You've been bitten by Salizzar, haven't you?"

Suddenly, the doorbell began ringing once again. Clayton flashed a sly grin as he replied, "Bitten by Salizzar? Ridiculous. Ah, saved by the bell!" Clayton got up from his chair, walked over, and opened his front door.

"Hiya, Unc. Sorry I'm late. I had to stay a little longer at the shop than expected. Problems with a lady's perm. Where's your Mercedes? Did you pick yourself up an older Jeep station wagon for four-wheeling out on the beach?"

Clayton smiled at his niece. "No. The Jeep's not mine. My car's in the garage."

Zoey walked right past Clayton into the house. She immediately spotted Ian seated on the couch as she blurted out, "Oh, I didn't know you had company."

Ian spoke up, "The old Jeep's mine."

Just steps behind his niece, Clayton too entered the living room. "Not to worry, Zoey. Ian over there, he's why I invited you over this evening. Well, he's not the only reason." Clayton chuckled. Zoey crossed the living room over to the couch. She immediately sat herself on the opposite end from Ian.

Clayton made his way back to his chair and plopped down into it as he spoke. "Well, now, introductions are in order."

Ian twisted slightly to his left so he could better see who he was about to be introduced to.

"Ian, this is my niece, Zoey. Zoey, dear, this is Ian. Ian McBride. I met him yesterday at the book signing. Ian's a private investigator whose services have been contracted by a family of one of the victims regarding that ugly business that's been going on in Astoria."

Zoey, who was already looking directly at Ian, smiled a bright smile as she stood up and approached him to within an arm's length. Ian then also stood up. Zoey was the first to extend her right hand and speak. "Very nice to meet you, Ian."

Ian reciprocated in kind as he extended his right hand. "As it is to meet you, Zoey." The two shared a very cordial handshake.

Zoey then turned and reseated herself back onto the opposite end of the couch. She then spoke up. "Okay, Ian. It's easy enough to figure out why you'd want to speak to my uncle about that club and its owner. What I can't figure out is what do I … Why am I here?"

Clayton stood up and walked over to the dining room table. It was sparsely set with just the three plates that he'd previously set out to the now-adjacent pizza boxes. "How about we save the questions until we've enjoyed some pizza before it gets any colder? I'll get the wine. Nothing goes better with pizza than a glass of red wine."

Ian wasn't certain about this declaration. He always felt beer was the companion libation of choice with pizza, but as a guest, he kept that to himself.

Zoey and Ian both slowly stood up and walked over to the dining room table. Clayton went into the kitchen and returned with a newly-opened bottle of wine and two glasses. He then left them once again for just a moment, then returned with a glass of his own ... already filled.

The three seated themselves at the table, and Clayton raised his glass. "Here's to the best things the Italians ever gave to the world: pizza and Chianti. Well, if you don't count art and the Renaissance, that is." They all laughed.

"Zoey, I told Ian that you have a hair salon downtown. He's going to attempt his hand at undercover work to somewhat infiltrate the world of that nightclub The Morgue. But as I'm sure you'd agree, he's going to need to significantly change his appearance in order to have any chance of success."

Zoey nearly choked on her pizza as she looked at Ian, clearly trying to imagine him in a place like that. "Yes, well, Unc … I'm not a magician." she blurted out. She then followed her previous statement with the standard disclaimer. "No offense intended."

Ian smiled as he looked at Zoey over his glass of wine as he replied, "None taken."

Zoey began looking Ian over, "Well, he's already pasty-white like the rest of us this time of year. So he's got that going for him. I suppose if we got him the right clothes. And definitely dyed his hair jet-black. Chopped it a bit to give it sort of an edgy look. And maybe … I don't know … pierced one of his ears, and gave him a dangly earring. Something like an upside down cross. That and add some dark eyeliner. Who knows? Maybe. Understand, I've only been there once. But most of the people that go there, they're pretty over-the-top even by my standards." Zoey laughed.

Ian looked directly into Zoey's eyes. "Could you … Would you be willing to help me with all that? I'd certainly pay you for your time and effort."

Clayton remained silent. He had a smile on his face that indicated he was to some degree enjoying this.

Zoey kept looking Ian up and down as if she was sizing him up in more ways than one. "Yeah … Yeah, I could pull this off. That is, if, like you said, you're willing to pay me for my time. And you're willing to buy all the clothes needed. You know, like biker square-toe boots, black pants, maybe leather. And a black shirt of some kind and …"

Ian smiled as he interrupted her and answered, "Absolutely!" But what he was really thinking was, *Good God. I'm gonna look like Billy Idol meets Johnny Cash.*

Zoey, still looking directly at Ian, took a deep breath. "Just one more thing."

"What's that?" Ian asked without hesitation.

Zoey continued, "To not draw too much attention to yourself, I mean to have any chance at pulling this off, you're gonna need someone with you. You know, arm candy. A person to play the role of a willing donor. I know, sick, right? But that place doesn't just attract Goth types. There's usually a bunch of vampire role players lurking around.

Some of them get pretty into it. You know, they take it pretty far with the cutting and sucking on each other and all that shit."

Ian tried hard to conceal behind a grin his obvious virginity regarding the subject as he replied, "Donor? Oh yeah, of course. Donor. That's not a bad idea for appearance's sake. But who would I …? I mean … I'm not from around here and don't know any …"

Zoey blurted out, "Well me of course. This all sounds so mysterious and kind of fun!"

Clayton suddenly frowned at the thought of his niece willfully putting herself in harm's way. He interjected, "Fun or not, it's potentially very dangerous. Zoey, do you understand me?"

Zoey glaringly flashed her eyes at her uncle. "I can handle myself."

Ian looked from Zoey over at Clayton. Clayton gave Ian a reluctant but slow, approving nod.

Ian looked back at Zoey and replied, "Okay, that sounds really good. When do we get started?"

Zoey fired back instantly, "How about right away? How about tonight? You can follow me back to my shop. I can color your hair. We can discuss where to go shopping tomorrow. To get you the clothes you're gonna need. And maybe some for me too, right?"

Ian smiled and nodded.

Zoey continued, "I'll take the day off tomorrow. You can add a day's pay to what you're gonna owe me. Besides, now I have a date for Halloween, assuming that's at least one of the nights you plan on checking the place out. Seems like it would be a natural. That place's gonna be crawling with creatures of the night on that night, I promise you." All three laughed slightly at that. Though Ian was getting more than a tiny bit concerned regarding what this was all going to cost him in terms of money and anything else.

Ian interjected, "Yeah. I'll … I mean we'll definitely want to be there on that night for sure."

They all finished their dinner, and then Zoey told Ian they should get to her shop before it got much later. He agreed. Zoey and Ian said their goodbyes to Clayton and began heading to the front door.

Clayton spoke up. "Ian, hold on for just a … Zoey, go ahead to your car. Ian will be right out. I just want to speak with him for a moment. I won't keep him but a few minutes." Zoey did as Clayton asked.

Clayton took hold of Ian's shoulders. "You take care of that little girl. She means a lot to me."

Ian smiled as he answered, "I will, Clayton. You have my word."

Clayton cleared his throat, "Yes. In answer to the question you asked of me earlier, to which I lied. The one you suspect you already know the answer to." Clayton pulled down the collar of the black turtle-neck shirt, which revealed two small puncture wounds on the side of his neck. The area surrounding the punctures appeared to be very red with dozens of white and blue wavy, streaked veins emanating from the wounds in all directions. It wouldn't have taken a medical professional to see that what Ian was looking at was most likely a progressively spreading infection.

Clayton spoke, "As you can see, I have a lot at stake in this. As do you. I've been bitten only the once but by an ancient: Salizzar. I know he's an ancient because of the rapid progression of the effects that I am fighting even as we speak."

Clayton then rolled up the right sleeve of his shirt, revealing to Ian razor-blade self-inflicted wounds. Ian quickly deduced that Clayton had been bleeding himself and adding his own blood to his wine. The very thought sickened Ian, though he did a fair job of concealing it.

"You take every caution, Ian. I've armed you with knowledge

that may only be the tip of the proverbial iceberg. Remember this above all else. Blood to vampires is more intense of an addiction than heroin is to a junkie. Blood is more than merely food to them. Do you understand? As for me, if Salizzar is destroyed, I should recover."

Ian fired one last question. "Clayton, you said that most real vampires are captains of industry and the like. As such, they would be under much public scrutiny. Someone like that would never risk going out roaming the streets to hunt their prey, would they?"

Clayton smiled, clearly pleased that Ian was such a quick study. "That's right, Ian. It's commonly understood that many business tycoons and high-profile famous people have their connections to receive their drugs of choice. In the case of ultra-wealthy vampires, both their food and their drug of addiction is human blood, which I suspect is distributed perhaps world-wide via a very sophisticated underground coalition, a network whose customers, mega-wealthy vampires, can and will pay any price to receive shipments of blood on a regular basis. Salizzar's nightclub may very well be a human blood-bank and body-parts processing and distribution center. He and his followers may harvest and sell organs to both vampires and humans alike. Anyone who seeks human organs for either cannibalistic food or for organ transplants that can be attained without having to go on any waiting list. I suspect if I'm correct in my vast assumptions that he would sell to anyone who can pay his price and remain totally discreet. Besides Salizzar's nightclub, there may be many such body parts factories and underground blood banks located all around the globe."

Upon hearing that, Ian thought about what Officer Ned Parker had said, that the club might be a front for drug trafficking and perhaps even a black market distribution center for human organs. Ian pondered for a second. *Ned was spot on with his theories. Well ... likely mostly right anyway.*

Clayton and Ian said their goodbyes. The rain had momentarily subsided. Ian walked out to meet Zoey at her car, which was a late model, silver Honda Accord. Ian walked up to the driver-side door and Zoey lowered her power window.

"Ian, just follow me back to town. But if you lose me, my shop's about a half block down from Marsh's Free Museum but on the left-hand side of the street. You'll see our sign. New Wave Hair Salon."

Ian smiled. "Sounds good. I'll follow ya. No worries. I'm pretty sure I know almost exactly where your shop is."

CHAPTER 10
Change

Ian immediately spotted Zoey's car, which was parked directly in front of her shop. He parked on the opposite side of the street, switched off his Jeep's ignition and headlights, then slowly exited the vehicle. The rain that had been not much more than a heavy drizzle during his drive had suddenly begun to come down in ever increasing intensity. Strong winds driving an incoming cold front seemed to have come from nowhere. The wind was blowing hard inland from the sea, dropping the temperature nearly instantly from what had been strangely, almost eerily mild to nearly frigid conditions. Ian quickened his pace as he began crossing the street, all the while attempting as best he could to wick away from his face the wind-propelled waterworks that stung his eyes and blurred his vision. Although the weather had all at once become bad enough to have passed itself off most anywhere else as the beginning of a storm of consequential magnitude, Ian knew as he crossed the street and walked briskly up to the front door of Zoey's hair salon that this was typical for the Washington coast, especially in the latter part of October.

Even though Ian was being relentlessly pounded by the torrents of harshly cold wind and rain, and was becoming increasingly soaked and chilled to the bone, he paused for reflection there at the front door before knocking. The pain and stiffness in his neck that he'd first suffered a couple days ago had begun creeping back on him once again. Ian surmised it was mainly due to tension. He couldn't help but question himself regarding the wisdom of further involving a young woman in what could prove to be a very dangerous endeavor. But despite his trepidation and confliction pertaining to the chain of events which were about to unfold due to involving Zoey, Ian felt he had reached a Rubicon Crossing, the point of no return, as he knocked on the door.

On some level beyond Ian's intellectual grasp, he'd been instantaneously intrigued, almost captivated by Zoey beyond mere sexual attraction from the first time he'd laid his eyes on her.

Standing at the front door waiting, and now completely drenched and shivering, Ian thought, *Come on, Ian. Just keep it professional. Like I have to worry about that. What would a hot young gal like Zoey want with an old fart like me? Christ, it's cold!*

Just then, the door to Zoey's shop opened. "Oh, God, Ian, I hope you haven't been standing here in the rain long! I had to run to the bathroom."

Ian smiled as he replied, "No, no. Just been here a moment. Boy, it sure is coming down!"

With a quick smile, Zoey motioned for Ian to come in. "Well, Ian, I invite you to enter of your own free will. That's something I got from my uncle. He always says that when inviting anyone into his house. Guess it sorta rubbed off on me." Zoey chuckled.

Ian went inside and immediately removed his jacket, which was completely soaked through. Seeing just how wet he really was, Zoey spoke up. "Ian, now don't be shy, I insist that you slip out of your shirt and jeans. I have an industrial clothes dryer in the back room. We do a lot of laundry around here. Well, mostly just towels. But anyway, it gets really hot and dries real fast. It's hell on delicates."

All of the blinds were pulled shut, but Ian, normally more than a bit timid regarding getting undressed to any level in front of a new, especially female, acquaintance, was to say the least reluctant. "Uh, do you have, like, a changing room or something?"

Zoey laughed. "Changing room? Ian, this isn't a clothing store. Now take off your wet clothes and hand them to me." As Ian began to comply, he noticed that Zoey was hardly even wet. She was still wearing the same clothes; all but the waist-length black leather jacket that she'd kept on while at Clayton's house. She was wearing the same oxford grey button-front knit, black belted dress, slightly more than mini-length. Beneath that she wore black fishnet leggings topped-off with black Doc Martens-style short-top, brass-buckle boots. Having had a daughter, Ian knew of Doc Martens. He mused, regarding his intense observation of her, *No bra. No panties. Not even a thong could hide itself under that dress. She must have got here just moments before the downpour.*

"I was lucky. The hard stuff didn't start coming down till I got inside." Zoey said while retrieving Ian's pants and shirt from him. She then headed for the back room. Ian, with what he guessed must be a pretty silly expression on his face, just stood there in the middle of the salon for a few befuddled, uncomfortable minutes. But that was instantly eclipsed by his now significant embarrassment at the sight of himself in a mirror sporting his somewhat less than bright white, v-neck t-shirt and equally less than originally white tube socks and blue and white striped boxer shorts. All of course not to be outdone by his current wet-dog disheveled hair. But worst of all, his t-shirt was damp enough to highlight where once not so many years ago dwelled washboard abs. They appeared to Ian to have somehow graduated from a six pack to a love-handle enhanced pony-keg.

Zoey came through the backroom doorway. Upon seeing her coming his way, Ian immediately did the best he could to suck in his gut.

Ian rather nervously spoke up, "It's certainly warm enough in here, thankfully, since I'm ... Well ..." Ian looked down at himself to try and make light of his situation, and it worked. Zoey laughed at the sight of him standing there in the middle of her shop in his present state of attire, or rather lack thereof.

"Yes, well, I have to keep it nearly uncomfortably warm in here for the blue-hairs." Zoey said while still somewhat giggling.

"Blue-hairs?" Ian asked, momentarily confused.

"Little old ladies. Blue-hairs." Zoey blurted out.

Ian smiled. He couldn't believe that one got by him. He'd heard that expression before dozens of times. "Oh yeah. Of course. Blue-hairs." he said, trying not to sound too naïve or ignorant. "For a second, I thought you were referring to some birds that flew into your shop to get warm. You know, Blue-Haired Biddies I think is their ornithological name." They both laughed, Ian a bit more than Zoey. "I ... I used to be a zoologist. But I was never that into birds," he said, attempting to clarify his attempted humor.

Zoey flashed Ian a quirky look as she rolled her eyes just slightly and grinned, "Okay. How about we get down to business?" Ian nodded.

"Take a seat," Zoey said as she pointed to the chair at her workstation.

Ian sat down. Zoey immediately grabbed a comb and scissors. She gave Ian's head a look over. "No need to waste time with a shampoo or wet your hair any more than it already is." They both laughed.

Ian replied, "No, I should think not."

"You know, Ian, when you talk, you sound a lot like my uncle. Half the time, I don't know what the hell he's talking about." Again, they both laughed.

Ian interjected, "Oh, I seriously doubt that's true. I guess I've never really considered what I sound like when I speak. But as for your uncle, he's without question a brilliant man."

Zoey smiled, "Brilliant. Oh yeah. That's for sure. He, like, knows everything." She tied a hair-cutting cape around Ian's neck and covered him appropriately. She then began cutting and chopping at his hair. Zoey kept at it, taking momentary pauses to examine her progress, until she was satisfied with what she'd achieved, all the while intentionally keeping Ian's chair turned away from the station's mirror.

"All right, I think that's good. Now, I'm gonna apply some color: black." Zoey began running her hands through Ian's hair, which to Ian felt wonderful.

"Actually, I really hate to change your hair color. The smattering of salt mixed with brown looks really good on you." she said, still running her fingers through Ian's hair.

Ian blushed ever so slightly from the compliment.

Zoey continued, "Anyway, I just so happen to have some of that five-minute men's coloring in the back in a few of the basic colors. Occasionally, we get a man in that wants to color his gray away but is too embarrassed to buy the stuff for himself." She began to laugh before she spoke again, "God knows how they ever get the courage to buy condoms." Zoey stopped laughing, then continued, "The color doesn't last near as long as what I'd typically use for women, but for a short time, a couple of weeks, it does the trick. I'll be right back."

When Zoey returned, she had a box of hair product in her hand, which she set down on the counter of the station. She noticed that Ian was rubbing his neck and slowly twisting it from side to side.

"What's wrong, Ian? Stiff neck?" Zoey asked as she opened the small box that contained the hair coloring.

"Yeah, it comes and goes in intensity. It's been bugging me for a couple-few days now," Ian replied, still rubbing and stretching his neck.

Zoey looked up from the bottle and application paraphernalia that she'd just removed from the box. "I'll see what I can do for that after we've got you finished here. Among my many talents, lucky you, I'm also a masseuse."

"Really." Ian said, sounding impressed.

Zoey continued, "Yeah, I've got a little massage table in the back. It's actually starting to become an important part of my business as an additional revenue stream, as Clayton puts it. My uncle paid for my schooling. You know, beauty school over in Astoria. Later, he even paid for me to go to school in Portland to also become a massage therapist. God, I mean, he even bought this building and fronted the money for me and my partner, Todd, to open this place and live upstairs. There's a two-bedroom apartment up above. I've been paying him back. I pay my uncle rent and all. So far, it's been good. The truth is, Clayton's done … He's always been there for me. My parents were both killed in a fire when I was just a baby. Clayton sort of adopted me and moved me here from San Francisco after they died. My dad and Clayton were brothers. Yep, that's my story."

Zoey put on the disposable plastic gloves that came with the box of hair color. She then began shampooing the coloring into Ian's hair. Ian somehow felt compelled to share a bit of his past with Zoey since she'd shared so much with him.

"I'm a widower. My wife and daughter were killed in a car accident a couple years ago. They were hit head on by a drunk driver."

Zoey instantly stopped working on Ian's hair. She took one step back to better look straight into his eyes. "Oh, God! I'm so sorry! I mean, in my case, I never really knew my parents, but you …"

Ian lifted his right hand from underneath the large, bib-style cape. "No. No, I mean thanks, but it's quite all right. I'm doing much better with dealing with it all. I have my work, and that keeps me busy. And I have my dog, Scout. He keeps me company and …"

"You have a dog? Really? What kind?" Zoey asked.

"I've got a large German Shepherd. You might say he's my best friend."

Zoey started spreading the color evenly all over Ian's head as she interjected, "You know, I think I could really dig having a dog. That is, if I could get over the fear of being bitten. Clayton tells me I'm afraid of dogs 'cause I was attacked – bitten – by one when I was very young. I can't quite remember the incident, but whenever I see a large dog, just knowing it's got those huge fangs, sort of … I don't know … freaks me out. Stupid, right?"

Ian thought to himself, *Strike one.*

Zoey continued, "But I think all I would have to do is get used to being around the right dog, you know, and I'd be fine. 'Cause I really do love animals."

He mused, *It's a hit.*

Ian paused for a second then spoke. "I think you'd get along great with Scout. He's as gentle as a big ole teddy bear. That is, unless someone was to attack me or something. If that was the case, I've no doubt he'd shape-shift quick from teddy bear to grizzly bear. He was trained as a police dog." Ian thought about what he'd just said. *Shape-shift. That was a weird way to put it. All the talk earlier with Clayton about vampires has me thinking with monsters on my brain.*

Zoey spoke up, "Well, it's settled then. Bring him. Bring Scout with us when we go shopping for some club clothes for you tomorrow. It's time I get over such a silly phobia. That a deal?"

Ian smiled as he replied, "Deal."

After glancing at the clock on the wall, Zoey said, "Okay, it's been more than five minutes. Let's rinse this out of your hair and see what we've got." She took Ian's hand and led him over to a chair at a hair-wash station. Ian sat down in the chair, and Zoey tilted the chair back and gently lowered his head back into the sink. Ian winced just a bit due to his stiff neck. Zoey then began rinsing the residual product out of his hair.

"Boy, that neck of yours is really tight, huh?" Zoey said with a sympathetic tone in her voice.

Ian replied, "Yeah, it's getting worse I think. Maybe you've got some Tylenol or Ibuprofen. Or better, a straight shot of tequila?"

Zoey laughed. "Like I said before, once I've finished with your head, I'll work on that neck." After she finished rinsing Ian's hair, she reached up and opened the wall-mounted cabinet above the sink, pulled out a plush white towel, and began drying his head.

Zoey looked Ian's hair over carefully. "Now, Ian, don't over comb your hair. In fact, don't comb it at all. Just run your hands through it after showering. The way I've cut it, well, it's supposed to look sort of messy."

Ian was beginning to grow slightly concerned regarding how much all of this after-hours special service was going to wind up costing him.

"Okay, now get your butt up from that chair and follow me back to the massage room," Zoey said with a commanding voice that would accept no arguments.

Ian got up from the chair and they both headed for the back room. Ian noticed that Zoey had gotten some dark hair-dye on her clothes.

"Zoey … Oh, Christ, I'm sorry. I see some of the hair dye on the left sleeve of your …" Ian exclaimed while pointing to the area of concern.

Zoey examined the sleeve. "Damn it." she blurted out. "Oh, well. What the hell. This thing's old anyway. I should have known better and changed out of it." She continued staring at the dark, Rorschach-test looking spot. "Well, I should at least try dousing it real good with Spray-n-Wash and throw it in the washer before the stain totally sets in."

Ian nodded his head in agreement as he spoke. "Zoey, I'm really sorry."

Zoey replied, "No biggy. Totally my fault!" She took a deep breath, then spoke. "Ian, go ahead back to the massage room. It's the room behind the first set of hanging beads. If you pass through a second set, you've gone too far. That's our little laundry and kitchen. Anyway, the light switch is just to the left. Go ahead and get undressed. You can cover yourself with a sheet." Zoey looked at Ian and giggled, "That is, if you're shy. You'll see a stack of folded sheets in an open-face wall cabinet just off to the right of the massage table. When you're ready, lay face down on the table. You'll see where your face goes: in the hole." Ian's mind boggled at the possibilities of Zoey's last words.

He was speechless, but went ahead and followed her instructions, or rather, orders. He mused, *Get more undressed than I am already? Okay, I guess.*

Zoey headed towards the back of the shop ahead of him. Just to the far left side of the room, about ten feet before the center beaded doorway, was a door that she opened, revealing a staircase. Zoey turned her head back towards Ian as she began heading upstairs.

"I'll be quick. I'm gonna just get out of these clothes so I can get it washing right away." Ian smiled as he continued on past her, heading towards the beaded doorway.

Everything in the massage room was as Zoey had described. Ian found the light switch and switched it on. He started to get undressed, then remembered that his shoes were still near the front of the shop where he'd initially gotten out of his wet clothes. Ian walked briskly back to where he'd left them, grabbed them up, and carried them back to the massage room. He then proceeded to get further undressed. Ian laid his boxer shorts, t-shirt, and socks on the floor on top of his shoes underneath the massage table. The room was neatly decorated with wicker furniture, chair, and an open-face shelved wicker cabinet that was filled with, besides white towels, an impressive assortment of oils, lotions, and potions. Suspended from the ceiling, directly above the massage table, was a banana leaf-styled ceiling fan.

The wall across from the initial beaded entryway was wallpapered in a picturesque tropic surf and sea motif similar to one Ian had once seen on the wall of a travel agency.

Sitting on top of a two-shelved, nightstand-type wicker desk adjacent to the room's only chair was an ornate brass Buddha incense burner and a box of incense sticks. On the second shelf below that was a small boom-box stereo. Ian chuckled as he thought, *Probably gonna have me listening to the sounds of whales copulating.*

Ian climbed onto the table and lay face down. He managed with a little difficulty from the awkward position he was in to adequately cover himself with a white sheet. Ian placed his face down into the padded facial hole.

Ian began feeling overwhelmingly silly, but just when he considered getting up from the table, Zoey parted the beads. "Let me just get my clothes started in the wash, and I'll be right with you."

Moments later, Ian heard the washing machine start up. Next he heard the gentle sound of the beads being disturbed yet again. He lifted his head and turned it sideways to see Zoey, who was now standing above him. She had already squeezed out some lotion into her hand from a bottle that she then sat down onto the table beside the incense burner.

Zoey was wearing only a loose-fitting men's white knit tank top, which revealed her totally tattooed left arm, all done in Asian-pictorials. Ian had never been much into tattoos, especially on women. But he noticed instantly how beautifully the body art had been done by what had to have been a master tattoo artist. All the ink on her arm, its colors and designs, reminded Ian of a movie he'd once seen that featured members of the Japanese mafia, the Yakuza.

Ian noticed almost immediately that the arm holes in the shirt Zoey wore were much larger than any woman of her small stature would require for proper fit. They vividly revealed with nearly each movement of her arms the sides of her firm breasts. Zoey was additionally wearing pink sweatpants that Ian thought revealed a perfect, athletic-like, firm hind end. Printed across the back of the pants in bold white letters was the word PINK. Her bare feet revealed that her painted toenails exactly matched her black fingernails.

Zoey's nose had a small, round, silver stud affixed to it. Ian guessed her ears had at least a half-dozen small silver loops on each, and he could see through her thin shirt that she had a small pin through her navel. Whenever Zoey turned her back to Ian and bent over slightly, Ian could see that the small of her back sported a tattoo comprised of a black and white Yin and Yang symbol that was semi-encircled by two symbolically contrasting black and white arrows. Ian would normally regard Zoey's body piercings and body art as superfluous at best, but somehow, they all seemed natural on her.

Zoey began massaging Ian's neck. At first, it was as painful to Ian as relieving, but after a few minutes, his neck began to loosen up just a bit.

"Stress has really done a number on you." Zoey said while working.

"Yeah, I guess. Well, in my profession, I have to keep a lot of things bottled up," Ian said while thinking to himself, *The secrets I keep. God, if she only knew.*

"Well, Ian, like a good bartender, you can tell your masseuse in confidence all your dirty little secrets." Zoey then giggled, "but don't say a word to your hair-dresser. They're gossipy as hell." They both laughed.

Ian thought to himself for a second of what Zoey had just said. He immediately related it to the Yin and Yang tattoo on the small of her back. To Ian, metaphorically, that was Zoey. Somewhat an enigma of polarized contradiction. Ian mused as her hands continued working their occasionally painful magic, *A little hard on the outside but very soft on the inside.*

Ian exclaimed, "Wow! You're really good. If I live through this, I think it's really gonna have helped."

Zoey laughed as she replied, "Yeah, well you know what they say. No pain, no gain."

After about fifteen minutes of working on Ian's neck and back, Zoey issued another order. "All right, time for the flip side. Turn over."

Ian suddenly became embarrassed. He'd become aroused by Zoey's looks and healing hands.

"Oh … um … Ya know, I don't think that will be necessary. I mean, my neck's feeling much better and …"

Zoey interrupted, "Turn your ass over so I can get to the sides of your neck and front of your shoulders. It's all connected. It's all part of the same series of muscles that are spasming."

By her tone and insistence, Ian knew, to his chagrin, that Zoey would accept no further arguments to the contrary. So he very slowly turned over, all the while trying desperately to mentally deflate his present condition by thinking of anything he could that was sexually repulsive. It didn't work.

Oh … God. Ian thought as he laid there with his knees both bent, a feeble attempt at trying to conceal his arousal.

Zoey had witnessed this maneuver by men in Ian's condition more than once, but she intentionally concealed her knowledge with a poker face that could have rivaled even the most prolific gambler. She decided to play with him. "Ian, you're simply gonna have to lay your legs down. They've got to be positioned perfectly straight in order for me to do a good job of rubbing all that stiffness out … from your neck." Zoey had to turn her head away from Ian for a second, so he wouldn't catch her giggling. Realizing that the situation was unavoidable, Ian began slowly lowering his legs.

Zoey spoke, "Now, there's a good boy. I'm going to rub long and hard. Up and down … on your neck and shoulders. Gotta get all that tension released." Once again, she had to turn her head away to regain her composure.

Ian could no longer stand not knowing how apparent his condition was. Reluctantly, he looked down towards his lower self. "Oh, Jesus. I'm sorry!" he blurted out.

Zoey laughed. "Relax, Ian. It's only natural." She began rubbing the sides of Ian's neck. "Your neck … There's a knot right here." She began concentrating her efforts on the left side of Ian's neck and shoulder. She continued, "The muscle right along here is really in spasm. By comparison to the other side of your neck, it actually feels a little swollen. Are you sure you haven't injured it recently?"

Ian thought about the wrestling around he'd done back at Harmony Falls. "Yeah, come to think of it, I did take a bit of a nasty fall up in the woods the other day."

Zoey shook her head, indicating that she thought it was more than just tension. "Try to relax as much as possible. This might hurt more than just a little while I try and work the knot out."

Zoey bore down on what she felt was the epicenter of the problem and Ian winced from the pain. She then walked to the head of her table. When Ian looked up at her, Zoey looked directly into his eyes with a sly grin on her face. She said, "You know, if you'd like, when I've finished working on your neck and shoulders, I could help reduce the swelling in your other problem as well." Ian was speechless as he gazed up into her deep, jade green eyes.

One hour later:

Ian stood next to Zoey at the opened front door of her shop. The rain had stopped a while ago as abruptly as it had begun. Ian, not knowing exactly what to say, cleared his throat then began to speak. "Well, um … my … uh … neck …" His speech was interrupted as they both couldn't help but laugh.

Ian continued, "Uh, yeah. Well anyway, my neck … ha! Yeah, it feels much better. And, um, thanks for drying my clothes."

Zoey giggled slightly, "My pleasure, Ian. I'm glad you're feeling better." Then she got serious. "Now, a couple of things. Are you going to tell me your real name? I could tell by the way my uncle introduced you, by the tone of his voice, that your name … he like invented it. Like a name from a character in one of his books. Or am I wrong?" Before Ian could say a word, Zoey continued, "That and … how about tomorrow? What time do you want to pick me up? We're gonna have to go to Astoria. There's nothing like what you're going to need here in town."

Ian was both startled and impressed by Zoey's calm, casual demeanor when asking him about his name. *She certainly is perceptive.* After an uncomfortable pause, he answered, "Yes. Yes, of course. Going to Astoria works. It would be great. I've got an appointment over there at around ten, so say around nine? Would that work?" Zoey nodded. But then she lifted her eyebrows and crossed her arms, clearly indicating that she was still waiting for her initial question to be answered.

Ian continued, "As far as my name. Okay. My name really is Ian. Clayton came up with the last name McBride. My real last name's McDermott."

Zoey smiled. "Well, Ian McDermott, if that is your name? Nice to meet the real you." she laughed.

Ian smiled. "No really. I swear! I'll show you my driver's license if you don't believe …"

Zoey held up her right hand with her palm facing Ian. She laughed as she spoke, "Stop. I believe you."

Ian continued, "Okay. Now that that's out of the way, great. Until tomorrow then. You have a good night. Uh … bye." Almost instinctually, Ian leaned forward to kiss her, but he caught himself before it was too obvious. He didn't want to be presumptuous, so he opted to just turn and walk out into the night across the street to his Jeep.

CHAPTER 11
Research

When Ian arrived back at his trailer, Scout was very glad to see him. But Scout didn't bark, almost as if he knew that it was late, and he didn't want to wake their fellow campers. Instead, Scout wagged his tail feverishly and began leaning against Ian, nearly demanding that Ian take a few minutes to pet him. Ian was glad to oblige.

After paying some much deserved attention to his four-legged friend, Ian got undressed down to his boxers. He set the alarm on his cell phone to go off at 8:00 a.m. the next morning, then placed his phone on top of the cabinet next to the sink. He reached up and switched off the overhead light and climbed into bed. After a few seconds, Ian gently patted his hand on the bed beside him, signaling Scout to hop on and join him. Scout instantly did just that. Within minutes, they both were fast asleep.

8:00 a.m. came way too soon for Ian. The alarm's incessant buzzing reverberated in his head. Ian first tried ignoring it by covering his head with his pillow, but that offered little to muffle the noise. Finally, after a few very uncomfortable minutes had passed, Ian made the long reach over to the counter. He snatched his phone, checked the time, then switched the phone's alarm off.

Ian slowly stood up and began stretching out his back and

shoulders. He had even more than his usual morning aches and pains that he'd grown accustomed to. Ian thought, *This damp, coastal climate isn't doing my arthritis any favors.* He pulled on a heavily-wrinkled, khaki-colored, cotton polo shirt and the jeans that he'd worn the day before … and the day before that … he then sat down on the edge of his bed and put on his at one time fresh socks and tennis shoes.

"Well, Scout, it's a good thing I'm going clothes shopping today 'cause if I don't buy some new threads, and if we don't make it to a Laundromat soon, I'm gonna have to use my clothes as camp-fire starter." Ian laughed at his attempt at humor. Scout barked twice.

After Ian and Scout had both finished with their typical morning routines, they climbed into the Jeep to embark on the day's adventures.

"Scout, what a beautiful morning. It can't rain all the time." Ian said as they drove out of the RV park's driveway onto the main road. Remembering a large advertising billboard when he'd first driven into Astoria that proclaimed radio station 97.8 AM - KNUZ to be the number one talk and news radio station for Astoria and the surrounding area, he promptly switched his Jeep's radio on and dialed it to AM 97.8.

The morning news broadcast was in progress, coming over his radio with excellent clarity. Ian proclaimed to Scout, "Boy, I tell ya, seems even when nothing else will come in, you can always get Christian or talk radio. I guess neither God nor the news will be denied."

Ian was half-listening to the local weather forecast when news came on that immediately caught his attention.

A man fishing in the Columbia River near Warrington found a body floating near shore. Astoria and Seaside Police both responded to a 911 call from the fisherman, who placed the call by cell phone just moments after discovering the body.

The yet-to-be-identified body was reported to be that of a young woman in her early twenties. The body was severely mutilated. Due to the body matching the same general condition of others, now seven in total, all nearly absent of all vital organs and blood, the women appear to have fallen victim to the serial killer or killers ... now dubbed the Vampire Slayer... or Slayers.

The bodies of the victims found over the last few weeks have been discovered in the water and on the banks of the Columbia as far up river as Clathlamet, Washington, and now as far down river as Warrenton, Oregon.

We will continue bringing you up to the hour reports on this headline story as it unfolds.

Ian switched off his radio, frowning and shaking his head. The weight and magnitude of what he was about to get directly involved in finally had become real to him. He couldn't have been more impacted by what he'd just listened to if he'd been hit over the head with a ton of bricks.

After ten minutes of driving south on the peninsula, they arrived at the downtown Long Beach business core. They drove a couple of blocks further on Main Street, then proceeded to pull over into a parking spot directly adjacent to Zoey's shop. Ian checked his cell phone. It was 8:52 a.m.

Just as Ian started to unbuckle his seat belt, he spied Zoey exiting her shop. She smiled and waved as she looked over at Ian, then crossed the street and walked directly up to the passenger-side of his Jeep. Ian had already climbed out and was waiting for Zoey curbside.

"Hi, uh, good morning," Ian said somewhat sheepishly.

"Hi yourself." Zoey cheerfully replied. Due to her apparent good mood, Ian's confidence immediately elevated.

"Well, Zoey, are you ready for the day's adventure?"

With a large grin, she replied without hesitation, "You bet'cha Ian. I'm always up for shopping ... and spying."

Ian and Zoey smiled at each other, and he opened the car door for her. She got in and immediately buckled herself up. Scout, who had been lying down in the back seat, suddenly leaned his head over Zoey's left shoulder, which startled her. Scout soon put her to ease by panting and gently nudging her shoulder, clearly indicating that all he wanted was for her to affectionately acknowledge him, which she did at first with a reluctant pat on Scout's head; soon, that led to Zoey gently stroking Scout's head and husky chest.

Ian slowly walked around his Jeep from the curb to the driver's side of his rig, opened the car door, and slid into the driver's seat. He smiled as he saw Zoey was now actively petting Scout, who had nearly worked himself into the front of the cab, semi-laying between the two front seats and draping himself over the center console.

"I see that you've met Scout," Ian said pridefully.

Zoey looked up from Scout and smiled at Ian. "Well, we haven't been properly introduced." Then she looked directly at Scout. "Hi, Scout, my name's Zoey."

Scout barked once almost as if he was proclaiming that he understood her introduction. A couple of seconds later, Scout barked two more times as if he were reciprocating Zoey's courtesy with his own self-introduction.

Ian exclaimed as he pulled the Jeep away from the curb and began their trip to Astoria, "Oh, I didn't tell you, Zoey. Scout here's a genius." Ian and Zoey both laughed, but Ian meant what he'd said.

Ian continued, "Zoey, I hope you don't mind, but I've got to meet up with a guy, Officer Ned Parker, one of Astoria's finest, up at ... well, up at the Astoria Column of all places. The Column's become sort of our rendezvous spot."

Zoey paused before she replied, "Good spot. I mean to meet and talk with your connection. Nobody can sneak up on ya. You know, that you can't see coming."

Ian continued to be intrigued by Zoey's rapid ability to connect dots though he still wasn't quite ready to tell her everything.

"Well, it's not as ominous as it sounds. Ned's just helping me a bit with some information and the like."

Zoey smiled, shrugging her shoulders and rolling her eyes just a little as she interjected, "Whatever. It's cool by me."

CHAPTER 12
In the Bag

Ian, Zoey, and Scout were just pulling into the Astoria Column's parking lot when Ian spotted Officer Parker's car. "There he is," Ian said in a low voice, then pulled into a spot a few places down.

Ian was cognizant that Zoey had noticed the policeman obviously wasn't in a police car, unmarked or otherwise, and he decided to address that.

"Yeah, Officer Parker … Ned … is driving his own car. This entire operation – well, if that's what you'd call it – is supposed to be totally off the books. Sort of like a …"

Zoey interrupted, "Like some kind of black-op?"

Ian looked over at her, then after a couple of silent seconds looked deeply into her eyes. "Yeah, well, even though that phrase sort of makes this all sound over-the-top intriguing, I guess that sums it up as good as any. Are you okay with all this?"

Zoey said with a blank face as she stared at Ned's car, "Sure. It's like I'm playing some character, like a spy in a suspense thriller. You know, like a book or movie."

Ian thought about the irony of Zoey's statement. *If Clayton gets his way, that's exactly what this is.*

Zoey glanced over at Ian and smiled reassuringly. She then looked away, back towards the plainclothes police officer, who had just exited his car.

It had just begun to rain. Ned quickened his pace as he headed towards Ian's Jeep.

Ian spoke, "Zoey … Ned … he's a good guy. I think you'll like him."

Zoey replied, "Well, that remains to be seen. I'm usually not big on cops."

They both noticed straight away that Ned was carrying a brown paper bag in his right hand. And the way he was carrying the bag so close to his body made it immediately noticeable that he was trying to keep it and its contents as dry as possible. Ian motioned for Ned to open the door and get into the back seat, which he did, sliding in next to Scout. Scout paid Ned little attention, almost to the point of ignoring him.

Ian turned as far around in his seat as he could to better face Ned and noticed immediately that Ned had a scowl on his face. Ian quickly spoke first. "Uh, hi, Ned. This is my friend Zoey. She's sort of … well on this … she's my partner. Feel free to speak your mind. Whatever you need to tell me, you can say in front of her."

Ned looked Zoey up and down for a moment before he spoke. "Okay. If Ian vouches for you, you must be okay. And by the looks of Ian's hair, you must have had something to do with that, am I right?" Zoey smiled as she nodded. Ned looked over Ian's new jet-black, spiked hair and nodded in approval. "Ian, don't get me wrong, it's perfect. Your hair. Now all you need are some threads that match the look."

Zoey spoke up. "That's exactly what we're going to take care of today!"

Ned somewhat ignored Zoey as he continued to look directly at Ian. "Ian, did you get my text? Well, since then, there's been another body turn up …"

Ian interrupted, "You mean the one found by the fisherman in Warrenton?"

"No. This is another young woman whose body was found across the river in Washington about twenty miles upriver."

Ian shook his head. "Jesus Christ."

Ned continued, "Yeah, well, that body was also completely drained of blood, but there's been a new twist. That is, if the body recovered is a victim of the same lunatic. This one was found absent its head and hands."

Ian thought to himself about the decapitations back at Harmony Falls. *Christ … not decapitations.*

Ned shifted a little in his seat and cleared his throat before continuing once again. "Uh … um, yes. Well, if this new, yet-to-be-identified body is a victim of the same person or persons, they're getting smarter. A body missing its head and hands … Well, that makes identification extremely difficult to say the least, as I'm sure you can imagine. No teeth, no prints. And so far, nobody's come forward with another missing person's report that might match up."

Ned finally turned his attention to Zoey as he looked at her measuringly. He then turned his head back towards Ian. "All right, Ian. I don't know your partner here, and maybe it's best that way. I suppose since you trust her …" Ned reached into the heavily-crumpled, wet paper bag that he'd set on the seat next to him. He brought a small electronic device out of it. "Ian, this is a portable police scanner. All you've got to do is plug it into your cigarette lighter. It's already set to our channel. This might come in handy if you decide to do some snooping around Salizzar's nightclub. You know, it'll let you know when officers are doing drive-bys and such. I don't need it back." Ned handed the scanner to Ian.

Ian replied, "Thanks. Good idea." He couldn't help but notice there was more in the brown bag.

Suddenly, a deep scowl overtook Ned's expression. "The Feds are getting involved. FBI specialists. They're gonna be flying in from the BAU, Behavior Analysis Unit, out of Quantico. They're going to be setting up camp at the station in about a week, maybe less. I hear they're gonna be sending us an agent in advance of their full team anytime now. That is, unless something turns on this thing. We've already got a couple agents from Portland poking their noses around, crawling up our asses. I figure your best play inside the club is day after tomorrow. Halloween night. That joint's no doubt gonna be packed full of mainly out-of-town weirdos. As arrogant as either Salizzar or some crazed follower of his has seemingly been, despite all the increased heat that's on him, that night, regardless of how cliché, will just be too tempting. The smart money says the perv won't be able to resist making a big statement, if you get my drift. Anyway, we're gonna be patrolling that place all night. Maybe even get one or more of our people inside. Regardless, even with Salizzar no doubt assuming we'll have a very high profile police presence, my money says that narcissistic fuck … he'll try and make a move anyway. Maybe his last one, his grand finale. You know, before he just up and disappears. A guy like him, with his kind of money, power, and connections … I don't figure him to stick around much longer just to run a piece of shit nightclub."

Ian didn't say a word but totally agreed with Ned's assumption that Salizzar wasn't going to stick around much longer.

Ned paused and took a deep breath. He then slowly slid his hand back into the brown bag. Zoey began to fidget nervously in her seat as her eyes, just as Ian's, had become fixated on Ned's brown bag. Then very slowly, reluctantly, Ned began extracting from the bag, its content. Zoey was the first to catch a glimpse of what that was.

"Oh God!" Zoey nearly shouted, then in one deft motion turned around and sank down deep into her seat.

Now completely out of the bag, Ned grasped firmly in his right hand a large black handgun. An ominous-looking weapon whose handle and trigger were conspicuously wrapped in silver duct tape. Ian's eyes bugged-out at the sight of the large pistol; he immediately presumed the handle and trigger were taped so it could easily be peeled off to effectively eliminate any traceable fingerprints. He thought, *Wait a minute. Even if Salizzar's guilty as sin, I'm nobody's vigilante or hit man.*

After seeing the gun and watching his master's reaction, Scout was now standing in the seat next to Ned, growling in a very threatening manner. His lips were fully drawn back, baring his fiercely formidable canines, waiting for either a word from Ian or just one more move from Ned.

After what seemed an eternity but in fact was no more than seconds, Ian mustered enough presence of mind to nervously speak. "What ... what the hell are ... What're you planning to do with that?"

Ned sat frozen, looking directly into Scout's glaring eyes. The large dog was now shifting his weight from paw to paw and growling furiously. Scout began shaking from an adrenaline-charged, all-out commitment to defend Ian.

By the expression on Ned's face and the sweat beading on his forehead, he obviously thought he was about to become brunch for a very large, very angry German Shepherd.

Ned began to speak fast. "Oh ... oh my gosh! What this must look like. No ... God no! This gun's for you, Ian. I mean, I thought maybe you'd be better off, if push ever came to shove, having a gun with more stopping power than that pea-shooter of yours. The tape is just for your protection, Ian. Your anonymity regarding any connection with ..."

Ian relaxed his posture, one that had had his back fixed to and pressing back hard against his steering wheel. "Scout, it's okay. CUT!" Ian said in an elevated but calm voice.

'Cut' was the vocal command that Charlie Redtail had taught Ian. The signal for Scout to back down immediately and halt any further aggression. If Ian would have said the word 'strike', Officer Parker, in less time than it would take a pin to drop, would have been requiring a new right hand and a tourniquet.

Ned looked impressed, with Scout as well as with Ian. Zoey, though no longer readying herself to attempt an escape, finally spoke in a noticeably rattled voice, "Gun? Ian, you never mentioned anything about you having … you packing a gun."

Ned smiled at Scout as he slowly reached towards his jacket's inner breast pocket. "Ian, tell your dog it's okay. I'm just getting something out of my coat for ya." Ned didn't think a second misunderstanding of his intentions would bode well for him at all.

Ian looked at Scout. "It's okay boy."

Ned slowly retrieved a business-size sealed white envelope from his jacket, then equally as slowly handed it forward to Ian. Ian, understanding the contents of the envelope would likely be additional operational seed money, stuffed the envelope into his jacket's inside pocket without examining it.

Ned spoke, "That's just some dough to help with expenses."

Ian replied, "Thanks!"

Ned opened the Jeep's door, pausing before making his exit. "That's the last of it. The last payment you can expect for your services. Services that have yet, I might add, amounted to nothing. So if you're not just taking the chief and this town for a ride, and don't misunderstand, I'm confident you're not, then if you're ever gonna get into that club and check things out, you better do it quick. Halloween

130

night's a natural. Anyway, get in there if you're gonna before the Feds get further involved. Hey, one more thing. One that nobody outside of the department and the coroner's office knows. The night before you came to town, a hooker was found dead in a parking lot not far from Salizzar's club. By the looks of things, the crime scene reports indicate suspicion that she might have been a jumper 'cept somebody got to her first. But here's where it gets really weird. Her body up and vanished last night from the funeral parlor. It's been kept there in the basement mortuary for a couple-few days waiting for an autopsy by a Portland forensic specialist. Yeah, her body, the only one not missing all its vital organs, was snatched. There's been that and the recent Warrenton body and all the others. But get this. I had a lady come into the station in total hysterics. Says she and her quadruple extra-large, ex-professional football player husband … They were attacked down at the docks by … and get this … what she called a devil monster. She said her husband was abducted. So far, nothing's checked out regarding any missing man beyond he might have just up and left her. But other than the part she said about him being taken by a devil monster, I believe her."

Ian thought to himself, *Taken by a devil monster? Maybe he was.*

Ned took a deep breath then continued, "Anyway, the gal … the possible jumper that disappeared from the mortuary … We did get a positive ID on her. Her name was, let me think, Brenda Peterson. Yeah, that's it. A runaway hooker known on the streets of Portland as Lucy. She and a couple other pros lived in a shitty apartment downtown, just off Burnside. She ran away from home at sixteen. Not much of a rap-sheet. Had a couple priors for prostitution. Originally from Eugene. Mom died a few years ago from cancer. Dad left the family high and dry a couple years before that. I tell you all this only 'cause shit's getting way weird. Out of control. It's gonna quickly turn into a media circus if we don't cut the balls off this dog soon." Ned turned towards Scout. "No disrespect intended." Ned then turned his attention back to Ian and continued. "You two keep your heads down, and mind ya, be careful. Stay in touch. Good hunting."

"Ned. That hooker you were just talking about. So, she died around three days ago, right?" Ian asked.

Ned paused before he replied, "Yeah, that's about right I guess. Why you ask?"

"Oh ... I don't know. No reason really," Ian said as he thought, *Three days ago ... Hmm, power of three.*

CHAPTER 13
Hide and Seek

Zoey was seated at the small kitchenette in Ian's trailer as she and Ian began to examine all of the fruits of their full day of shopping.

Though purchased for Ian, Zoey held up against her chest a black, crew-neck t-shirt, one that sported some death metal band's name and logo that Ian had never heard of. Ian was ignorant to the specific meaning but understood the concept of the theatrics regarding the band's use of the pentacle and witchcraft-like symbols.

Zoey smiled as she spoke, "This is gonna look great on you. You better not wear any of this garb around town other than of course the regular jeans, shirts, socks and underwear you bought for everyday. Anyway, all these club rags … You need to hide this look from anyone around here. This is your secret club persona."

Ian nearly laughed as he thought to himself, *Wear any of that crap anywhere other than that club. Ha! I plan on burning it all when this is over.*

He tried desperately to maintain an open mind. He did a fair job of mustering an almost believable, unassuming expression as he looked the shirt over. Under normal circumstances, Ian wouldn't have been caught dead in it but he thought, *Ah what the hell? These aren't what you'd call normal circumstances. Wearing this ridiculous shit won't kill me, but if we don't blend in, that could get us both killed.* Ian decided it was time to turn the focus from the freaky frocks to more pressing matters.

Ian blurted out, "Zoey, I want to get inside that club."

Zoey, a bit taken aback, looked up from the shirt that Ian was still holding next to his chest as she replied, "Uh, yeah. That's the whole idea."

Ian smiled as he set the shirt down onto his little dining table. He momentarily shook his head and continued, "No ... I mean yes. That's the idea, right. But what I mean is, I want to get inside and check things out during the day. Mainly the ground, or rather the wharf-level floor. I'm not so interested in the club upstairs. That's probably pretty normal. Weird, but well, you know what I mean." Ian thought regardless of what Clayton said about vampires and sunlight, he'd still rather take his chances while the sun was still up.

Zoey looked curiously at Ian. "Are you saying ... Now let me get this straight. You want to sneak ... You want to break into that joint?"

Ian, with a slight grin on his face, nodded somewhat timidly.

Zoey paused for a protracted moment. After giving Ian plenty of time to have added to or retracted from what he'd just conveyed, Zoey said, "Why Ian, I had no idea you were such a rebel."

Ian grabbed his coat, then began helping Zoey slip hers on as well as he spoke. "Let's get going. We haven't much time. It'll be getting dark in a couple hours." Zoey was slightly unnerved by the nervous tone in Ian's voice.

She spoke up with intended levity, "Yeah, we should get there before the dead wake up hungry."

Ian, slightly unsettled by Zoey's comment, looked directly into her eyes as he thought, *If she only knew how right she just might be.*

Zoey picked up on Ian's befuddled expression and responded,

"What? That was funny, right?" Ian didn't answer. He just half-smiled as he nodded.

It was 3:15 p.m. when Ian, Zoey, and Scout reached their destination. Ian parked his Jeep one block north and two streets up from the area of the waterfront where Salizzar's nightclub was located. He cracked open a couple windows of his Jeep. "You stay here and hold down the fort, Scout," Ian said while opening Zoey's door and helping her out of the vehicle. Scout panted and wagged his tail but began pacing back and forth in the back seat. Ian could see that Scout was behaving a little nervously.

Zoey spoke up. "Okay, here we go. But Ian, please go over the plan with me one more time."

Ian and Zoey began walking down the sidewalk, heading towards the waterfront. Ian took a deep breath and began to go over his makeshift plan. "Uh, well, like I said during our ride here, this is going to be pretty much a 'wing-it' ordeal. I don't know if we stand any chance of getting into the joint, especially without being seen. His warehouse may … It probably has a security system, like his house, the former Flavel House Museum. If so, we're done before we get started. We certainly don't want to get arrested for breaking and entering."

Zoey glanced over at Ian. "No, we don't want that. That would totally fuck up our cover."

Ian replied, "Yeah, it would. That would be totally fucked up. I mean, it would certainly fuck up everything. Which would be really fucked." Zoey started laughing at Ian's overused, forced F-bombs. It was more than apparent that the F-bomb was not at the top of Ian's small arsenal of seldom–uttered, descriptive expletives. Ian was trying to be funny and also trying to act a bit more in tune with his new look.

Zoey laughed as she said loudly, "FUCK YEAH!"

135

Ian and Zoey walked briskly across a cross-walk. They were heading north on the waterfront boardwalk still with a block to go to get to their destination. Ian continued telling Zoey his semblance of a plan. "Maybe, if we get lucky, there will be some way inside. You know, like a window around back that's not locked. Something. I just hope besides doors being alarmed … I hope the place isn't armed with motion detectors or a gauntlet of a spider-web of laser beams or whatever."

Zoey looked suspiciously at Ian. With a smirk on her face, she said, "Oh, this sounds like a good plan. What could possibly go wrong? Spider-web of laser beams … come on … James Bond." Zoey rolled her eyes and giggled quietly to herself.

Ian smiled and shook his head slightly as he replied, "Yeah, what could possibly go right?"

A few moments later Ian and Zoey stood on the north end of the nightclub's deck-style parking lot, which was part of the expansive river front dock system that collectively covered at least a half-mile of Astoria's waterfront. The large warehouse that served as The Morgue nightclub had been built nearly fifty years ago by the Bumble Bee Seafood Company as part of their tuna and salmon processing and canning operations. Bumble Bee had shut down their canneries in Astoria over thirty years ago. Ian had read about it in one of the coastal informational brochures on Astoria that he'd picked up shortly after arriving in the area.

The large warehouse-turned-nightclub had to be, by Ian's estimation, over twenty thousand square feet and spanned from the nearest terrestrial road all the way to the very edge of the river side of the dock. Ian mused, *Lucky guy … or whatever you are. You could fish right from any window on the river side of the joint. Oh well. No matter. I don't imagine you eat fish.*

Ian couldn't help but admire the waterfront dock system, constructed of enormous timbers fashioned to be enormous wooden planks which served as the dock's foundation. It was all supported by hundreds of huge, coal-tar, creosote-coated pylons, which were collectively engineered by design and placement to afford maximum strength and support to the docks.

Ian noted the construction was somewhat similar to turn-of-the-century train trestle bridge supports. He surmised the entire docking system was probably originally constructed not long after that period, but it was very apparent that it had been continuously well-maintained and no doubt upgraded in many ways over the years.

Ian marveled at the dock's construction as he silently thought to himself, *This entire suspended waterfront was certainly built to stand the test of time and the elements. Imagine the relentless battering from storms, the continuous wearing away at the pylons from this incredibly powerful tidal river. Amazing.*

Ian noticed that there were spacings between some of the massive planks large enough to actually see the river's edge not twenty feet below. Ian quickly deduced by noting water markings on the pylons that it was nearly low tide. He smiled as he took a deep breath. The faint wafting smell of fish entrails mixed lightly with an even lighter hint of salt in the air was both fabulous as well as nostalgically fragrant to Ian. It reminded him of visiting Fisherman's Wharf in San Francisco with his parents when he was a boy. The smell of salt in the air was of no more surprise to Ian than was the smell of fish as he mused, *The mouth of the Columbia, where it dumps into the open ocean, is less than five miles from here by way the crow, or rather the seagull, flies.*

With that thought, Ian paused for a moment to watch the seagulls hang-glide the winds. Occasionally, one would land on top of the nightclub, using the high vantage point as a lookout for any fish in the river that might venture too close to the water's surface for its own good, or any potentially meaty mussels attached to rocks and pylons that might become exposed by the rapidly-ebbing tide.

Ian couldn't help but visualize some mental similarities between the gulls and perhaps other predators that might be residing in that building, ones that might be watching him and Zoey right now, just waiting for them to venture close enough that they might swoop down and snatch them up for a late afternoon snack.

Ian's attention was suddenly diverted from the gulls and the warehouse. He smiled as he spotted a couple of otters frolicking in the water. They too were going for a fish or a mollusk meal as they dove deep down into the river's cold, dark water. Ian noted that the otters were experiencing much more immediate success than the patiently watchful gulls.

Ian held Zoey's hand for one peaceful moment. But unfortunately, that moment ended all too soon as he gazed upwards at the fast-moving clouds that had momentarily parted just enough to reveal a glimpse of the sun, which was in the final approach to its daily descent behind the western hills. Ian wished he and Zoey were back at Long Beach, where they could be enjoying the sun setting into the sea rather than fearing the dusk and then the absence of light that it would bring.

Ian shivered at the realization that they had maybe thirty minutes before darkness began to engulf the river city of Astoria, inviting its creatures of the night to come out to play.

CHAPTER 14
Seek

Ian began to privately rethink his initial approach to the nightclub. Any attempt of a hopefully clandestine investigation of the place might be in vain, especially this late in the day. *In vain.* Ian shuddered slightly at the irony of his word choice as he thought of its homophone. *Yeah, this could end up in 'vein' all right.*

He decided it was time to let Zoey in on what he was contemplating. Ian began speaking just above a whisper. "Okay, the way I see it is, there's probably no way to get inside the place without getting confronted by someone or tripping an alarm. That is, unless …" Zoey looked at Ian with a confused expression on her face.

"Unless, what?" she prompted before Ian could collect his thoughts and elaborate.

Ian continued, "That is, unless there's some kind of doorway, like a trap door that gains access to the place from the river below. You know, between the pylons. Hopefully not too far from shore at low tide anyway. Trap doors like those are usually pretty common in dock warehouses. You know, so they can lower goods onto skiffs for transport out to tugs and ships. Warehouses and waterfront bars sometimes used trap doors many years ago even for unsavory things like shanghaiing."

It seemed to make sense to Zoey, as she nodded her head in agreement.

Ian glanced at Zoey as he spoke. "Okay then. Follow me." He began walking across the suspended parking lot towards the street. Towards land. He headed to the very edge of the dock, which he guessed would be the nearest point that might afford any chance for them to make their way beneath the dock. That would put them around a hundred yards from the warehouse, hopefully not too far for them to work their way over into position directly under the nightclub.

It seemed to be a good idea, and there was almost no pedestrian or vehicular traffic around. As they arrived at their intended destination, Ian was pleased to see that the tide was indeed low enough and far enough out to allow them to get under the docks. There was a small gate in the dock railing, one that, if opened, afforded access to what appeared to be a galvanized steel dock ladder that was permanently affixed onto the side of the dock for access beneath it.

But it was obvious from the warning sign attached to the small gate that it was for maintenance personnel only, and access by anyone else was strictly prohibited. Any trespassing violation would subject the perpetrator to arrest and at the very least a hefty fine.

Ian thought about the warning for a moment, then looked around and saw nobody in sight. He opened the gate and climbed down just far enough to see beneath the dock and ahead to what they might be facing. What Ian saw immediately put a frown on his face. It wouldn't be easy going at all. There were planks attached to pylons that appeared to serve as a series of catwalks that led off in several directions.

One of the catwalks looked like it would at least get them under the warehouse, but the going looked tricky to say the least. Ian also noted that all around, bolted to pylons, were numerous KEEP OFF warning signs, which underscored the foolishness of them proceeding any further with his idea. He continued down the ladder until he was standing on a small platform. From there, he had access to the catwalk planks. Zoey had also climbed down and stood beside him to see for herself all that Ian had been checking out.

"Well, we didn't come all this way for nothing, did we?" Zoey nudged Ian gently.

Ian grinned slightly, then took a deep breath. "No. No, I don't guess we did. And what the hell ... what could possibly go wrong. Besides falling off the catwalk down onto the muddy river bottom, which will probably act much like quicksand, trapping us until the tide comes in and drowns us. Or if we make it a bit farther out, then fall, we could easily be impaled by one of those many broken planks and poles that you see protruding from the river bottom. Or if we make it further out yet, you know, where the water is, that sorta speaks for itself. Other than all that, like I said ... what could possibly go wrong?"

Zoey gently placed her right hand on Ian's mouth, stopping him from continuing with any more morbid potentialities. She then smiled brightly as she spoke. "Or ... or we could be just fine."

Somehow, Zoey's reassurance was all of the encouragement that Ian needed to muster up some confidence.

Ian took a deep breath, than spoke. "Okay, I'll go first. Keep your hands ... hold firmly onto something at all times. If we go slowly, you're right. We should be fine."

Ian paused for a moment and pointed ahead of them. "You see those planks way ahead of us? They're so barnacle-encrusted, it tells me that sometimes the tide's so high they are occasionally, at least partially, underwater. Let's hope that's not gonna be the case today. Either way, they're gonna be slippery as all ..."

Zoey interjected before Ian could complete his phrase. "Slippery as slimy snot on a door-handle." Ian thought, *Not how I would have described it, but yeah. Slippery as that.*

141

Without any further thought of the danger or the possibility of being discovered and arrested, Ian and Zoey proceeded, with Ian leading the way.

Ian turned his head to glance behind him. Zoey was no more than three feet back. They were walking on planks that were little wider than a balance beam, all the while trying to hold onto, when possible, the intermittent support pylons and sparsely affixed 4x6 inch makeshift hand-rails. Ian whispered, "Zoey, be especially careful. It looks like just ahead it gets even more sketchy."

"Yeah, I see that," Zoey replied in a low voice but loud enough for Ian to notice that her stress and apprehension was beginning to elevate.

Just when Ian began strongly considering that the risk was getting too great to proceed any further, he spotted it. There was indeed a trap door devised to enter into the warehouse from beneath the docks, as well as a galvanized steel access ladder that went from the catwalk all the way up to the hatchway.

There was a second ladder that went in the opposite direction from the ramp down to just a few feet above the river's surface at what would be nearly low tide. The trap door and ladders were obviously devised for loading small boats directly from the warehouse and to facilitate human transit between warehouse to tugboats or ships by way of 'river taxi' motorized skiffs.

In his excitement, Ian unintentionally left Zoey behind in his hurried efforts to reach and check out the trap door. Once he reached the trap door's metal ladder, he began to climb up the approximately ten foot distance until he was able to reach the hatchway.

Ian held firmly to the ladder with his left hand. He then took a deep breath and slowly exhaled as he began to push upwards on the heavy-hinged 3x3 foot wooden door. To his near amazement, Ian felt the door lift. It wasn't nearly as heavy as he'd expected it to be. He winced at the noise that he'd instantly created. It was as if the trap door had been suddenly awakened from a deep slumber as its rusty hinges squelched upon their awakening. The hinges gave off a duality of high and low pitched noises, which reminded Ian of the piercingly vile sounds created by cats in the thralls of coitus.

Ian immediately surmised due to the ease that the door lifted that it must be assisted by some form of counterweight system. He only lifted the trap door up a few inches before he reversed his actions and closed the hatch as he listened for an alarm to go off. He heard nothing. It didn't occur to Ian that the place might be armed with a silent alarm.

Zoey was standing on the platform directly beneath Ian. Both of her hands held almost painfully tight to the cold, steel ladder. The tide had begun coming in, and the wind had picked up, creating waves that had begun sloshing and pounding the pylons all around below her. What had been only moments before little more than atomized river mist on their faces had quickly turned into white-cap kicked-up heavy spray that was rapidly getting Zoey soaked.

Ian knew that if the wind was to get much stronger along with the rapidly incoming tide, they could easily be stranded, unable to walk on submerged planks, the very ones that they'd just used. Under the best of conditions, getting back to shore from where they were was going to be challenging to the extreme.

But even with the very real hazards that loomed heavily on both of their minds, when Ian looked downwards, he couldn't help but smile. Zoey was already grinning. She'd witnessed Ian lift the trap door even though it had been just a few inches. They both, without uttering a single word to each other, understood well that this hatchway would indeed get them inside. But with that, if they chose to proceed any further, things were about to get very serious.

Ian looked directly into Zoey's bright eyes. "Well, wadda-ya say? Shall we do this?"

Zoey, with an excitedly confident look on her face, nodded her head as she said emphatically, "Yes!"

CHAPTER 15
Hide

Ian and Zoey both breached the hatchway. They stood for a moment silent and still just inside what was effectively the skylight basement of the warehouse.

Ian looked around to see if he could spot some sort of counterweight pulley system, one that allowed the hatch-door to open with such relative ease. He could see none.

That's bizarre. That hatchway door's gotta weigh at least … Ian's train of thought was interrupted as Zoey spoke just above a whisper, "Ian, how come even as dark as it is in here, everything looks shiny. Like, brand new. And do you smell that strong chlorine smell …?"

Ian's eyes almost instantly begun to burn and sting. "Bleach. The place has been totally scrubbed down with bleach," Ian said as he thought, *The place is clean, all right. Too clean. Like they knew we were coming, and … Nothing cleans up blood and guts better than bleach. Just splash it around all over. It renders any DNA that might have been missed in the cleanup totally unviable for testing. Smart … no loose ends.*

The lighting was dim but not too bad. The few windows that there were on the dock-floor level of the warehouse had long ago been soaped out, but they did afford some light from the outside world, and Ian was thankful for it. He'd brought a flashlight for just such an occasion but had forgotten it back in his Jeep.

Zoey spoke up again. "Look at all this equipment. It all looks like it was just installed. I guess for kitchen use. The place must serve food. But this looks way beyond what you'd typically see in the back of any restaurant I've ever been in. Looks more like stuff you'd see in a cannery or ..."

Ian interjected, "Meat packing plant."

Zoey nodded as she replied, "Yeah. Weird."

Ian began looking closely around the room. He spotted a stainless steel walk-in freezer and opened it up, but it was totally empty other than a dozen meat hooks that hung from long, steel, clothesline-like poles.

Ian closed the door to the freezer and panned his eyes across the large area. All of the countertops and huge deep sinks were made of stainless steel. There were no ovens or stovetops of any kind. No microwaves or heating methods that he could see, but there were plenty of stainless steel knives, meat cleavers, and various other blades or saw-toothed paraphernalia all devised to chop, saw, or cut through meat or bone.

Ian thought about what Zoey had said. Maybe it's all for food preparation. But then he noticed, strangely enough, there was no food stored anywhere. No restaurant-sized cans of anything. Just then, all the pieces came together and hit Ian right between the eyes as he stared intently about while Zoey was looking closely at all the knives and meat-cleavers.

Ian suddenly exclaimed, a bit louder than he'd intended, "This is no restaurant preparatory kitchen ... or storage facility. Well, not for any restaurant."

Zoey frowned as she raised her right index finger and placed it to her lips, signaling Ian to quiet down. Ian nodded, then continued but in a much softer voice, "This is the old fish cannery room. That's true. But that's not what it's used for now."

Ian thought, *This room's for food preparation all right. Food preparation of the ghoulish kind.*

Suddenly, they both heard the sound of an opening door, and then someone's footsteps down the staircase from above. Both Ian and Zoey had seen the stairs when they'd first climbed up through the floor-hatch doorway, but they had appeared to lead to nowhere.

Zoey quickly motioned for Ian to follow her as she pointed towards the walk-in freezer. Without hesitation and as quietly as they could, they made their way to the freezer, opened it, and went inside, closing its door behind them. Ian was glad the freezer was a brand new model. The door opened and closed silently, and he knew that since it was a very new model, with safety laws being what they were, it would not lock them inside.

Inside the sub-zero freezer, it was intolerably cold. Zoey, whose clothes were already wet, began shivering almost instantly. The freezer's door had a small glass window designed to afford easy viewing for any person of average height.

Ian motioned to Zoey that they should both crouch down on opposite sides of the doorway so as not to be readily spotted by anyone looking through the freezer's window.

Suddenly, light shone into the freezer. Someone had switched on the overhead neon lights to the room. Even inside the freezer, they could both hear the buzzing sound made from the neon light ballasts warming up. The light flickered a bit and became brighter by the second. Ian could almost hear his heart pounding and definitely felt his stomach turning as he heard someone walking around in the room. Zoey stared at him in wide-eyed dismay. After a few moments which seemed like forever had passed, the lights went out, and they heard heavy steps ascending the stairway and fading away.

With no intentions of doing any further investigation, Ian opened the freezer door and they both hurried over to the floor hatchway. Ian reached down and took hold of the handle. He quickly and silently began lifting the hatchway until it was completely open. But Ian was confused, because this time when he tried to open the trap door, it was at least as difficult to lift open as he'd initially assumed it would be.

Ian felt a cold shiver run up his neck and spine as he thought, *Oh shit. Lifting is much easier than pushing from beneath. There's no way I pushed it open that easily on my own. Someone must have helped me open the hatch."*

Ian signaled for Zoey to go first and get out of there as quickly as possible. She began her egress from the warehouse via floor-way. Once she reached the catwalk planks, she looked up at Ian who was still climbing down the ladder from the trap door. "Ian, you forgot to close the hatch."

Ian looked down at Zoey as he continued his descent. "Trust me, it doesn't matter. I'll explain once we've gotten the hell out of here."

The tide had continued coming in while they'd been inside the warehouse. The water's surface was now only two feet beneath the wooden planks. Due to the rising tide and the increasing strength of the wind, waves were starting to breach the surface of the planks. Green seaweed slime and barnacle-covered planks were slippery enough when dry, and they were now drenched – which made them now slippery to the extreme. The going was treacherous and seemed to be getting worse by the minute. So much so that both Ian and Zoey each kept their horrified thoughts to themselves – that it was a very real possibility that they'd never make it back to land again.

Ian had Zoey go ahead of him so he would at least have a chance to save her if she began to fall. As Ian slowly made his way forward as best he could, he began thinking about the very real prospect of their possible demise, a prospect that by percentage, like the tide, wind, and weather, was increasing exponentially by the moment.

Due to Ian's education and training, he began nearly instinctually intellectualizing how if they did fall and sink to the depths of the dark, icy-cold waters of the Columbia, in mere minutes they would be overwhelmed by the effects of hypothermia followed by near certain drowning regardless of swimming ability, or in his case lack thereof. That hours later, the gases would begin their process of expanding their guts, effectively bloating and inflating them to the point of sufficient buoyancy to resurface unless their bodies became caught on some submerged snag. But with any luck their former selves would eventually float up to the river's surface and ride the tides and currents into shore like flesh and bone boogie boards.

CHAPTER 16
Recuperation

Fortune smiled on Ian and Zoey. Against all odds, they both made it back to land after the longest short walk of their lives.

They climbed up the ladder that led to the dock level, and hurried back to the Jeep, dripping wet and cold to the bones. Once there, Ian and Zoey were greeted by a very excited guard dog. Scout had been a good boy while they were gone. Ian petted his dog and even kissed him on his head, as he thanked Scout for being so good for so long. Ian started up his Jeep and cranked the heater on full; he continued for a moment petting his best buddy. Then all at once, Ian was hit square between the eyes by another epiphany. If they hadn't made it back, what would have become of Scout? Ian suddenly felt terrible about that previously unconsidered possibility.

During their drive back from Astoria to Long Beach, the weather rapidly turned from bad to full-on coastal storm, about the time they were nearly halfway across the Astoria-Megler Bridge which spanned across the Columbia River connecting Oregon and Washington. They were traveling on the area of the bridge that was as straight as an arrow. Typically, its road surface was suspended around thirty feet above the river, but due to the high tide, torrential rain, and approaching gale-force winds, occasional waves were breaching the sides of the bridge's sea-wall railing, making driving precarious at best.

Ian was getting a little nervous regarding the intensity of the wind; it had begun gusting so hard it was nearly pushing his Jeep into the oncoming traffic lane seemingly at its whim. That, compiled with his windshield wipers near-failing efforts to keep up with the pounding, torrential rain, and a heavy fog that seemed to have come from nowhere, made seeing where he was driving extremely difficult.

By the time they'd made their way into Long Beach, the wind had died down a little. It was still blowing in gusts that Ian estimated had to have been in excess of fifty miles an hour. Zoey, after having not spoken for nearly twenty minutes, decided to break the ice.

"So Ian, are you hungry? I'll bet Scout is." Ian hadn't thought about it in light of what he'd just driven through, but upon hearing Zoey's question, he realized that he was starving.

"Yeah, I could eat," Ian said casually, not wanting to sound desperate as he glanced over at Zoey. He spoke again, this time smiling, "You got a place in mind? Somewhere that allows filthy, soaking wet people I hope."

Zoey looked like she was concentrating for a moment. "Yes, as a matter of fact, I know someplace that would be perfect on such a gloomy, stormy night. That is, if they're still open."

"You mean if they haven't closed due to the storm? You sure you don't want to change into dry clothes first?"

Zoey fired back, "No. Are you kidding? Nobody around here closes due to a little weather. And we're all dirty and wet most of the time. Ha! God, really. Inlanders!" She laughed.

The truth was they were dirty, but their clothing had dried to the point of not looking as wet as they felt.

Zoey spoke. "If we did go and change into dry clothes, by that time, every place will be closed." Ian looked at the time on his cell phone. He realized she probably was right as he mused, *After what we've survived today, how ironic would it be if we end up dying from pneumonia.*

As they approached the downtown area, Zoey quickly pointed towards a side street in the direction of the ocean. "There, Ian. Take that street. It will take you to the beach access drive. Near the end is the tallest building in town – the Seabreeze Motel. Yeah, it's a real skyscraper. Three stories. At the top is a good lounge and restaurant that looks over the ocean. Even in this fog and rain, with the flood lights shining out at the dunes, you'll be able to see the waves hit the shoreline. It's really beautiful! Don't worry about the way we look. This is the beach. Nobody cares. But if it makes you feel better, we can eat in the lounge."

Ian smiled as he replied, "Sounds good to me. We can get something to go for Scout. Until then, I've got a bag of doggy snacks in the glove box. I'll give him some when we park. That will tide him over. That is, after I've taken him for a quick walk to stretch his legs and relieve himself."

As he drove, Ian thought about how very attractive Zoey was, even with her still nearly-soaked stringy hair and wet, dirty clothes. But also how very young she was and how it was becoming more than obvious that she liked him, as he did her.

Just then Ian remembered that he had a semi-clean dry towel in the very back of his Jeep; as they pulled into the parking lot of the motel he glanced at Zoey. "Hey, I've got a dry towel in the back of my rig. We can use it to dry off." Zoey began squinting her eyes and puckering her lips in such a way that it reminded Ian of someone who had just sucked on an under-ripened persimmon.

"Um, not to be rude, but that would have been really useful information about forty minutes ago." Zoey said with an intentionally cocky tone to her voice.

Ian smiled and shrugged his shoulders as he replied, "Sorry 'bout that."

The intensity of the storm had lessened considerably. It was still raining steadily, but not all that hard. It was now only a bit more than typically breezy. Ian silently marveled at how quickly and extremely the weather changed at the coast.

Ian quickly exited the Jeep, ran to the back and opened the tailgate door. He grabbed the towel, then rapidly rejoined Zoey in the front of the Jeep. They dried themselves off and wiped away dirt smudges on their faces with the towel as best they could. Then Ian gave Scout a handful of doggie snacks and cracked his driver's side window.

"Okay, fella. I hate to leave you again. But I promise, I'll bring you back something special to eat." He and Zoey exited the Jeep and proceeded with haste across the parking lot into the motel.

Once inside the lower lobby, Ian pressed the button for the elevator and they both stepped in. Zoey immediately punched the button for the third floor. The door closed, and they were on their way up. It was a relatively slow, jerky ride.

On their way up, Zoey said, "Ian. After thinking it over, I think we probably *should* eat in the lounge. You know, with the way we look."

Ian smiled and laughed just a bit as he replied, "Yeah, I think you're probably right."

The elevator door opened, and they both stepped out. Ian noticed immediately that there were only three directions that a person could take. Straight ahead led to the third floor rooms of the motel. To the right was the entrance to the restaurant, and to the left was the Sand Bar.

Once inside the cocktail lounge, it was obvious that it was a seat-yourself establishment. Zoey took the lead. Holding Ian's left hand, she led him across the lounge to the ocean view tables. The place was decorated to the nines with Halloween lights and decorations. There were small, colorful pumpkins and gourds placed at each table.

There was only one other person in the lounge. He looked to Ian to be in his mid-to-late seventies. He had white hair that semi-circled his pattern baldness, and an equally white though shortly-cropped beard. He wore weathered, khaki dungarees that were supported by a set of wide, careworn, orange suspenders and a black and grey plaid flannel shirt.

Ian immediately surmised that the man was most likely a local. A commercial fisherman would be a better than fair money bet. Ian further deduced he was likely the captain of his own vessel. That hypothesis was based on the fact that the man's hat bore some nautical-looking embroidered insignia. That, and Ian was pretty certain that it said 'Captain' just under the insignia.

Ian caught the man looking him over. He figured it was because he was wet and dirty, and especially because of his spiky, jet-black hair, so Ian wasn't all that surprised. But on closer examination, Ian realized the man's attention was not so much on him. He was more focused on Zoey.

The man spoke in a loud voice. "Zoey, girl, watch-ya doing out-en-bout. Ain't a fit night fer man ner beast."

Zoey instantly tore her eyes from gazing out the window at the ocean and looked towards the man. Zoey smiled as she spoke. "Oh, hi Ray. Better question, what are you doing out so late? Where's Molly?"

Ray spoke, "My Molly, she's up river ..." The man let out a throaty couple of coughs indicative of a smoker of long standing. He then continued, "She be up river in Longview, visit'n er sister fer a few days. At dat home fer' old folks. We moved her into er when her husband passed on a couple month back."

Zoey looked over at Ian, who was still casually looking at Ray. She spoke directly to Ian. "Ian, I'd like you to meet Captain Ray. Ray McGuire. Ray, this is a friend of mine. Ian Mc... McBride."

The older gentlemen was silent for just a moment. Ian spoke up, "Nice to meet you, Ray. Uh, Captain."

The captain looked Ian up and down for a second. "Yes, well, any friend of this little gal'za friend a-mine. Say, you got some head a hair, don't-cha, young feller? Zoey-girl, she cut yer's and make er all shiny-black like dat? She cuts me Molly's, right good."

Ian was too embarrassed to answer. He just smiled as he panned his eyes around the room, double checking that there were no other people within listening distance other than the three of them and the bartender.

The bartender was a young man that Ian guessed was just barely old enough to be serving alcohol.

Without saying another word, the old sea captain finished his food, got up, laid some money down on the table, tipped his hat at Zoey, then turned and walked out of the lounge, leaving Ian and Zoey the only patrons in the place.

Ian and Zoey made small talk for a couple of minutes before the bartender came over to their table to take their order.

"Hi guys. So you decided to come out and brave the weather?" the young man said. Zoey smiled. "Aren't you ... I mean weren't you little Joey Patterson?"

The young man smiled back at Zoey, recognizing her as well. "Yeah, that's me. I mean, without the little part. Everyone calls me Joe now. You used to babysit me and my sister years ago, right?"

Zoey was smiling widely. "That's right. And you were a handful!" The young man and Zoey laughed. Ian grinned as he mused, *Small towns.*

"Now here you are working at the tall building." Zoey smiled at Ian as she continued, "All the locals call this place the 'tall building' since for years it was the tallest building in town – and still is if you don't count the large, newer time-share vacation club located just across the road. That place was built just a few years ago and is about the same height I'd guess."

The young man said, "Yeah, here I am working part-time mostly on this side of the restaurant in the old Sand Bar. That is until they get a replacement bartender. Roger, the normal bartender …" Joe looked directly at Zoey. "Zoey, you know him, right?" Zoey smiled and nodded her head, yes.

Joe continued, "He up and quit the other day for no real reason I know of 'cept he had been calling in sick a couple shifts before. Last time I seen him, he told me he'd been feeling real bad for the last couple weeks, and no kidding. He looked pale as hell. One thing I do know is he'd been working himself to death. He recently took a second bartender job over in Astoria. I don't know what place. Janice, the manager, she told me it was especially odd for him to up and suddenly quit like that. That even though he only worked four shifts a week 'cause of how good he was and how long he'd been here and all, she and the owner had decided they were gonna soon be putting him on the company medical plan. Anyway, man, if he is real sick, he sure quit at a bad time 'cause he might really need insurance as expensive as it is to see doctors and all. Anyway, she says to me that it wasn't like him. Not at all. That to the best of her recollection, he'd never taken a day off for being sick in over three years. I told her that I'd heard from more than one person that there's a real bad bug going around. Anyway, when they fill the spot with an experienced person, I'll be back over in the restaurant bussing tables. Only reason I'm here tonight is I'm the only newer help they got that's twenty-one. All the people with seniority, they only want to work the busy shifts, if you know what I mean. For the tips." Both Ian and Zoey smiled and nodded.

Joe caught his breath. He'd been speed talking, and it had nearly taken his breath away. "Well, you guys want some drinks? And maybe something from the kitchen? This place has got real good food." Ian and Zoey took the opportunity to look the menu over.

"Uh, I've been studying the drink cheat-sheet all day. I'm sure I can make just about any of the drinks real good. You know, like screwdrivers or rum and coke or anything from a pre-mix. 'Course, wine or beer … that's easy. But I'm up for trying, I mean making, anything you want."

Right out of the gate, Ian liked the young man. He was obviously nervous, but to his good fortune, it was a very slow night.

Ian spoke up. "I'll have a Jack Daniels and Coke, in a tall glass." He figured there wasn't much chance the young man could screw that up.

Zoey, also not wanting to apply any pressure on the young man, decided to keep it easy as well. "I'll have a glass of the house Cabernet Sauvignon."

Joe looked at Zoey with a momentary blank expression on his face. But then as if a light just switched on in his mind, a large smile came over his face as he replied, "We've got that."

As Joe started to turn to go back to behind the bar, he paused to speak to Zoey. "Say, um, if you like my service and all, and if it wouldn't be too much trouble, maybe you could fill out that little card there and well … give me a good score." He pointed to a card that was placed next to the small, basic condiment caddy on their table.

Joe continued, "Anyway, the manager, Jill … She's really into reading those. She gives people more hours if they get lots of good scores. They're like a score card about service, friendliness, and knowledge of what we have on our menu. Stuff like that. If you give me a good score, maybe they'll let me work this side tomorrow. Halloween. Even if the weather stays bad, it should be real busy. Lots of tips."

Ian smiled and nodded while Zoey replied, "Of course. We'd be happy to, Joe."

Joe smiled as he replied, "Awesome! I'll get your drinks and come back and take your food order. You do want food too, right?" Both Ian and Zoey smiled and nodded. As Joe turned and walked away, Zoey grinned and rolled her eyes slightly as she looked at Ian. Ian returned her smile with a big one of his own. He then winked and nodded once, indicating to her that this was a good, laid-back choice.

Ian leaned over the table slightly towards Zoey before he said, "The young man, our bartender, Joe. I like him. He's trying his best. That's all that should be asked of anyone." It was more than apparent to Zoey that Ian truly meant what he was saying, and that touched Zoey's heart.

Ian relaxed back into his seat and began glancing over his menu, but then looked up from it for a moment as he said, "Well, I'm finally more dry than wet. How about you?"

Zoey grinned as she replied, "Yeah, finally. I'm good!"

Ian began looking once again at his menu as he spoke. "Okay, since you've been here before probably lots of times, what's good?"

Zoey replied, "Well, it's all good. But if seafood's your thing, I've been told their fried oysters and razor clams are real good."

Ian smiled. "The razor clams. Now that sounds perfect! I had oysters recently, but I haven't had a mess of razor clams in ... seems like ages. How 'bout you? What'll you be having?"

"I'm gonna have their soup and salad. Clam chowder ... in a bread bowl."

Ian smiled and gazed outside for a moment at the weather before speaking. "Hot chowder on a cold, wet night. That sounds good too. Maybe I'll have a cup of chowder with …" Ian looked over his shoulder. Joe was back with their drinks.

"Here ya are, guys," Joe said while he placed their drinks on the table. "Ah heck. I forgot the little napkins for these to sit on."

Zoey immediately spoke up. "No, Joe, we don't need 'em. This is just fine."

Joe smiled. "Okay, then. Can I take your food order?"

Ian smiled as he spoke. "Yes, Joe. That'd be great. Zoey's going to have a bread bowl of your clam chowder and a salad."

Joe looked from Ian over at Zoey, then asked, "What kind of salad? I've got this one … We have um … Caesar … or … our house garden salad. And if you want like … like a fancy seafood salad, we've got crab or shrimp Louie's. I hear they're real good."

Zoey smiled as she glanced at Ian then up at Joe before speaking. "I'll just have a garden salad with bleu cheese dressing on the side." Joe smiled and nodded his head as he made his notes.

He then looked back over at Ian. "Okay, uh … For you, sir. What will you be having then?" Ian couldn't help but nearly laugh at the way Joe would slide back and forth from sounding like a kid talking on the street to trying to sound like a professional waiter.

"Well, Joe, I'm going to try your fried clams, and a baked potato with everything … which I might add has come highly recommended." Ian flashed a grin at Zoey before returning his attention to Joe. "And I'll also have a cup of your clam chowder."

Joe was slowly jotting their orders down, making certain he didn't forget anything before he spoke. "Okay, I'll get your orders turned into the kitchen and … Oh, I know. Can I get you some waters?"

Ian looked over at Zoey, who shook her head before replying, "No, Joe. I think we're great here." Joe smiled, turned, and began walking away off towards the restaurant side of the establishment.

Ian picked up his drink. He then looked over at Zoey. "Here's looking at you, kid." he said in his best Bogart impersonation, trying to be both funny and flirtatious.

Zoey smiled and giggled as she lifted her glass. "Cheers." she said as she posed her glass towards Ian's.

They both took sips of their drinks before Ian cleared his throat and continued speaking. "Zoey, I don't know. I mean, I really don't know exactly how to say what I'm about to."

Zoey, a little confused and now slightly uneasy, replied, "It's been my experience to try and not overthink things. Just say what's on your mind."

Ian smiled and nodded, then took a deep breath before he continued, "All right. Here goes. Tomorrow night, we very well may be facing some really dangerous people. It's not too late for you to back out. The fact is, you probably should. I mean today was … well … we were lucky to have not gotten killed. And it would have been hands down totally my fault."

Zoey reached across the table with her right hand and took Ian's left. She remained silent for a moment just holding Ian's hand, then she spoke. "Ian, I'm in this all the way with you. I mean … you know … tomorrow night."

Ian, with a dry, I'm-not-bluffing poker-look on his face, continued, "Well, I want you to listen to me. And after you've heard me out … That is, if you don't think that I'm completely crazy … You may want to change your mind. But first …" Ian reached into his wallet. He pulled out six one-hundred dollar bills. He folded them up and handed them to Zoey.

Zoey looked at the money in her hand. "Ian, this is too much."

Ian fired back, "Like hell it is. This is half of what Ned gave me today. This is really dangerous stuff. Besides, you've missed work, and anyway, I'll hear no more of it." Zoey sat back in her chair, smiled, and respected Ian's wishes. She said no more on the subject of money.

Ian continued, "Okay now that that's settled, I, like the Astoria Police, am convinced that the killings across the river are absolutely directly connected to that guy Salizzar and his nightclub cronies. You already know that." Ian paused for a second. Zoey, with a blank look on her face, looked directly into Ian's eyes as she nodded.

Ian continued, "But what you don't know is … That is, what I and your Uncle Clayton suspect about Salizzar himself is …" Just then, Ian was interrupted. Joe was back with Zoey's salad and Ian's cup of soup.

"Here you are." Joe said with a particularly pleasant tone to his voice. Ian suddenly remembered his promise to Scout. "Say, Joe, would you please put in an order to go for your four-piece chicken strips and fries? I have a hungry partner waiting for us."

Joe smiled back. "Sure, you bet." Ian speculated that Joe was happily anticipating that now an even larger tip might be coming his way.

CHAPTER 17
Warning

Ian never found the right moment again at the bar to tell Zoey just exactly who, or what, he suspected that Salizzar might actually be. The mood was too good, and they were enjoying relaxing in each other's company too much for Ian to potentially spoil such a good time with any more bleak or crazy sounding talk. By the time Ian and Zoey were ready to leave the restaurant lounge, their clothes were dry, but they were neither dry, nor feeling any pain.

Just before leaving the restaurant lounge, Zoey told Ian in no uncertain terms that she'd like to go to his place, that they couldn't be alone at hers because her roommate Todd would be there and the walls were thin. Ian was happy to oblige. Once they'd climbed into Ian's Jeep, he fired up the engine, then turned halfway around in his seat to face Scout, who was very excited to see him. "Scout, I've got something I think you're really gonna like, boy. Oh, and is it okay if Zoey sleeps over tonight?" Scout barked twice and began wagging his tail.

Ian opened the Styrofoam to-go carton that he'd carried with him from the restaurant and set it on the armrest between the two front seats. "Here, boy, this is for you."

Zoey laughed and gave Ian a bad time regarding his choice of dog food to feed Scout. "Uh, Ian. That's pretty expensive dog food you're giving Scout, don't ya think? Spoil him much? Ha!"

Ian replied, "Yeah, nothing so pedestrian as AttaBoy or Alpo for my fella." Ian petted Scout on the head while Scout munched away on his dinner.

Once Scout had wolfed down his meal, Ian put the Jeep in drive and began heading towards the main street of Long Beach. Just as Ian was turning left onto the main street of downtown Long Beach, he and Zoey spotted a fire truck that sped on past them, lights flashing and sirens blaring. Ian drove his Jeep over to the side of the road and came to a stop. The speeding fire truck was followed seconds later by two police cars that also had their lights flashing and sirens screaming. One behind the other, the fire truck and the two police cars sped as fast as they dared through downtown, heading north up the peninsula, the same general direction that Ian and Zoey were headed.

Zoey looked at Ian. "Wow, there must be some sort of emergency on ahead." Ian nodded. Once the last police car in the small emergency caravan had passed them, Ian pulled his Jeep away from the curb and started driving, heading north on the main street through town.

Within minutes, the fire truck and police cars were so far ahead of Ian and Zoey that they soon disappeared from their view. Just moments after that, they could no longer hear their sirens.

Ian continued driving north on the peninsula's main road for several miles. It was Zoey who first spotted even in the dark, rainy gloom of night a massive plume of smoke that was billowing up from an area not far ahead of them. Minutes later, it became apparent that the smoke and fire glow was coming from Oscar's on the Ocean.

Once they pulled into the RV park's office parking lot, Ian could see clearly what was burning, making him nearly physically ill. The RV park owner, Oscar, seemed nearly beside himself as he spoke with the police.

Ian looked at Zoey, who had a slightly confused look on her face as he began to speak with a shaky voice, "The fire ... that's my ... that was my trailer. Looks to me like probably someone's trying to send a message, don't ya think?"

Zoey couldn't even answer. She just sat with tears in her eyes, staring across the park at the burning trailer.

All of the other campers and many onlookers were gathered as close to the fire as the police would let them. They watched the firefighters as they fought to keep the fire from spreading. It was obvious there was nothing that could be done to try to save Ian's trailer or any of his belongings inside.

Ian climbed out of his Jeep and walked around to the passenger-side of his rig. Zoey rolled her window down.

Ian cleared his throat before speaking. "Well, it wasn't much, but the trailer and its contents were all I've got ... had." Ian thought about all of the money he'd stashed inside the trailer.

Just then, Ian's cell phone began chiming. Ian reluctantly answered. "Yeah."

"Ian, this is Clayton. I just heard about your trailer from one of my ... people. Are you and Zoey ... Is everyone all right?"

Ian took a deep breath. "Yeah, thankfully, none of us were there when ..."

Clayton interrupted, *"Okay. Forget about that old trailer and whatever clothes and personal belongings you've lost. I take care of my friends. I've already booked you a room at the Ebb Tide Condominiums just up the road a little ways from where you are. In your room on the nightstand, you will find an envelope with enough cash in it to replace your losses and any cash you may have lost as well. Of that, I'm confident."*

Before Ian could say a word, Clayton hung up. Ian thought, *Who is this guy? Clayton reminds me of some sort of a mafia godfather. What in the hell's really going on?*

A police officer walked away from the crowd and approached Ian.

"Hey, your name McDermott? Are you Ian McDermott?" the officer asked. Ian remembered that before Clayton suggested he use 'McBride' as an alias, he'd already registered at the RV park under his real name.

Ian replied, "Yeah. Yeah, that's me."

The police officer continued, "Oscar, the owner of this park, tells me that's your trailer on fire over there." The police officer pointed with his chin towards the trailer inferno. Ian didn't reply. He just nodded slightly. "Okay. Anyway, Mister McDermott, we caught the two scumbags that did this to yer trailer. Neither of 'em from around here." The officer pointed over at his car, in the back of which were two men who appeared to be in their mid-twenties.

"We've got at least five eyewitnesses seen 'em do it. Hell, they didn't even try to run once me and my partner got here. They just stood their ground, empty gas cans in hand with spaced-out looks on their faces. Every time my partner'd ask them why'd they do it? Why'd they torch 'yer trailer, they just mumble, 'he commands it.' Doper freaks. Meth-heads, more likely 'un not. We'll get them over to the hospital in Ilwaco, have 'em piss checked and tox-screened for illegal substances. Didn't find anything more than a little grass on either of 'em. But trust me, it ain't a little pot that's gotten 'em that loopy. They're both fly'n higher'n kites. Both look like they've got injection marks on the sides of their necks. Weird place to be shooting up, but anyway ... I hope your trailer was insured."

Ian thought, *Insured? Uh ... NO! Other than liability, who insures an old piece of shit trailer?*

Zoey got out of the Jeep and stood next to Ian. The officer tipped the brim of his baseball-style uniform hat. "Hey Zoey."

Zoey somberly replied, "Hi Dan."

The police officer continued, "Well, I'll need you to stop by the station or call us, and we can mail you some forms you'll need to fill out primarily for your insurance company's requirements. And of course so we can formally bring charges against those scumbags. Assuming, of course, that you're gonna press charges. Hell, truth is, once we ran 'em ... we found that those two losers both have a laundry list of petty crime convictions. If you choose to press charges, they ain't going nowhere but a short stint in jail then straight to prison. Hell, we've got enough even without you pressing charges to put 'em away. Vandalism, reckless endangerment, arson, destruction of property ... On and on. Not much of anything that any lawyer can do for those two. We caught 'em red handed. We've got plenty of eye witnesses. Trust me, you ain't gonna have to testify. That's pretty much a guarantee. I mean, what would anyone need or want you to say or prove? Other than that you were the owner of the trailer. And you can do that by phone-interview and faxing in whatever license, title and registration documentation we'll be need'n."

Ian spoke. "Sure. Yeah, I'll press charges. Of course. I'll either drop by your station or ..."

The police officer continued, "This is where I'd like to say good night to ya, but I know that'd be a cruel joke. So I'll just say take care."

Ian couldn't help but smile at the officer, who had been very nice. Once again, Ian thought, *Small town cops sure could teach their big city counterparts a thing or two about manners.*

Ian looked into the Jeep at Scout, who was noticeably upset. He smiled at Scout in a wordless gesture intended to hopefully ease his furry friend's stress. Ian then looked directly into Zoey's jade-green eyes. With all the intestinal fortitude that he could muster, almost jovially,

166

he asked, "Well, Zoey, tell me about the Ebb Tide Condominiums. Is it a nice place? Knowing what I know of your uncle, I expect it is. Clayton booked me a place there. How he knew about all this that quick is beyond me."

Zoey didn't even looked surprised as she replied, "My uncle knows pretty much everyone on the peninsula. Not much gets by him. Well that, and he's pretty addicted to listening in on his police band radio, which he says he does for research." Ian smiled at Zoey's statement while nodding his head in agreement.

Ian replied, "Yeah, I don't suspect much at all around here gets past Clayton. Anyway, when we get there and settle in, I've got some things I want … that I need … to tell you. Very important things that, well, that you, more than most, might even believe. That is, if first you don't come to the conclusion that I'm certifiably insane."

Zoey smiled widely at Ian as she spoke. "Don't worry, Ian. I already think you're crazy!"

CHAPTER 18
Tell-Tale Heart

Ian stood waiting in the office of the Ebb Tide Condominiums. At first glance, it appeared to be an impressively expansive and aesthetically pleasing condominium complex. It seemed more of a motel than a condominium in the classic sense of the word, primarily due to the sign in the office that stated they offered condo suites for rent by the day, week, and month, though Ian suspected that some units likely served as permanent residences for a fortunate few.

Ian looked around the office and began admiring the Halloween decorations that were on the walls, front desk, and even hanging from the ceiling.

Zoey and Scout had remained in the Jeep, which was parked in one of the guest registration parking spots located directly in front, and in clear view of, the condominium office.

Ian waited patiently while an elderly couple that had arrived before him continued going through the process of getting checked in. They were on their sixtieth anniversary and proud to tell anyone who'd listen. Ian couldn't help but admire the couple who genuinely seemed in love even after all those many years of marriage. But the thought also saddened him as he reflected momentarily on the loss of his wife, Janet, and his daughter, Sue Ann, just a few short years ago. One horrific instant ended for all time any further anniversaries he'd ever celebrate with his beloved wife; never would there come the day when he would walk his daughter down the aisle to proudly give her away to a new son-in-law so they too might one day be celebrating their sixtieth anniversary.

Before time allowed any further melancholy to set in on Ian, the couple completed their business and left the office. Ian knew that he was already reregistered, so checking in was little more than a formality and wouldn't take long.

Behind the desk was a middle-aged, heavy-set blonde woman, still very attractive. One of those ladies that just a few years and pounds ago would have turned every man's head when entering a room. She was wearing a brass-embossed name badge that bore the name Sharon.

Ian liked the name Sharon; it was his mother's name. Sharon McDermott. She had raised Ian on her own. Ian's father, Skip "Skeeter" McDermott, had been a career Navy pilot who died in a military training exercise due to a mechanical failure when Ian was just three years old. Ian never personally knew his father, though everyone he'd ever spoken to had said he was an exceptionally good man and one hell of a pilot. His mother never remarried. Ian couldn't even remember his mother going on any dates, although she was a very attractive woman, especially on the rare occasions that she'd make herself up.

She'd been a chain smoker for as far back as Ian could remember, smoking nearly non-stop up to the day she died from emphysema nearly ten years ago. Ian believed that the reasons she smoked so much and drank vodka every day was that she'd never recovered from the loss of her husband. That depth of grief and what it can do to a person was something Ian understood all too well.

Suddenly Ian was snapped back to the present when the front desk lady, Sharon, smiled at him and said, "I'd bet my bottom dollar that you're Mister McBride, am I right?" For an instant, Ian was taken by surprise and caught slightly off guard. He'd momentarily forgotten about the cover name that Clayton had suggested he use. But he quickly remembered and also surmised that Clayton had probably given her his general physical description.

"Um, yes. That's me. How'd you guess?" Ian replied somewhat sheepishly.

Sharon smiled, apparently pleased with her power of deduction. "Clayton didn't tell me you were such a handsome buck." Sharon flashed Ian a flirtatious smile.

Ian didn't know what to say. "Um, well, I don't know how I could possibly be much to look at after being out in this storm ... and the day I've had. But thanks." Ian thought, *Add to that, my ridiculous 'Dee Dee Ramone' punk rock hair style.*

Sharon then handed Ian a card key. "We've got you in one of our best ocean view units up on the third floor. Here's a map of the place." She set a small map on the counter for Ian to view and began pointing to it as she explained how to read it.

"As you can see ... you're ... here, and your room is in Building Three ... right there. Oh, and the hot tub and pool are in the building right next to the office. Pool towels are available here at the front desk. The pool and hot tub are open for adults only, from 9:00 to 10:00, day 'er night. Clayton told me you had a dog, no problem there. Besides the dog, he also said you might be here by yourself or you might have someone with you." Sharon pointedly looked out the office window at his Jeep. "I see you have a VERY YOUNG someone with you." She grinned cheekily and winked at Ian.

"Pets are okay with a deposit." Ian started instinctually to reach for his wallet. "Don't sweat it sugar ... Clayton's paid for everything. You're all set."

Ian smiled. "Um, say...Do I need to give you the make and year of my ..."

Sharon interrupted Ian. "Nope. Clayton knew your license plate number and gave me everything about you that we need. Say, Mister McBride, how do you come to know our local famous author anyway? You a writer too?"

Ian smiled. "No. No, I'm not a writer. How do I know Clayton? Well, that's a good question. Clayton and I, we go way back. Hundreds of years, it seems." Ian snickered slightly.

Sharon gave Ian a funny look regarding his vague and somewhat provocative answer.

Ian continued, "Anyway, I'll find my way from here and thanks, Sharon, for your wonderful service." Sharon smiled large and let out a small sigh as Ian turned and left the office. But then all at once, she blurted out, "Oh my goodness, I almost forgot. For some reason Clayton booked you a rental car. Is your Jeep not running well? Anyway, here're the keys. It's parked right in front of where you'll catch the elevator to go to your room. It's a black Toyota Camry. Real nice car, those Toyotas."

Sharon tossed the keys to Ian, who snatched them out of the air almost effortlessly. Ian grinned, "Yeah, my Jeep's not been running very well. Uh, okay then. Thanks!"

Ian climbed into his Jeep and smiled at Zoey. Scout was just about in her lap as she continued petting and loving him up. "You two sure have hit it off." Ian said.

Zoey glanced at Scout and then up at Ian as she grinned. "Yep, he's one of my two new favorite men. So are we … Are you all checked in?" Ian smiled back at Zoey.

"Yep, we're all checked in."

Zoey smiled and giggled slightly as she replied, "Good, 'cause while you were in the office, I called my shop. I've taken the next couple of days off. Todd's gonna cover my few scheduled appointments.

Besides," Zoey giggled and took Ian's hand, "I've got to start earning all that money you paid me."

Ian half laughed as he replied, "Oh, I'm pretty sure we're both going to earn our money tomorrow night." Just after he said what he did, he realized that Zoey was trying to be flirtatiously funny. Ian smiled. It was music to his ears that Zoey had cleared her calendar for the next couple of days presumably to be with him.

Ian started his Jeep and began driving to Building Three to get to their room. It wasn't until he'd driven past Buildings One and Two that he realized just how large the condo complex really was. "Zoey, we'll go to your apartment first thing in the morning so you can pick up some clothes and whatever stuff you'll need. Me, well obviously I've got to pick up some things. Clothes, toothbrush, and lots of basics. Ironically, the only clothes I've got left, well, besides what's on my back, is that outfit you bought me for going to the club. For some reason, call it fate or whatever, I put those clothes in that brown bag in the back seat."

Zoey smiled. "Well, we'll get you some duds tomorrow, like you said. Can't have you going all around town looking like some Goth clubber." Zoey and Ian began laughing.

Ian replied as he shook his head, "No, we can't have that."

Once they'd driven over to their building, Ian spotted the rental car. "Oh, Zoey, there's our new wheels for the next day or so." Ian paused and pointed to the car as he continued, "That Camry right there. Clayton arranged for it. He must have surmised that those two thugs that burned down my place … they must have followed me at one time or another back to my trailer. Your uncle's just helping us out so we're not so easily spotted, I'm guessing. I figure my cover … our cover … is basically blown. But regardless, I'll continue to go by Ian McBride. That car and the alias can't hurt."

Zoey cleared her throat. "Uh-um … it looks like a nice car." she said while looking it over.

Ian replied, "Yeah, Toyotas are nice. But also common. They don't stand out. It's a smart choice. I owe your uncle big time." Ian mused, *Maybe too big.*

After riding the elevator up three floors, Ian, Zoey, and Scout entered the condo unit. Even at first glance, the place was noticeably very nice. About what Ian had expected from the outward appearance of the place. The entire unit was nicely furnished with nautical-themed knick-knacks. There were seascapes in the form of nicely framed prints on nearly every wall. The furnishings were all fashionably quaint. As Ian began walking through the condo, he took note that there was a small but complete kitchen equipped with all the usual accoutrements. It had a serving counter that was accessible from the living room. On the living room side, there were three bar stools. Directly adjacent to the kitchen was a small dinette table positioned up against the wall with two nice chairs. In the living room area, there was a queen-sized bed located near a sliding glass door that offered access to an outside deck. Next to the living room bed and end table was a modest couch and an equally modest coffee table. The couch, even at a cursory glance, was easily recognizable as a foldout hide-a-bed.

As Ian took stock of the condo, he was happy to note that it had a nice gas fireplace positioned directly in front of the living room's bed. The curtains were open, revealing through the sliding glass doorway a small table and chairs, and a partially tarp-covered gas barbeque out on the deck.

Ian opened the sliding glass door and stepped outside onto the deck, which offered a fabulous view of the ocean. Zoey joined Ian for a moment but then signaled for Ian to follow her. They headed past the kitchen through an open doorway that led down a short hallway.

Scout had already made himself at home and was lying on the hearth in front of the gas fireplace that Zoey had switched on just moments after they'd arrived.

Zoey showed Ian that the condo had two full bathrooms and two nicely-furnished bedrooms. Ian realized that Clayton had reserved him some kind of master suite unit; the place had a lockable door just down from the first bathroom that could be closed, separating the front unit from the back two bedrooms. The condo was designed to be one large master suite, or separated ... dividing it into two separate rentable units ... one with a kitchen, and one without.

Ian and Zoey returned to the kitchen.

Ian thought, *This place, even in the off-season, must have cost Clayton at least a couple hundred a night. Boy, am I in the red with him. My debt's rising high as the tide.*

"Wow! This place is awesome!" Zoey blurted out as she walked from the kitchen into the main living room. She then walked over to Scout and stood with her back towards the fireplace. Ian remained in the kitchen. He opened the refrigerator and immediately noticed that it had been stocked with champagne, two different wines (a red and a white), a six-pack of bottled beer, and assorted cheeses. Ian smiled and began shaking his head as he gazed at the contents of the refrigerator. He abruptly exhaled as he thought to himself, *That Clayton ... the guy thinks of everything.*

After a moment of silence, Ian replied to Zoey's declaration of approval. "Yeah, this place is something. Your uncle's outdone himself with all this. Would you believe he even had the refrigerator stocked with ..." Before Ian could say another word, he spotted a manila envelope that was stuffed to obesity sitting on top of the microwave oven. The envelope had Ian's name written on it.

Ian paused for a moment, remembering Clayton telling him he'd take care of everything. Ian was certain the envelope contained money. Suddenly, more than ever, Ian began feeling like a captive bird in a gilded cage.

Ian opened the envelope. He was right; it was full of money. But it also contained an Oregon driver's license with his picture on it as well as all of the essential basic information. The license showed his last name as McBride. Ian marveled at the fake ID's detail, which was perfect in every way. Ian quickly put it in his wallet as he mused, *This would fool any expert. How does he get such things? And in the speed that he does …*

Also within the envelope was a note from Clayton.

Ian, I hope this money helps ease the pain of your losses. I strongly suggest that you put your Jeep into a storage facility of mine early tomorrow morning. It's called Stoker's Storage, and is just up the street at 101-2 Pacific Avenue. The code to enter the security gate is: 999666. No need to stop at the office to check in or anything. My manager is expecting you. Regards, Clayton.

The envelope contained much more money than Ian would have ever guessed. It was stuffed to its capacity with rubber-banded thousand dollar groupings of one-hundred dollar bills. In an instant, Ian calculated that the envelope contained twenty thousand dollars.

Ian almost staggered from the kitchen into the living room and flopped down on the edge of the bed. Zoey saw the large envelope that Ian held in his right hand. She also couldn't help but notice the expression on Ian's face; it looked like he was in at least mild shock.

Ian spoke before Zoey had a chance to ask any questions. "Your uncle and I have entered into a business partnership of sorts. He's going to write about my investigations. Clayton either must have gotten some kind of advance royalty and he's sharing it with me, or …"

Zoey spoke in an excited tone, "Wow! By the size of that envelope, that must have been some kind of advance. I mean, I know he's done very well in the past and is still pretty famous … but…" Zoey giggled then asked, "You two aren't into something shady, are you?"

Ian smiled reassuringly as he spoke in a calm voice. "No. No, nothing like that. I'm telling you the truth. At least what I've told you, and as I understand it. Come here and sit next to me … I'll tell you a tale. One that you're going to find hard, if not impossible, to believe. But I swear, hand to God, it's true."

Zoey left the comfort of standing in front of the warm fire and set herself just a few inches away from Ian on the edge of the living room bed.

"Okay Ian, shoot! Just know I can take and even understand just about anything. I'm no Mother Teresa. Just don't … just don't ever lie to me."

Ian smiled slightly while he nodded his head, acknowledging what Zoey said.

"All right. No lies. Here goes. All I ask is that you wait until I've said everything that I need to say before you either ask questions or want me to call you a taxi."

Zoey laughed at that remark, "Taxi? Where do you think you are, New York? There's no taxi service. Well, I guess there's sort of the one, but … Oh, never mind. Tell me what's on 'yer … Just go ahead."

"Okay. You know I told you a little about the town of Harmony Falls. You know, where I was before coming here. Well, without going into too many boring details, suffice it to say a friend of mine died. Let me back up. I was helping local law enforcement somewhat like I'm doing with Ned. Anyway, I was helping them investigate a situation that started with some hikers who'd been missing then later were found dead. Presumably killed by an animal or animals. There was that, and there were some other non-fatal attacks on a logger and some kids … And, well …"

176

Ian paused to look Zoey in her eyes to see if she was following him. Zoey nodded her head slowly as she spoke. "Yeah, got it. Keep going."

He continued. "Anyway, it wasn't an animal. Well it was … Oh man, this is hard to explain. Me and Sheriff's Deputy Charlie Redtail, we caught the murderer. But after he'd also killed the local sheriff. A good man. Sheriff Bud O'Brien."

Zoey spoke in a gentle voice, "It's okay, Ian. Tell me everything."

Ian took a deep breath, cleared his throat, and regained his composure. He continued, "Anyway, the thing is … The thing about the killer is, he wasn't … I mean … Ah hell, Zoey, I swear to you and God above the guy wasn't human."

Zoey looked intensely into Ian's eyes as she replied, "No duh. The guy was a psycho ... a monster!"

Ian started laughing as a purely nervous reaction. "Monster. Yeah, he was a monster all right. A fucking WEREWOLF! I shit you not!"

Zoey stood up, running her right hand through her hair. "Werewolf? Did I hear …? Ian, did you just say the murderer was a WEREWOLF! And you're not speaking metaphorically? Or … some such shit …?"

Ian took another deep breath as he shrugged his shoulders. "Yeah. You heard me right. I know. I know. Had I not been there and seen it with my own eyes, I mean you have every right to think me a crazy or compulsive liar or WHATEVER!" Ian couldn't help but nervously raise his voice.

Ian paused for a couple of seconds to calm himself down, then continued, "But whatever you think of me, it won't change a thing. I've told you the truth to the best of my ability. And now here's another one to swallow. Your uncle and, well, me too I guess, we believe that Salizzar, and maybe some of his cronies, are not only cold-blooded killers but ..." Ian paused as he mused, *Cold-blooded killers who happen to kill for warm blood.*

Zoey stared up at the ceiling and took a couple of slow, deep breaths before she spoke in an over-exaggeratedly calm voice, "Actual vampires. Let me get this straight. You and my uncle got your collective heads together and have come up with the theory that Salizzar's a real vampire? Fangs and all?"

Ian said, "Zoey, it really doesn't matter if you believe me or not. Just try and accept this much. I have witnessed events that go way beyond what any person with a rational mind would ever consider other than laughably possible. Things totally contrary to science regarding all accepted laws of physics. And believe me ... you don't experience anything like what I've seen and barely lived through ... without it rocking your entire belief system and changing you; opening your eyes wide to a world that you never would have ever realized exists all around you. Everywhere and nowhere, depending on what you allow your eyes to see. What I mean is, what I'm trying to say is this, I'm willing to at least consider the possibility of things now that just a few weeks ago I would have immediately dismissed as utter superstitious nonsense. I tell you, I can no longer be so quick to dismiss extreme possibilities. But mainly, what I want you to know, to fully understand, is regardless of whether they're actually blood-guzzling vampires in the cinematic sense of the word or just crazy vampire wannabes, these are likely ruthless killers either way. That is, if they are in fact the perpetrators of some or all of those recent murders across the river. Now, I tell you this because for one last time, it's not too late for you to back out. Actually, there's a part of me that wishes you would. The night we first met I told you about how my wife and daughter died in that car crash. Well, now with the loss of my trailer, not that it was much, you can probably understand that I have nothing much left at stake to lose, present company excluded."

Ian glanced over at Scout for a second, then focused back on Zoey as he continued, "Anyway, what I'm trying to say is that you've got your entire life left to live, and you're doing great ... and ..."

Zoey stopped staring at the ceiling. She took a deep breath, then looked at Ian. "I believe you, Ian. I mean I believe you're telling me the truth to the best of your understanding of the facts. Clearly you've experienced more loss than most people can take. I know about loss ... My parents and all ..." Zoey paused. Suddenly, she changed the tone of her voice from extremely soft to that of strength.

Zoey collected her thoughts then continued, "That was then and this is now. The way I see it is simple. If Salizzar or any of his nut jobs actually drink human blood or eat flesh or ... Well, that in my book makes them vampires real enough. I have a firm grasp on how dangerous tomorrow night might get. The very fact that they probably are the ones behind the murders and are behind those punks that destroyed your trailer and things ... uh ... duh. Yeah, these are ruthless, dangerous guys. But, if you think that I'm going to let you go into that lion's den tomorrow night by yourself, then there's no doubt about it. You are crazy! Hopefully, all this worrying is for naught, and we'll end up having a happy Halloween. But if it all goes to shit ... the very worst case scenario is we'll go down fighting together. And that's all I have to say about that." Zoey held her right hand palm-out towards Ian. "I'll hear no more of this tonight. Now, get undressed 'cause it's payback time, and by the looks of that envelope, maybe I can earn a bonus or two." Zoey giggled just a little as she leaned over towards Ian, closing the gap between them. She then closed her eyes and gently pressed her lips against his.

CHAPTER 19
All Hallows Eve (I)

Zoey was up early and moving about the condo, sipping a cup of coffee that she'd made just minutes before. She sat down on the bottom edge of the bed next to Ian, who was still sleeping on his back, and began gently tickling Ian's left foot which was protruding from the bedding. Scout had replaced Zoey in her spot in bed the moment she had gotten up. He was wide awake but had continued just lying patiently next to Ian.

"Wake-ee wake-ee, sleepy head. Happy Halloween!" Zoey said, looking for Ian to stop snoring and open his eyes. "It's time to wake up and smell the coffee."

Ian lazily opened his eyes and smiled when he saw who'd woken him from his slumber. Zoey was wearing only the v-neck white undershirt that he'd been wearing the night before.

Zoey spoke up in a cheery voice, "Well, before we go shopping, I have a very special place to take you, one that's fun to visit anytime. But on Halloween, the place is perfect! Just the right amount of weird mixed with a bit of creepy! My very favorite store, or museum depending on a person's point of view, in Long Beach or anywhere for that matter. I know you've seen it from the outside, but that's nothing. It's high time you've seen the awesome spectacle that is Marsh's Free Museum and met their famous resident, Jake the Alligator Man. You haven't really seen Long Beach until you've wandered through Marsh's."

Ian didn't have to be sold. The truth was, anywhere with Zoey was an adventure, and he loved unique, interesting stores, and museums.

"But first, how about we go and hot tub?" Zoey excitedly proclaimed.

Ian, still a bit foggy, thought about that for a moment, then replied, "Uh, that's a good thought, but neither of us have swimming suits."

Zoey laughed. "That's not a problem. I read that it's adults only in the hot tub for quite a while yet. My bra is a black sports-style one, and my panties look pretty much like regular black colored swim-suit bottoms. And you … You've got those boxers. They could pass as swim-shorts, no problem."

Ian looked down under the covers at his boxers. They were a dark blue-plaid. Ian thought, *Huh … shouldn't be a see-through problem … I guess.* He'd always bought the kind that had no fly. Ian further mused, *Having a fly in underwear's stupid. Like I'd stand there trying to pull my dick out of some 'cockamamie' fly-hole instead of pulling my shorts down to take a piss.*

"Okay, what the hell. I'm in." Ian exclaimed as he got up. He then immediately joined Zoey in having a cup of coffee. Once Ian had finished his coffee, he got dressed and took Scout out for a doggie-walk. Upon returning, he had the pleasure of watching Zoey slip out of his t-shirt and slide on her bra and panties before proceeding to get fully dressed. Watching Zoey undress then shimmy her slim, sexy body back into her clothing gave Ian thoughts of instigating an alternative agenda to hot tubbing. Thoughts of perhaps a morning round three, but he suppressed his voyeuristically-driven lust, and the two of them proceeded towards the condo's front door.

Ian looked at Scout as he spoke. "You stay here and be a good boy. We won't be very long." Scout barked once and wagged his tail.

Ian and Zoey climbed into the rental car and drove across the parking lot from Building Three over to the pool and spa building next to the office. After parking the car in front of the pool building, Ian went next door to the office. He immediately spotted neatly-folded pool towels piled on the corner of the front counter, Ian picked up two towels and exited the office unnoticed.

Ian met up with Zoey, who had just exited the car and was heading to the pool and spa building's front door. Zoey held the door open for Ian to catch up and enter with her.

Ian looked up at the sky as he said just loud enough for Zoey to hear, "Well, at least it's not raining. Not much more than a gentle breeze out today either. I hope this nice weather holds."

Inside the pool building, straight ahead of them was the indoor heated swimming pool. They both spotted the hot tub at the same time. It was located outside the building through sliding glass doors in a fenced-in patio area. Even from a distance, it was easy to see that it was a large, very nice spa that was totally privatized by a six-foot cedar fence all around it. There were tables and chairs for outside lounging. The weather was uncommonly warm for the time of day and month of the year. Ian guessed it to be in the mid-fifties. The sun had even begun periodically playing peek-a-boo through the clouds.

They had the place all to themselves. Zoey immediately began taking her clothes off, all but her underwear. Ian did the same. They set their clothes on a chair that was in the line of sight of the hot tub just beyond the sliding glass doors.

Zoey opened the sliding glass doorway as she said, "Last one in's a rotten egg." She giggled as she headed towards the chrome handrail and stepped into the ground-level mortar-and-tile spa.

Ian was right behind her as he paused for a second to close the sliding glass door behind him.

Once in the spa, Ian was pleased with the temperature of the water, which he guessed to be around 102 degrees. Higher temperatures than what the spa was currently set at tended to wreak havoc on his blood pressure in little to no time at all.

Zoey spotted the button to turn the jets on, which was mounted waist-high on one of the fence posts. She exited the spa just long enough to push down the large, red switch. Zoey then quickly bounded back into the spa, this time not bothering to enter on the side that had the handrail. She almost landed in Ian's lap.

There was a little delay in the jets coming on, but seconds after Zoey got back into the spa, they did.

Ian blurted out, "Wow! This is great!"

Zoey excitedly replied, "Oh yeah. You got that right. This is wonderful! Ian, would you be a dream and sit behind me and rub my shoulders? I've got a small kink in my neck. Not used to their pillows."

Ian was more than happy to rub any part of her. Zoey's stiff neck reminded Ian that his neck was fine now. Even with the stress of what they might be up against, Ian thought to himself, *Just having Zoey with me for a couple days has worked wonders.*

Ian began massaging Zoey's neck and shoulders. Occasionally, she would emit a quiet, low groan, clearly indicating when Ian was dead on the mark. After ten minutes of massaging with her back up against him, and her bottom pressed up against his crotch, Ian could bear the pressure no longer. He began slowly moving his hands first down her back, and then to the sides of her shoulder blades. Ian kept moving his hands slowly forward until he held both of Zoey's breasts cupped gently in his hands. Zoey leaned back and kissed him on the side of his neck. She sighed softly, clearly indicating that she didn't want Ian to stop.

Within moments, Zoey was reciprocating. She began working her right hand around behind her until she found home. Zoey began slowly massaging with her finger tips up and down Ian's now fully erect penis. Zoey guided Ian's left hand around and between her legs. She continued holding Ian's hand gently beneath her own as she began slowly stroking herself with Ian's hand, guiding his every movement. First on top of her panties, then with a little adjusting, Ian's hand and Zoey's both shimmy-slipped down inside them. Zoey let out an exquisite moan.

Without saying a word, she slipped her panties down, intentionally maintaining them just around her right ankle. She then turned around to face Ian as she skillfully began sliding Ian's boxers down to his knees.

"My God … You think we should?" Ian uttered in a half-hearted objection as he became ever more intensely fever-driven until succumbing to his glandular-charged madness.

Before Ian could even begin to clear his head and attempt some semblance of rational clarity, in one deft motion, Zoey slid him inside her, taking within her the full length of his swollen phallus. Seated on top of Ian, face to face, she began performing perfectly-timed rhythmic pelvic undulations. After a protracted period of lovemaking to the point that neither could hold out any longer, Ian and Zoey came to simultaneous, exquisitely gasping, anaerobic-sexercised climaxes.

After nearly a minute of their sharing large smiles, hugging, and laughter, Ian was able to finally catch his breath. He spoke while gazing starry-eyed into the deep green pools of Zoey's eyes, "Happy Halloween."

Zoey giggled as she replied, "Happy indeed."

She slowly climbed off of Ian's lap. It was then that Ian saw it. Startled and instantly embarrassed, he blurted out, "Oh my God!" Ian pointed up to what he was looking at – a camera mounted on a pole that undoubtedly surveyed by remote the entire spa and surrounding lounge area. Zoey couldn't help herself. She burst into laughter as she said, "Oh my God is right. Hopefully we didn't give anyone too much of a show. Thank goodness the jets were on and I left my top on."

Ian too began laughing as he replied, "Yeah, not that that fooled anyone regarding what we were up to. Who knows if that camera even works and whether anyone's even watching the TV monitor." He'd noticed it was an old camera, and it was very salt-air weathered.

Ian pulled his boxers back up where they belonged. "I think I'm getting … I mean I got a bit overheated. I better get out."

Zoey smiled at Ian. "I've had all the fun I should as well." She pulled her panties back on. They left single file out of the spa, just as the jets turned off. Ian guessed they were set to run no longer than thirty minutes at a time.

They went inside the pool building and began drying off. Ian stepped into the men's bathroom and removed his wet boxers before getting dressed. Zoey did what amounted to the same over in the women's room. Once they left the pool and spa building, Ian returned the towels to the office and put them in a wet-towel hamper. Ian was relieved once again to see no one behind the counter. But when he turned to leave, he distinctly heard the faint clapping of someone's hands. Ian turned to see a young twenty-something man now standing behind the office counter. The young man didn't say a word. He just grinned at Ian and continued slowly clapping. Ian's face instantly turned radish-red as he turned and rapidly accelerated his pace and got out of the office as quickly as he could … all the while thinking, *So much for hoping the video camera didn't work.*

Ian began laughing by the time he joined Zoey, who was already in the car that he'd left unlocked.

Zoey asked, smiling, "What's got you in such a good mood ... As if I didn't know."

Ian took a deep breath as he replied, "Oh, nothing. Nothing at all. Ha! It's all good!"

Once Ian was settled in the car and had started it up, he glanced for a second over at Zoey. "How about first off ... that is after we get cleaned up, I'll drive the Jeep, and you and Scout follow me in this car just down the street to your uncle's storage facility where I can stash the Jeep for a day or so."

Zoey interjected, "My uncle owns a storage facility?"

"Uh, yeah. Apparently he does. I've got a feeling Clayton has his fingers in lots of pies. Anyway, after we store my rig ... you, Scout, and I can then head up town to look into buying some clothes and stuff."

"Yeah, that'd be great! Then we can go by my shop so I can pick up a few things for tonight. And ... and after that, we can walk across the street and venture through Marsh's so I can introduce you to my boyfriend Jake. Maybe pick up something to eat somewhere along the way ... sound like a plan? I mean, there's probably no need to go to Astoria too soon, right?"

Ian enthusiastically replied, "Sounds great!"

Ian and Zoey returned to the condo where they took a shower together and got cleaned up as best they could. They had no choice but to put back on their soiled clothes.

After cleaning up, the three of them left the condo for the day's adventure. Moments after Ian turned his Jeep in at the storage facility, he joined Zoey and Scout in the rental car. Zoey had already gotten out from behind the steering wheel of the car and switched to the front passenger seat. With Ian at the helm of the car, he, Zoey, and Scout began heading towards downtown Long Beach.

Ian's phone rang. He immediately answered it while driving.

"Hello." Ian knew he was taking a small risk talking on his cell phone while driving, since the state of Washington had some tough laws against such activity.

"Hey, Ian. Ned. So, you ready for tonight?" Officer Ned Parker asked.

Ian glanced for a second over at Zoey then trained his eyes back on the road while he replied, "Yeah, I'm … I mean we're pretty much ready. Zoey and I."

"Good. That's good. There's been a small change in plans. It shouldn't affect what you'll be up to. But me and an FBI agent from the BAU, we're also gonna be undercover inside the club tonight. We might try and have a look-see around the ground floor skylight basement and such before we join the party upstairs. The FBI agent I'll be with is a good looker. I'd guess her to be in her mid-thirties, but she looks younger. Hey, I'll look like a cradle-robbing club-fuck just like you." Ian didn't laugh. He didn't find much humor in the comment. It struck home harder than Ned would ever know.

Ian replied, "Okay. Well, as long as neither of us screws up the situation for the other, all should be fine. It's good to know that there will be some professionals on hand backing us up should the situation get ugly."

"Yeah that's what the chief decided when he came up with the idea. Okay then, let's bag us this Salizzar asshole and as many of his cronies as possible. Especially before the Feds take over with full jurisdiction. Right now, the Feds are in an observe-and-advise-only capacity. So far, our department gets the collar, but that could all change soon."

Ian interjected, "Yeah, that is if we can be sure there's good cause that Salizzar and/or his people or some club regular are the guilty party. I mean if evidence is clear and present."

Ned fired back, *"Yeah, right. That is if the scumbag's … I mean if there's sufficient evidence that the pervs are guilty, of course. But they're guilty, mark my word. Of that you can be certain. Oh, and once again, Ian, and this comes from the chief, don't you in anyway unnecessarily put yourself or that little missy in harm's way. Got that?"*

Ian replied, "Understood."

"Okay, later then …"

"Later," Ian said. He then hung up by switching his phone off.

The stage was set and the ball was in full motion. Zoey looked over at Ian as they headed down the road. "That was that Astoria cop … Ned, wasn't it?"

Ian replied, "Yeah. He just wanted me … wanted us … to know that he'd be undercover at the club tonight as well. He and a lady FBI agent … his arm candy." Ian smiled as he said that, remembering the term that Zoey had used at Clayton's the night they first met.

"FBI? Wow! This is suddenly getting very real, isn't it?" Zoey said, sitting further back in her seat.

They arrived in downtown Long Beach. Scout sat up in the back seat and barked once as he spotted a man walking his dog on the sidewalk in front of a store called Stormin' Norman's: Kites, Clothing, and Gifts.

Ian remarked, "Maybe I can get a couple sweatshirts in that place?"

Zoey looked over. "Stormin' Norman's? Yeah, they've got lots of sweatshirts, but most of them will have 'Long Beach, WA' embroidered or screen-printed on them. But that's cool, if you're into that. Like my uncle would say, that's as good a place as any and better than most."

Ian proceeded driving up the block before pulling the car over into a vacant parking spot on the main road, directly in front of Marsh's Free Museum. Just across and up the street two buildings was Zoey's shop.

"Hey, why don't you two men just wait here? I'll be back in just a few minutes with some clothes for tonight and a few essentials."

Ian smiled and nodded. But before Zoey exited the car, Ian spoke up. "Hey, um, why don't you meet me inside?" Ian pointed over towards Marsh's.

Zoey replied, "Yeah, sure. Cool. Leave the car unlocked, and I'll put my stuff in when I come back. Then I'll meet you inside. Nobody's gonna mess with your car with Scout on guard." Scout barked twice as if to say, *You got that right.*

Zoey left the car and walked briskly, haphazardly, across the street, not bothering walking the few feet further up the street that it would have required for her to use the nearest crosswalk.

Ian wanted Scout to have plenty of fresh air, so he opened the two back windows a couple of inches. It hadn't rained so far and it didn't look like it would again anytime soon.

"Okay, buddy. I'm gonna go into that store right over there." Ian pointed to Marsh's. "Don't accept gifts, especially food, from any strangers, or go with anyone if someone was to open the door." Ian half-believed Scout could understand every word.

"You take care of yourself, and be a good boy. I don't know why I always tell you to be a good boy. You're always a good boy, aren't ya, fella?"

Scout got up on all fours, wagged his tail, and barked twice. Ian reached back and began petting his friend, then reached into his inside jacket breast pocket and retrieved a zip-lock plastic baggy half-full of doggy treats. He gave three small bone-shaped biscuits to his very appreciative furry friend as he said, "Don't worry, boy. I'm gonna pick you up some proper dog food today while we're out and about."

Ian then exited the car and proceeded towards Marsh's Free Museum. Once inside, he quickly understood why Zoey so fervently wanted him to see the place. For Ian, a former zoologist turned cryptozoologist now reinvented as a paranormal investigator, it was like being a kid in the proverbial candy store … it was love at first sight.

Fifteen minutes later, after browsing around, Ian was staring intensely into a wood-framed glass display that housed Marsh's curiosity of considerable notoriety, Jake the Alligator Man.

Ian was marveling at the detail of what he surmised in an instant to be a very convincingly clever hoax. Truly the work of a mummification and taxidermy master. Jake reminded Ian of some of the curiosities that he'd seen before in his line of work. In some ways, he was like the Jackalope and supposed Big Foot hand that he'd once seen in Idaho displayed inside a glass case at a truck stop restaurant and curio shop. Ian suspected Jake to be a master craftsman's clever amalgamation of a mummified shrunken head seamlessly fused to a likewise mummified body of a small alligator. But he wasn't completely certain of his theory. Jake appeared even at close examination to be very real.

Ian mused, *If only I had some sort of hand-held x-ray machine. Or … Oh, well. Some mysteries that bring a smile are better off left to the imagination. P.T. Barnum would have loved this place.*

Zoey finally managed to pull Ian away from Jake. She began leading him all around the place, which was filled to the brim with curiosities of every kind. Stuffed two-headed animals. Taxidermy corpses of African and Amazonian creatures of all persuasions. A stuffed bear, a lion, and a large shark. Collected shells, rocks, toys, and gift items of more variety than Ian could wrap his brain around. If they weren't in somewhat of a hurry to get to more pressing shopping and with a specific agenda for the day and night, Ian could have spent at least another hour looking through the place and, more likely than not, purchasing a number of unique things. But alas, the clock was ticking.

Ian reluctantly spoke up, "Well, lions and tigers and bears, oh my. This place is AWESOME! But we should hit a couple of stores that sell clothes and … well … deodorant, toothpaste, and the like. Oh, and dog food. Don't let me forget dog food."

Zoey nodded in agreement, then kissed Ian on the cheek. She took his hand and began leading him out of the store, but not before Ian purchased a bumper sticker that bore a picture of Jake on it that read, 'I brake for Jake - the Alligator Man.' Ian told the cashier that he didn't need a bag. He just stuffed the bumper sticker into his pocket, and he and Zoey were on their way.

After several hours of shopping with frequent stops back to the car to check on and occasionally walk and water Scout, Ian had purchased enough clothes and basics to get by for some time. It was 1:35 p.m., and they were all getting very hungry.

Zoey came up with the idea that they visit a local deli and pick up some sandwiches and drinks, then drive out onto the beach so they could gaze at the ocean. Ian thought that was a great idea, so they did just that.

"Wow, it must be high tide. Look at the size of those breakers. And it's not even windy." Ian exclaimed between bites of his turkey and Swiss on sourdough sandwich. In addition to the sandwich he was busy polishing off, Ian held in his lap a round Styrofoam container, one that only minutes earlier had been filled with the best Washington coast version of New England style clam chowder that he'd ever tasted.

Zoey was in the final stages of enjoying her Shrimp-Louie salad. Ian didn't have the heart to feed Scout merely dog food while they were picnicking. Scout had already gobbled up his nearly two pounds of thin-cut, slow roasted roast beef. He was lapping up the remaining contents of a twelve-ounce bottle of water that Zoey had poured for him into one of his two newly purchased dog dishes.

191

After finishing their lunch, the three took a walk on the beach very near the shoreline. The thin clouds had parted, and the sun was shining bright. At the ocean shoreline it was pretty brisk out, and it seemed to be getting colder as the day went on, not warmer. Ian estimated the temperature to be at best in the mid-fifties, but the occasional sun-breaks against their faces felt warm and wonderful.

Ian spotted a nice-sized stick that was the perfect size for throwing. He picked it up and tossed it up the beach with all his might. Ian was disappointed that Scout didn't pick up on his attempt to play with him. But then Ian noticed that Scout wanted to play, he just wouldn't. At first, Ian was confused, but then it dawned on him; Scout wanted to fetch the stick in the worst way but simply would not do it without being commanded to do so.

Ian looked excitedly at Scout. "Go get it boy!" Without a nanosecond's delay, Scout sprang into action. Within seconds, he was in full galloping stride. He reached the stick in half the time Ian would have guessed possible. Scout grabbed it in his powerful jaws and with no hesitation began racing it back to Ian.

Zoey tried as best she could to get Scout to return the stick to her. She shouted, "SCOUT! COME ON BOY! BRING ME THE STICK!" She laughed when she realized that there was no way Scout was bringing her the stick, even as much as he liked Zoey, and that was very obviously a lot. Scout paid no attention to her calls as he immediately returned the stick to Ian. Scout then set himself right at Ian's feet and waited patiently for Ian to throw it again. Ian played fetch with Scout time and again over the next twenty minutes, but then Ian realized how late it was getting. He said with a beaming smile, "Well, as much as this has been the best day I've had in ... in years, and I sincerely mean that, Zoey." Ian paused to catch his breath before continuing, "We've got to get back to the condo and start getting ready for tonight."

Zoey actually frowned slightly before replying, "Yeah. This really has been. It's been awesome. Really! But you're right. Now comes business."

The three walked to the car and headed back to the condo.

Once back, Ian and Zoey got dressed in their would-be vampire clubber attire. Zoey did Ian's and her own exaggerated make-up. She then spiked Ian's jet-black hair with hair product. Ian checked himself out in the bathroom mirror. *Jesus fucking Christ. I look like the offspring of Billy Idol and Alice Cooper.*

Ian felt he looked ridiculous. He tried to take solace in reminding himself where he was going and for what reason, and that it was Halloween after all.

Knowing that it might be a very long night, Ian at first thought the best thing to do would be to leave Scout at the condo. But then he started thinking about his trailer burning down. Even though there was no perfectly safe place, Ian finally decided that he would take Scout with them. At least that way he could check on him periodically. *And, like Ned said, having a large, four-legged bodyguard might not be such a bad idea.*

Ian fed Scout and took him for a short walk. Then the three of them climbed into the rental car and headed for Astoria for the rest of the day and night. Ian brought two bottles of water and a doggie dish with them. Even though it would neither be very warm nor terribly cold in the car for Scout, Ian wanted him to stay plenty hydrated. Ian didn't think that Scout would relieve himself in the car no matter how much water he'd drink nor however long he had to be left alone. Ian thought, *What the hell. If I'm wrong, it's a rental.*

Astoria ...

It was just after seven in the evening and Ian and Zoey were both getting a bit hungry. They'd been driving around Astoria for the last couple of hours looking at buildings and businesses. The last ten minutes had been spent with them slowly circling the block, staring at every aspect of Salizzar's residence.

"Ian, are you getting hungry? I sure am, and I know the perfect place. It's pretty reasonably priced. I mean, it won't cost an arm and a leg or a large manila envelope full of cash!" Zoey was trying to get some sort of reaction out of Ian, who'd been nearly in a trance-like state for over ten minutes as he continued staring blankly at the mansion.

Zoey replied to her own last statement in the deepest voice she could, "Sure ... Sure, Zoey. Getting something to eat sounds great."

Her exaggerated levity in attempt to get Ian's attention worked.

"Oh yeah, right. Something to eat. Great. Let's go. Ian said, finally managing to turn away from his semi-hypnotic attraction to the cryptically creepy Victorian mansion.

Zoey instructed Ian to drive towards the waterfront less than a block away from where they were going to be this evening. Once nearly there, she finally told Ian where she thought they should eat. "There, Ian. Right over there's the Soggy Dog."

As Zoey pointed towards the place, Ian saw it as well. He pulled into a parking spot directly across the street from the establishment's front door. Ian looked at the sign above the door, which read, "The Soggy Dog Saloon and Brewery - Established 1995."

Zoey looked over at Ian. "I think you're going to really like this place. They make their own beer, and the food's great. Like all places around here, seafood's their specialty. But they've pretty much got every kind of sandwich, burger, or ... well pretty much everything. As you know, the city of Astoria's done a really good job of capturing a sort of San Francisco Fisherman's Wharf look. Well, like I said ... sort of." She giggled.

Zoey continued, "The Soggy Dog has a great view of the best part of the docks. It's really eclectically cool inside. The city even put in a trolley car that takes people up and down the connecting docks. It passes right in front of the place. Anyway, come on. Let's go in." Ian was feeling very reluctant to be seen in public given the way he was dressed and made up with black eyeliner, especially while it was still light outside.

Zoey continued, "Ian. You look great! Besides, this place caters to a lot of what you might call forward thinkers."

Ian mused about Zoey's description regarding patrons of the establishment, *Ah, artsy-types, musicians, and ... Well, nothing wrong with any of that. I should fit right in.*

Zoey continued trying to abate Ian's self-consciousness. "And besides, it's Halloween. They'll just assume we're here to eat and have some pre-function drinks before going out tonight to some costume party. And hey, that's about the truth of it. We don't want to get to Salizzar's too early but not too late either. Too late, and especially tonight, we might not even get in. I'm guessing that tonight, way beyond the place's usual crowd, there'll be a lot of people going there just because it's a freaky place with a creepy vibe. And with the string of murders, there will be some adrenaline and ecstasy cravers that will be going there for the assumed sexy danger factor. It's known as a meat market, which will always be packed on special occasion nights, no doubt especially Halloween. The place is the perfect choice for college-age party revelers from here to Seaside. Probably as far away as Portland. No doubt about it's gonna be totally packed with creatures of the night." Zoey giggled at her unintentional pun. Ian couldn't help but crack a smile. Zoey's unplanned zinger … in fact was, pretty funny.

Ian lowered the back windows a couple inches. The good weather was still holding, but the sky was beginning to look like that might change in the next few hours.

"Okay Scout, you know the drill. We'll be back soon." Scout didn't bark this time. This time, he just let out a slight whimper and a moan-like sound as he went from a standing position to lying down in the middle of the back seat.

Ian and Zoey exited the car then walked briskly hand in hand over to the entrance of the eatery. Ian opened the door for Zoey, and they entered. Inside, around ten feet directly ahead of them were three steps that led upwards and into the restaurant portion of the brewery. Off to their right, just inside the threshold, housed behind a large, transparent glass barrier, were a half-dozen tall, stainless steel tanks that contained whatever types of beers were presently being brewed. The sign said, 'Please Seat Yourself,' so they headed up the three steps to do just that.

Ian and Zoey found a table against the windows that looked out over the docks and the river beyond. From where Ian was seated as he stared upriver at the various waterfront buildings, though barely within his panoramic view, he could see just a sliver of Salizzar's nightclub a block away.

Ian then took his focus from gazing out at the docks to looking all around the restaurant as he thought, *Zoey was right. There's certainly a number of 'regular folks' in here, but there's also a lot of …* Ian became distracted and lost his train of thought as he glanced across the table at Zoey, who was beautiful to him in so many ways. Ian had an epiphany then; he'd been a closet bigot all of his life. He silently vowed to make a genuine effort to stop judging people based on their looks, whether conventional or unconventional. And the most shameful self-realization of all, judging on race or sexual persuasion.

Ian had been, for the most part, one who believed in judging individuals by their merits. Ian was at the core a scientist with degrees in zoology, anthropology, and paleontology, a man who understood that intellectually, racial bigotry or any form of homophobia was totally illogical and absolutely unfounded. But he also knew that once in a great while, he had his bad moments regarding usually well-suppressed, preconditioned attitudes due primarily to his upbringing. Ian's mother referred to most people of color in less than flattering vernacular, and touted heavily biased and prejudicially spun out of context biblical scripture regarding homosexuals. Ian thought of his mother for a moment. *Mom … She would have been the quintessential female version of Archie Bunker. What a loveable bigot she was.*

Ian smiled slightly as he continued reflecting on how far he'd already come in his goal of trying to be a better person. *I can honestly say that besides Scout, my best male friend in the world is Charlie Redtail, a Native American, and he's without a doubt in every way … the most honorable man I've ever known.*

"So what's got you smiling?" Zoey asked as she glanced up from looking over her menu.

Ian shrugged his shoulders as he replied, "Oh, I was just thinking about personal growth and the paths our lives take us. And that I'm definitely a work in progress. But mainly that … I'm just glad to be here with you."

Zoey smiled big as she replied, "Well, that's pretty heavy." She giggled for a second before continuing, "But seriously, occasionally being introspective and taking stock of oneself is a good thing … At least that's what my uncle Clayton tells me … a lot. Anyway, I'm happy to be here with you, too!" Ian marveled at Zoey's word choice and wisdom as he silently mused, *There's certainly more to this girl than meets the eye.*

Zoey cleared her throat and continued. "Uh, um. Okay, you should take a peek at your menu. I'm pretty sure the waitress that keeps glancing over at us while waiting on other tables is gonna be with us soon."

Ian didn't reply but nodded his head in agreement as he picked up his menu and began studying it. After only seconds, he placed his menu back down on the table. Zoey did the same.

"Wow, that was quick. You know what you want?" Zoey asked as she stared into Ian's eyes.

Ian replied, "Yeah. How 'bout you?"

Zoey happily blurted out, "I'm gonna have their fettuccini alfredo with scallops. Their fettuccini is awesome."

Ian grinned and replied, "That does sounds good. But I think I'm going with a good 'ole cheeseburger. The bleu cheese bacon burger to be precise. I've been eating so much seafood lately, a change of pace sounds good to me."

Zoey smiled then said, "It's a good thing I'm a seafood nut 'cause around these parts, well, when in Rome."

Ian nodded slowly as he replied, "Yeah, when in Rome, do as the Romans do. When in Astoria ... do as the ... astronauts do?" Zoey and Ian both laughed.

"Hello. Happy Halloween. Welcome to the Soggy Dog." the waitress exclaimed as she approached their table. She was a young gal, obviously in her early twenties, cute and petite, with long, medium-brown hair with blonde-streaked highlights, pulled back in a ponytail. She was wearing a black Soggy Dog logo printed t-shirt and black, denim jeans. Ian noticed right away that she was wearing large earrings fashioned to look like Jack-o-lanterns, and an inverted bull-ring style septum nose piercing.

"My name's Madison, and I'll be your server. Can I get you started with a drink? Today, we're featuring our galactically famous Indian Pale Ale for just $3.75 a pint."

Zoey glanced at Ian and flashed him a smile while nodding. Ian smiled at their waitress. "Yes. I mean, that sounds perfect! We'll both have the special, the Pale Ales. And I think we've already decided on what we want to order for food."

Madison smiled as she replied, "Sure, great. Shoot."

Ian looked at Zoey as he spoke. "Shall I order for us?" Zoey nodded.

He continued, "Okay, the lady will have your fettuccini alfredo with scallops, and I'm going to have your bleu cheese bacon burger."

Madison asked, "How would you like your burger cooked?"

"Uh … medium well would be great." Ian said with a smile.

Madison continued, "Can I bring you two some salads before your entrees?"

Ian looked over at Zoey, who was nodding. "Yeah. A couple of house salads sounds good. I'll have the bleu cheese dressing."

Ian glanced at Zoey, who spoke up, "I'd love a light vinaigrette."

Madison smiled as she replied, "Perfect!" She turned to go place their food orders, but then paused and asked, "Say, will you guys be staying for the band, The Stilettos? They start at 9:00. I hear they're really good. They're a band from Cannon Beach. I just read their promo sheet. It says they play mostly R and B. If you're already inside before 9:00, you won't have to pay the ten dollar per person cover charge."

Ian smiled at Madison, "Well, much as I … we … would like to, we're committed to being elsewhere tonight … just down the street, in fact." He looked outside towards Salizzar's.

Madison nervously looked around to see what ears might be listening. Satisfied that nobody could hear, she spoke very quietly, with an excited look on her face, "Are you guys going to The Morgue tonight?" Ian raised his eyebrows before he sheepishly nodded.

Madison continued, "So am I. When I get off work at ten that is. I'm meeting two girlfriends there. I've never had the guts to go in there before. I mean, the stories ya hear about the place. But no way they could be true. The flyer that they've put all over town says they've got some Portland death metal band playing there tonight. The band's called Sons A Witches. Anyway, it should be fun. I'll see you there."

Madison turned and briskly went off to turn in their orders and get them their beers.

Ian looked over at Zoey, who was slowly shaking her head. Ian felt as though Zoey was reading his mind; she knew that he desperately wanted to tell their waitress to stay the hell away from that place, especially tonight. But Ian also knew that he couldn't say anything of the sort. Not without potentially seriously jeopardizing, if not totally destroying their cover.

Ian looked at Zoey as he spoke. "I guess we need to make some kind of tentative plan for once we're in the place tonight."

"Yeah, at least some kind of plan would be good."

Ian took a deep breath. Then all at once, his face took on a serious expression as he spoke. "Okay, here goes."

Zoey scooted her chair closer to the table and leaned in towards Ian in response to his hand gesture to draw her nearer so he could speak in little more than a whisper.

Ian continued, "If Salizzar or any of his cronies are behind the recent murders and rash of missing persons, then there must be a reason for it beyond just a crazy lunatic serial killer doing it for some twisted sexual gratification or to get back at his mother for ... Well, you know what I mean." Zoey nodded.

Ian took another deep breath, exhaled, and once again continued

200

to expound his theory and plan. "Salizzar is a guy who's such an obvious prime suspect, he has got to be up to something much larger than any killer that kills simply for the thrill of it. And I mean something much larger than just running a nightclub for Goths and vampire role players to lure in victims to kill for sick kicks. I think he's got a specific agenda. I think he's in the – for lack of better description – the business of supplying blood and body organs through most likely an ultra-sophisticated black market network. I've even considered that he might be into white slavery, but due to the mounting body count, I think it's even sicker and more twisted than that."

Though Zoey said nothing in response, Ian saw for the first time a trace of noticeable fear on her face.

After a short pause, Ian continued, "I think this guy Salizzar – man, monster, or myth, whatever you want to call him – I think he's supplying others like him all around the world, in addition to supplying ultra-rich people who can afford to buy blood products or body organs for transplants without having to go on any waiting list."

Just then, their waitress, Madison, arrived to their table with their beers and said, "Okay, let me know if you like the beer. Your food should be up in just a few minutes." She smiled then turned and briskly walked to another table.

Ian immediately took a sip of his beer. He winced ever so slightly in reaction to its bitter hop flavor. He'd never been a big beer enthusiast.

Ian cleared his throat then continued, "Uh, um, anyway, I think Salizzar's got himself a factory going on in the basement of his club. With all that we saw yesterday, it would be a perfect set up. Bone saws, walk-in subzero freezer, all stainless steel countertops and sinks with high-pressure washer-sprayers. I think he's collecting blood and body parts, packaging them, and selling them to vampire-like wackos and maybe witch covens. People into cannibalism maybe. Very likely, he supplies people who need human organs and can pay to get them totally off the grid. Little doubt he'll sell his products to anyone who's able to pay his price and keep totally silent lest they quickly wind up dissected themselves. My guess is he sets up a factory for a very limited time, does his thing, makes a number of fast millions, then per his pre-planned exit strategy, he and his people disappear without a trace. When a guy's as well-funded and connected as it appears to me that he is, he can almost instantly become a ghost besides being a blood sucker."

Zoey gasped a bit, then took a three-gulp drink of beer. She slowly set her beer glass down, her hand was trembling slightly. After a few uncomfortably long silent seconds had passed, she finally spoke. "Oh … my … God! If you're even half right about any of it, he's gotta be stopped. Ian, we've gotta do what we can to stop him."

Ian slowly nodded as he panned his eyes around at the tables near them to see if Zoey's small outburst had drawn any attention. It hadn't seemed to. The music in the place was at the perfect volume to allow for discreet table conversation.

"Now, whether I'm right or not as far as a plan for tonight, I feel we've got to, for our own protection, operate under the assumption of worst case scenario that I'm, like you said, even half right. Under that assumption, I feel we should …" Ian paused mid-sentence as the man who had gone to the men's room just minutes before walked past them to his table, which also sparked Ian's thought.

Ian continued, "As for tonight, we can't be separated any more than necessary, for lots of obvious reasons. I think at least some of the abductions probably occurred right in the club itself. I've been thinking that over and over in my mind. I always come up with the same …" He stopped again as Zoey, who'd been staring unwaveringly into his eyes, suddenly turned her attention behind him as she spotted their waitress, Madison, who was rapidly heading towards them with their food.

"Here, guys. I hope you enjoy!" Madison exclaimed as she set their food down onto their table. "Can I get you anything else?" Ian had already noted that there was already ketchup, mustard, and Tabasco sauce at the table.

After looking at Zoey and seeing that she smiled and shook her head, Ian replied, "No, I think we've got all we need, at least for now."

Madison flashed Ian a bright smile, then turned and headed off towards the kitchen.

Ian took another even larger drink of his beer, this time with seemingly no displeased reaction to the beer's strong hop flavor. He smiled as he glanced at his glass, then looked back at Zoey and continued, "This isn't bad. Kinda grows on ya. Anyway, where was I? Oh, yeah. I think we should concentrate somewhat on the restrooms. Primarily the lady's room."

Zoey looked at Ian with a confused expression before interjecting, "The restrooms …?"

Ian fired back, "Yeah. Where else does a person leave their date and go, usually more than once throughout an evening, more than to the restroom? That is if their date's of the opposite sex, that is." Ian smiled, and Zoey rolled her eyes while she giggled. Ian continued, "Granted, often women will go to the lady's room in couples or even in groups. And presumably in a club like that, there will be couples of all genders doing all sorts of things in both bathrooms. But still … some … a lot will go alone, right? And when they do, once inside a private stall with all kinds of commotion going on and a background of loud music from the sound system or a band …" Zoey suddenly got the mental picture Ian was painting.

"My God, Ian. You might be right. What if there's some kind of trap door or something in the bathroom stalls in the women's ... well, and maybe in the men's room too for that matter. And ..."

Ian interrupted, "People are being shanghaied at least down to the basement for exsanguination and dissection."

Zoey covered her mouth as she exclaimed, "Good God, do you really think so?" Ian solemnly nodded twice.

He continued, "Something like that. A doorway behind the toilet that someone could grab a person from behind or a trap door in the floor that would suddenly drop an unsuspecting victim. Either way would serve as a perfect way to quickly abduct and disappear a person." Zoey again nodded her head in response to Ian's theory. "Oh shit ... I just thought of something."

Zoey looked deep into Ian's eyes as she spoke. "What?"

Ian continued, "I just remembered that I forgot that police scanner that Ned gave me. It's back in the ... it's in my Jeep. Oh well, we probably won't be just sitting around listening to it anyway." Zoey nodded in agreement.

After nearly a minute of silence, Zoey said, "Anyway Ian, about what you were talking about before. All anyone working at the club would have to say to any waiting boyfriend or girlfriend that might go looking around the club for their missing partner would be something like, 'I think they left cause they got sick.' Or, 'I think I saw them leave with another person.' Or, 'We didn't see a thing.' Shit, whatever. Nobody would be the wiser."

Ian didn't say another word for a couple of long, silent moments. He just sat thinking over his theory. As terrifying as it was, it made sense.

After a few long seconds passed, Zoey took a deep breath, exhaled, and spoke. "Ian, what you told me before about what happened in that town … What was it called, Harmony Falls, I believe you said?"

Ian replied, "Yeah, that's right."

Zoey continued, "Well, I too am willing to keep an open mind about what you call extreme possibilities. For certain, I believe there's much more going on in this world than meets the eye. And I believe in you. What I'm trying to say is, I believe something clearly unimaginably horrific happened to you and your friend Charlie. And you guys took care of business the only way you could. End of story. Now all that said, it's time we get out of here, walk up the block, and go and kick some vampire ass. Do we, like, need any special weapons … like wooden stakes or holy water? Stuff like that?"

Ian bit his lip and raised his eyebrows while shrugging in response to Zoey's question all the while thinking to himself, *Christ, according to Clayton, stuff like that wouldn't even help. Although it sure as shit took silver bullets back at Harmony Falls. Let's hope that Glock 9mm counts for something.*

CHAPTER 20
All Hallows Eve (II)

Standing at the top of a long, wide, Z-shaped ramp that led up
to the second floor, then forward to the front door of The Morgue,
was a very tall, extremely formidable-looking, middle-aged black man.
He had pronounced streaks of gray concentrated around his temples,
which sharply contrasted the mostly deep ebony color of his heavily
product-enhanced hair.

This near giant of a man was nattily dressed in a black silk tuxedo,
white wing-collar shirt, and a thin black leather bowtie. Over his shirt,
he wore a long, impressively substantial, serpentine-link gold chain,
which had a large, presumably solid gold pendent designed to look like
brass knuckles. The mammoth-sized man also wore large, diamond-
stud earrings, one in the lobe of each ear. His eyes were perfectly
hidden behind very dark lenses held within also likely solid gold wire
frame sunglasses. The imposing way the man posed himself with his
massive arms crossed left no doubt that he was at least one of the club's
bouncers and likely one of Salizzar's personal bodyguards.

The huge bouncer's tuxedo coat, though an obvious nicely-
tailored fit, was ever so slightly draping roomier on the left side than
the right. Ian quickly deduced that the bouncer was likely packing
more than just sheer muscle.

There was a very lengthy line of people waiting for their chance to get invited past the red velvet rope gate that served as a gateway to the front door and forward to the elevator beyond.

Ian quickly observed that unless you were a beautiful, Playmate-esque, pseudo *Elvira Mistress Of The Dark* vampiric type, or your name was among those on the clip-board list which was wielded like it had magic power by a pale-skinned dwarf, convincingly costumed from head to foot in the attire of a medieval court jester, getting inside was going to be challenging to say the least.

Ian couldn't keep from staring at the freakishly pale, bordering on semi-transparent Lilliputian, who even in the very low light appeared to have tiny, bulging blue veins that spider-webbed all around his forehead and cheeks.

The dwarf's appearance, though small in stature to the extreme, was to Ian nonetheless forebodingly frightening with his pointy ears, appendages that Ian reasoned had to have been surgically altered. And his teeth, though no larger than those of a child, appeared also to have been cosmetically fashioned to be like those of a shark, grotesquely filed to what appeared to be pin-point sharpness. All with the obvious intent of achieving the look of a devilishly demonic, folklorish, hell-spawn imp. There was something inexplicable about him, something mesmerizing that transcended just mere morbid fascination at the sight of the fiercely evil-looking elf.

Zoey noticed that Ian was staring at the little man, much longer than what would be considered polite by any measure. She tugged on Ian's right arm slightly, which broke his trancelike fixation. As Ian looked away from the midget, realizing why Zoey had broken his concentrated stare in the manner she had, he thought, *There's just something about that ... little devil.*

After waiting in the cold and drizzling rain for about ten minutes, it was becoming clearer by the moment that it was going to be a very long wait to move up in the line, let alone ever gain entrance. That was until Ian saw a man hand the dwarf a fat wad of cash. Fortunately, Ian had anticipated that this night might require a lot of green, so he reached inside his recently heavily-fattened wallet and pulled out three portraits of Benjamin Franklin. Ian folded the bills in such a way as to show off the sum of his offering intended for the little jester.

The maniacal-looking munchkin was standing near the front door with his back turned towards them. Then, as if the demon dwarf had eyes in the back of his head or could literally smell money, in less than three seconds he was standing hip-high alongside Ian. The dwarf never spoke a word; rather, with mouth open wide and his gums fully retracted, displayed a killer, shark-like, terrifying smile as he grabbed the money from Ian.

The monstrous miniature then pointed up to the large black man, who nodded back at him. The huge bouncer signaled Ian and Zoey with a wave of his massive hand to bypass all those ahead of them in line to proceed forward to the doorway to be admitted at once into the club.

Once inside the front door, Ian and Zoey were greeted by a veiny-faced blond albino man of no consequential size. He was also nattily dressed in a black tuxedo. He stood eerily glowing blue under a large, black-light illuminated podium. The man was checking everyone's identification before allowing them to proceed any further.

Zoey had given her driver's license to Ian earlier in the evening so she wouldn't have to pack her purse around and risk getting it stolen. Ian had subsequently locked it in the trunk of the rental car.

Ian handed the man both his fake driver's license as well as Zoey's real one. The man glanced at both for just a second. Ian figured it was mostly formality due to their ages, and the lighting that the black lights emitted was so dim he didn't figure the guy could read them anyway. *Unless, of course, he's got some kind of night vision.*

After less than two seconds had passed, the man looked at Ian as he spoke in a heavy Eastern European accent, "You and your date have a lovely evening, Mister ... McBride." When the man spoke, Ian and Zoey both couldn't help but notice he had Hollywood-styled stereotypical vampire fangs. Ian wondered, *Are his fangs permanent prosthetics? Or are they removable? Or are they unnaturally natural?*

Once Ian had retrieved their IDs from the man and had put them back in his wallet, they were instructed to go over to an elevator that was located just a few feet straight ahead of the entrance.

When they approached the elevator, Ian noticed in an instant that it was configured to only go up from where they were, which was technically the second floor. The next floor, the third floor actually, was the nightclub level.

Ian was more than happy that they'd only checked IDs and weren't patting people down, or worse, using a metal detecting wand. He had his trusty .32 Beretta that he'd years ago affectionately named Ole Caretaker strapped to his right ankle. After giving it more thought, Ian knew there was little to no chance at all of going with his first plan of trying to sneak in the large 9mm Glock that Ned had given him, so he'd left it in the glove box of the rental car and opted for his much smaller, easier to conceal weapon.

Once Ian and Zoey, along with a few other chosen ones, were inside the elevator, Ian looked over the control panel and quickly deduced that the elevator probably did go down to the daylight basement below via the insertion and activation of a key into the unmarked keyhole located just below the button labeled 'Level One'.

A young, beautiful woman, distinctly Gothic in appearance, quickly pushed the button marked '2' and soon, the doors closed.

Within less than ten seconds, they were up on the club level.

The moment the elevator doors opened, Ian, Zoey, and the other occupants quickly shuffled out into the club. There was a free-standing portable sign directly ahead of them that said, *Enter of your own free will - and please seat yourself.*

Once they were inside the club, it was immediately obvious the place was designed to look like a medieval European castle. Its walls and archways that led to various adjacent rooms were all constructed from imitation stone. Ian surmised the material must be similar if not identical to what Hollywood would use to construct a medieval-looking fortification on a movie set when painted Styrofoam wouldn't be structurally strong enough to serve the purpose.

There were wrought-iron chandeliers that sported imitation candles all over, torches that lined the walls, and corridors whose burning flames, upon Ian's close examination, were not flames at all, merely cleverly devised lighting effects that created a very convincing illusion of fire.

Ian thought, *Apparently, even vampires have to obey fire codes when building their clubs.*

As Ian continued looking around at the imitation suits of armor, period-perfect-looking furniture, and stained glass darkened windows … he thought, *Maybe this guy Salizzar's no boogieman. No more real than those torches. Maybe this club and his eccentric lifestyle just mark him as an easy target to pin the killings on. Still, the killer, or killers, could be freaky frequenters of this place. Come on, Ian. Stay focused. If it walks like a duck and quacks like a duck, it's probably a …*

"Hey, how about we sit over there in the corner? That little booth for two. It should offer a pretty good view of at least half of this place," Zoey said, almost shouting. The music was loud, almost intolerably loud for Ian.

Ian followed Zoey over to the table. She was right. It offered a good vantage point that would allow them to view much of the main room and what appeared to be the main bar. Ian felt lucky to have gotten a table at all. The place was filling up fast. It was just a few minutes past 10:00 p.m. Ian knew that was still very early by clubber's standards. At the rate people were pouring in from the elevator every couple of minutes, there would be no tables left and the place would be standing room only within an hour.

As Ian looked about the main room of the nightclub, he noticed that there were a few presumably private booths built into the walls. They had burgundy velvet, crescent-moon-shaped couches with lots of matching pillows. Their style was slightly Victorian, with diamond-tucked upholstery. And small, probably imitation Duncan Phyfe-style tables in their center. Ian surmised they were imitations and not actual antiques, since all of the tables appeared to be clones of one another. The booths had dark burgundy velvet curtains tied back with thick, golden ropes that if pulled shut would offer assured privacy.

One such booth already had its curtain closed, but not completely. Ian could see inside just a bit, primarily due to light emitting from the booth's table lamp, an incandescent candelabra.

What Ian saw going on inside the booth almost made him gag. A young woman was slitting her wrist with an antique-looking straight razor and letting another woman lap up her flowing blood.

Ian directed Zoey's attention to the booth. When Zoey saw what the two women were up to, she had to immediately and momentarily cover her mouth, fearing that she might get instantly sick.

Just moments later, a very tall, exceptionally-pale male waiter came to their table.

"May I get you something from the bar? We have a fine selection of licentious libations and of course pride ourselves on serving the best

Bloody Marys in town. We also have imported Romanian absinthe. It's been said absinthe makes the heart grow fonder." The waiter flashed a maniacal grin in response to his own lecherously-delivered levity. He too spoke in a thick Eastern European accent, but his was the voice that Ian felt could launch a hundred nightmares. It was devilishly deep and freakishly monotone. Ian loudly replied at a volume that he could only hope the waiter would hear, "I'll have a Jack-n-Coke. Light on the Coke. And the lady will have …"

Zoey smiled at Ian and nearly shouted, "That sounds perfect. I'll have the same."

The waiter nodded his head once as he replied, "Excellent!" He turned and headed towards the bar.

"Wow! It's so loud in here. That guy must have the ears of a …" Zoey didn't know how to finish her statement.

Oddly, to both Ian and Zoey, even as loud as the room was from the band that was playing in the adjacent room … and they were VERY loud. The waiter was easy for them to both hear and understand. Even odder was that he could so readily hear Ian. Zoey only barely made out what drinks Ian had ordered, and she was facing him directly and much closer to him than the waiter was. Zoey only agreed with Ian's choice because she didn't want to have to try and yell out her own choice of drink.

Ian thought that it was if the would-be Lurch spoke directly to his mind, more like thought transference than mere spoken words. But within moments, Ian recanted that thought as being ridiculous, merely his imagination getting the best of him.

The waiter was quickly back with their drinks that he held among others that he balanced on a drink tray. He said nothing as he first placed cocktail napkins on their table, then set their drinks down on top of the napkins. The waiter, still without speaking a word, quickly turned and left to deliver drinks to other tables.

Zoey suggested to Ian, more by hand signals than words, that they leave their coats at the table and take their drinks to walk around the place, primarily down the short corridor past the restrooms that led to the room where the band was playing. Ian smiled and nodded firmly twice, indicating that he thought that was a good idea.

Ian motioned for Zoey to take his hand. They began walking through the corridor that led past the restrooms and into the next room. Upon entering the band room, Ian and Zoey immediately understood why the name of the club was The Morgue.

The room was about two-thirds the size of the main room they'd just come from and was designed and filled with decor to look just like a real morgue. It had what looked like stainless-steel, refrigerator-styled cadaver drawers stacked one atop the other, three drawers high. They were all installed along the room's south wall.

Ian thought, *The steel drawers look genuine. Maybe this room during the day serves as some kind of demonic dormitory for the hell-spawned help.*

Ian walked over to the steel drawers and put his hand on one. It was extremely cold to the touch. He realized instantly that they were in fact refrigerated. The genuine article.

All along the sides of the room were what looked to be genuine gurneys and antique I.V. glass bottles with surgical-style rubber tubing attached, as well as various machines that appeared to have been devised for the purpose of voiding a human body of all blood in preparation for a quid pro quo infusion of formaldehyde, commonly known as ... embalming.

On its eastern wall, the mortuary room had a slightly smaller bar than the main room of the club. Located on the river side of the room was a stage that was being used to its capacity by the heaviest metal-looking group of musicians that Ian had ever seen. The entire middle of the room was comprised of a very large dance floor that was nearly packed with young twenty-something, vampiric-stylized and Gothic-attired raving party revelers.

The intense high-decibel level that the band and its scream-singing lead vocalist had achieved reached far beyond Ian's ability to tolerate what he considered to be nothing more than head-banging, hate-mongering, sweat-slinging, helter-skelter rabid noise rather than any semblance of what could be called music, regardless of its being labeled death metal or otherwise.

Zoey had already finished her drink. Upon noticing that, Ian quickly guzzled the remainder of his. He then took their empty glasses and set them on the nearest corner of the bar.

Ian considered for a second what it would probably look like to the surrounding crowd. *Old man can't take the music.* But at this point, it no longer mattered. Ian cupped his hands over his ears as he returned to Zoey's side.

Zoey noticed immediately that Ian was suffering severe decibel overload. She smiled at him and pointed towards the corridor from which they'd entered into the room, clearly indicating that she wanted to leave the band room. Ian knew that her decision to leave the room was mainly due to his distress and not her own.

Once they were back near the restrooms, Ian motioned to Zoey that he was going into the men's room. "I'm gonna go back to our table." Zoey nearly shouted. Ian smiled and nodded.

Almost shouting, Ian replied, "Wow, I never guessed it would be this loud."

Zoey smiled as she actually yelled, "Yeah, this is insane." Hearing Zoey say that made Ian feel not quite so ancient.

Before Ian and Zoey parted, he spoke nearly as loudly as he could,

"Hey, order us a couple more drinks if ya don't mind." Ian handed Zoey a fifty. "That waiter … He never asked for any money for the last round, so we must have a tab going. But just in case, here's some money for what we owe and …"

Zoey smiled large and nodded. She then turned and headed through the archway corridor back towards the main room.

The men's room door flung open, and a young man and a young woman came bounding out. Ian entered without having to touch the door. The restroom was admittedly beautiful. It had marble floors as opposed to the refinished hardwood flooring throughout the rest of the nightclub which well supported the club's castle-like motif.

The restroom's sinks and faucets were brass. It was packed nearly beyond capacity with heavily made-up and vampiric-costumed young men and very attractive young women.

Ian thought as he looked around the bathroom, *Some of these supposed women are likely she-males. But I swear they could pass anyone's discernment short of a full body search.*

There were no independent urinals, just one continuous brass troth that Ian estimated was around twelve feet long. It was slightly sloped from both directions and had running water streaming into it, causing all deposited urine to flow to the center and rapidly drain away.

Ian opted to check out and use one of the restroom's six fully-private toilet stalls. He zigzagged past a number of people of varying sexual persuasions and made his way over to the center stall. Ian noticed its door was not locked because it did not display the small occupied sign that the door was devised to display. Even still, Ian decided that he'd better knock to be safe. He loudly rap-tapped on the door with the knuckles of his right fist. Nobody answered, so Ian pushed the door; it swung open but only to reveal that the room was in fact occupied by a man who was sitting on the toilet and a woman who was sitting on top of him. She was facing him with her skirt hiked up to her waist, revealing her very shapely, naked hind-side. Neither of them had heard Ian's knocking on the door due to the ambient noise and their feverishly-engrossing activities.

The woman was moaning loudly and uttering very convincing sounds of genuine ecstasy while performing what to Ian appeared to be perfectly-timed rhythmic pelvic thrusts ... simultaneously bouncing her body up and down on the man's phallus like she was skillfully bareback riding a wild stallion.

Ian backed away from the bathroom stall a little ashamed. He realized that he had lingered watching the couple a few seconds longer than was appropriate by any civilized standards. He closed the stall door, took a deep breath, and went over to the stall on the immediate left. It was occupied, so he went further down the line until he spotted another one that indicated it was vacant.

Ian knocked louder on this door than he'd knocked on the other. Two seconds after he knocked, a young man came semi-staggering out of the stall. He had white powder residue under his nose, which came as no surprise to Ian. Street drugs of every kind abounded in the place. Cocaine and ecstasy were easier to procure than paper towels, as patrons huddled in groups around the sinks of the restroom-slash-pharmacy. Ian couldn't help but think, *You'd think the police could get this place shut down just for the rampant drugs if nothing else. But I guess in the vernacular of the locals – they've got bigger fish to fry.*

Once inside the restroom stall, Ian immediately locked the door. He then proceeded to relieve himself. Once he'd finished with his nature call, he began tapping on the wall behind the bathroom stall. Ian continued examining the seams of the wall for several minutes, though he couldn't find any type of obvious irregularity or apparent removable panel. He did notice that the wall seemed very thin, and he thought it might have had an unusually hollow sound when he tapped it hard. But due to the noise in the restroom, he couldn't be certain if there was anything out of the ordinary about it or not. The floor appeared to be seamlessly solid.

Ian exited the stall and made his way past a number of people over to a sink. He washed his hands and dried them under a hand blower, then left the bathroom and headed back to rejoin Zoey.

Once at the table, the room that had initially seemed horribly loud to Ian didn't seem so bad. He realized that he was rapidly adjusting to the volume but wondered if that was necessarily a good thing.

The drinks Zoey had ordered for them had already arrived. Zoey had already drank around a third of her drink. Ian picked up his glass and began taking small pulls from it as he once again began panning his eyes around the room.

Zoey spoke, "I paid for all of our drinks. The ones from before and these. I figured if we need to make any fast moves, that would be out of the way."

Ian smiled and nodded his approval as he replied, "Smart. Good thinking!"

Zoey winked at Ian for his compliment. She then pointed to the money the waiter had brought her back as change for the fifty she'd handed him. Ian picked up the paper money, leaving the coinage, and stuffed the bills into his wallet minus a five dollar bill that he left lying there.

Zoey spoke, "I already gave the guy a good tip."

Ian raised his eyebrows, grinned, and retrieved the five dollar bill and stuffed it into his pocket.

Ian checked the time via his cell phone. It was a little after eleven. Before Ian put his cell phone back into his front black denim jeans pocket, it began vibrating. Ian checked it again. Its screen notified him that he'd just received a text message.

Ian glanced up from his phone at Zoey for a few seconds. It appeared to him that she was panning her eyes around the room in every direction, likely looking for anything that might appear out of the ordinary.

Ian looked back at his phone and began checking his message. It was from Ned.

Just got here. I'm with FBI Special Agent Alisha Simmons. She's a hot-looking black gal. We look like we belong in a fucking Napoleon period Frenchy movie. Her idea. I thought I saw you in the band room minutes ago. We're now near the main bar. Come find us. Erase this message now.

Ian understood about erasing the message; in case his phone was to wind up in the wrong hands, it would blow Ned and Agent Simmons' cover and potentially put them all in greater danger than they might already be in.

Ian erased Ned's message. He then looked over at Zoey and motioned for her to lean over the small table to get as close to him as she could. When she did so, Ian spoke as loudly to her as he dared, "Ned's here. And he's with some lady FBI agent. They want me to head over to the bar so we can talk. I think we should go over to them together. Once we meet up with them, we should maybe look like we're all old friends. What do ya think?"

Zoey took no time to think about what Ian suggested, agreeing right away. "Sounds good. Let's go." She obviously didn't want to be left alone any more than absolutely necessary.

Ian and Zoey both quickly finished their drinks and began making their way through the crowded room over to the main bar. Once close to the bar, Ian spotted Ned and the FBI agent right away. Ned's description of how they were dressed, though crude, was spot-on. They were both dressed like attendees of a 1700's French Cotillion masquerade party with elaborate period costumes, wigs, hand-held masks, and all.

Ian walked up behind Ned, who was leaning against the bar attempting to look like he was making small talk with his date. Ian noticed immediately that Ned was spot-on about something else as well. Agent Simmons was very attractive indeed.

Ian tapped on Ned's shoulder. Ned somewhat overreacted as he jerked around to face Ian.

"Fuck me, Ian." Ned grabbed at his heart. "Ya didn't have to … Christ, ya nearly scared the hell out of me."

Due to the location of the main bar, which was directly behind a wall that separated them from the smaller bar in the band room, this was the least loud place in the entire club. But due to the music and the size of the crowd, it was still LOUD.

"Ian. Zoey. Allow me to introduce my friend Alisha." Ian, Zoey, and Alisha all smiled and nodded cordially in response to Ned's simple introduction, not wanting to go overboard with handshakes and such and draw much attention.

Ned then positioned himself close to Ian and began speaking into Ian's left ear just loud enough to be heard.

"The chief told me to tell you to stop your investigation at once since the Feds are actively in on this now." Ian stepped away from Ned for a second – he was a bit taken aback by what Ned just told him, but said nothing.

Ned leaned in to speak into Ian's ear once again. "That said, I personally think you can be very valuable to me and Agent Alisha here. And she concurs. So if you're still game, I'd like you and your partner there …" Ned glanced over and flashed a charming smile at Zoey, "to continue on regardless of what the chief said. For reasons I can't explain, at least not now, I'd … we'd like you to stick with us on this but just for tonight. Come tomorrow, you're cut loose. You okay with that? If not, I totally understand. But if no, I insist that you grab your lady friend and the both of you just turn around and get the hell out of here and don't look back."

Ian thought about it for a couple of long, silent seconds. He then looked intensely into Ned's eyes. With equal intensity, he looked over at Agent Simmons. She said nothing but nodded twice, clearly signaling her agreement with Ned.

Ian felt he'd come too far to not see this thing through at least regarding tonight. He took a deep breath and sighed as he exhaled. Ian then slowly, inconspicuously nodded his head.

Ned motioned for Ian to once again lean towards him so he could speak into his ear. Ian complied.

"Okay. This is how we're gonna play it. I believe we're gonna have a warrant to search this place and the Flavel House by mid-morning tomorrow as soon as the judge is in. But until then, I want to see for myself if that warrant's gonna be worth the effort to convince a judge to issue. Hopefully a judge that Salizzar doesn't already have in his pocket."

Ian nodded. "Yeah, I could see how that'd be tough with this guy."

Ned interjected, "Good! Then here's the plan that Agent Simmons and I cooked up. She's gonna join your gal, Zoey. You guys got a table?"

Ian replied, "Yeah, we've got one across the room. At least that's where our coats are parked. I hope it hasn't been taken."

"Good!" Ned said. He continued, "All right. In about an hour, Alisha will go over to join you guys at your table. She'll hang there for a while, appearing to be making chit-chat. At that time, you're gonna leave and rendezvous with me outside over on the south side of this place. You and I are gonna get into that basement from a side door near the back of the place. Almost no lighting on that side of the warehouse. It's good and dark. It should be pretty easy to avoid being seen."

Ian knew that besides the suspended basement that he and Zoey had entered into yesterday, there was a side door towards the river end of the warehouse on the dock level. But he had seen for himself that the door was locked, secured well by an extra heavy-duty hasp and very large padlock.

"Ned. I've seen the door you're talking about. It's really locked-up. I mean big time."

Ned backed away from speaking directly into Ian's ear to face him. He then flashed Ian a grin as he replied, "You let me worry about that. Now why don't you and your date go back to your table and try and look like you're having a good time for a while. Alisha and I are gonna do a bit of snooping around here in the club, especially around the shitters."

Ian wondered if Ned and the FBI agent had come up with a similar theory regarding the restrooms. Ian figured the way Ned said they were going to check them out, more likely than not, that they had. Ian looked over at Zoey, took her hand, and they both headed back to their table.

CHAPTER 21
All Hallows Eve (III)

The club was buzzing even more than before with all kinds of bizarre sights, some of which underscored Ian's naiveté regarding nightclubs of this nature.

All around him were seated and standing gothically-dressed, pseudo-vampiric, heavily partying role-players. But some, a scarce few to Ian's closely observant eyes, were perhaps … just perhaps … something else.

By this time, both Ian and Zoey had had a few Jack-n-Cokes so as not to appear to be doing anything other than partying and having a good time. With that, there were a few times that Ian thought his eyes might be playing alcohol-related tricks on him. Very occasionally, and totally randomly, he thought he'd seen something to the effect of an unnaturally quick movement by one or another of the more sinister-looking vampiric types who were mainly seated in private booths being utilized for even more seedy activities than the near club-wide illegal drug consumption and overt near-full-on copulations occurring on top of tables, against walls, and up against pillars. Activities such as he'd seen previously in the restroom had now migrated into the main rooms of the club.

Ian knew that the place could be shut down just for this alone.

But that wasn't why they were here. Ian knew he had to keep his eyes and mind on the much larger picture: serial killers and the horrifying likelihood of its intended result – human blood, and organ trafficking.

A number of minutes had passed since Zoey had excused herself to go to the lady's room both for natural reasons, as well as to do a bit of restroom sleuthing. She'd been gone now a bit longer than Ian was comfortable with. He was getting ready to head over towards the restrooms when he felt a presence looming just behind him. Ian abruptly turned nearly ninety degrees, almost causing his chair to tip over. He recovered his balance and stabilized himself just in time to see whom he knew in an instant by description to be the man himself. Salizzar.

Salizzar was dressed in a long, black leather coat with a turned-up collar. Visible beneath his unfastened coat was a white satin or silk shirt that had large, flowing ruffles, what you'd expect to see worn in a movie depicting a man of the aristocracy from the post-renaissance era.

Salizzar also sported a wide, black leather belt with a large, golden buckle. It was fashioned to look like the head of a dragon with fiery, ruby-colored eyes. Knowing at least a bit about some of the man's impressive wealth, Ian surmised that it was likely the buckle was solid gold and just as likely that the dragon's eyes were actual rubies.

Salizzar had long, jet-black hair that was pulled back into a ponytail. He wore ruby solitaire stud earrings in both earlobes. Ian noticed immediately that his eyes, which peered over the top of small, perfectly round, golden-framed blood-red lens glasses, matched perfectly the rest of his attire. His eyes appeared in the dimly-lit room to be as jet-black as his hair.

After what seemed to Ian to have been a near-eternal uncomfortable moment but in actuality was no more than seconds, the man spoke like so many of the others who worked for him, in a very thick Eastern European accent.

"Allow me to introduce myself. I am Salizzar. Welcome to my modest club."

Ian cleared his throat. "Um, good … Nice to meet you. I'm … My name's Ian. Ian McBride." Ian was nervous to say the least and wondered if he'd delivered his alias in a believable fashion.

Salizzar grinned impishly, "Yes. Well, Ian … Or would you prefer Mister McBride? May I join you? In the absence of your lady friend, who must be powdering her nose, so to speak."

Ian nodded as he motioned with his right hand for Salizzar to take a seat.

Salizzar sat down in the only other chair at the small table, the one that Zoey had occupied an uncomfortably increasing number of minutes before.

"Well then, Ian, how do you like my nightclub? Are you and your … companion … enjoying yourselves this fine All Hallows Eve?"

Ian thought to himself, *Companion. Interesting word choice. He's careful. A mark of intelligence and perhaps that of someone who has something to hide!*

He paused for a second before replying, "Yes, your club is quite nice. Not my normal cup of tea, mind you, though you probably already gathered that by my poor attempt at trying a little too hard to look the part. But … it is Halloween … and when in Rome. Anyway, we thought this might be fun."

Salizzar smiled as he spoke. "Yes, well, it's been said, Ian … McDermott … that a half truth is no more than a whole lie. You've in fact visited my place before, though admittedly not on this floor. Yet once again, you have entered my place freely of your own will."

At hearing Salizzar speak those words, Ian thought his heart was going to pound itself right out of his chest. Sweat began gathering in heavy beads across his forehead. His mind raced. He felt faint at the total realization, *He knows who I am. What was that he said? I've entered of my own free will! Clayton said something like that. That ... that means something ...? Christ, I can't remember.*

In one deft motion, Salizzar rose up from the table. "Well Ian, enjoy yourself. Oh, and it seems we have a mutual friend. One who poses as a writer of what I would consider to be comedy. Though unfortunately severely misguided, our mutual friend is not without influence. Therefore, I'm pleased to tell you that your money is no good here. That is ... for the rest of the evening. From this point forward your drinks or anything you wish, and also for your friends as well ... everything is on the house. But I grant you this night my hospitality and guarantee you and your friends' personal safety and protection from the crescendo of this evening's festivities ... under one provisional condition. In order for me to maintain my good humor, speaking in the local vernacular, I strongly suggest you re-plot your present laid-in course. I have as yet no reason to cause harm to Officer Ned Parker and the lovely FBI Special Agent Alisha Simmons nor yourself or your lady friend Zoey Collins. If you wisely heed my warning and cease at once all further efforts that might cause me, albeit only momentarily, any further consternation., I shall amply reward you. I am known to be very generous ... to my friends. But, if you feel you must continue hunting matters you cannot possibly fully fathom, well ... might I suggest you consider pursuing a not so formidable prey, lest you become preyed upon. Like, say, chasing the 'Green Fairy.' Absinthe is our house specialty libation. I have it flown in weekly from Prague. I shall have a fountain of it sent to your table immediately. Along, of course, with all of the necessary accoutrements to fully enjoy it.

For your sake, Mister McDermott, and that of your companions both bipedal and quadruped – hopefully, we shall not meet again under unsavory circumstance." Salizzar then turned and rapidly headed in the direction of the corridor that led past the restrooms and on into the band room.

Ian shuddered at the thought that Salizzar knew of them all, even Scout. He was very apparently as brilliant as he was, in a word, evil. Ian knew there was no mistaking the intent or extent regarding the threat he'd just been given as he thought, *I've got to get Zoey, and warn Ned and Alisha. Without more backup, we've gotta get the hell out of here.*

Just then, the tall Lurch-like waiter brought to Ian's table a transparent glass container filled with a light green elixir. The glass container had a transparent plastic ice tube inside it; obviously devised to keep the beverage contained within cold without becoming watered down.

Ian stared for a few long moments at the elixir-filled dispenser. His mind was racing, and he desperately tried to regain some composure. It was then at the pinnacle of his confusion and fear that two things happened simultaneously. Zoey came back to the table, and for that he was eternally thankful, and his phone began vibrating once again.

Ian quickly snatched it up. He had received another text from Ned.

Ian. Change of plans. I decided to check out the basement myself. Is Alisha with you guys? She said she was going to join you after first going to the can.

Zoey sat down and stared at the absinthe-filled container and the two fancy crystal glasses that had slotted silver spoons balanced on top of them. There was also a small China saucer that held several sugar cubes. She laughed as she declared, "Wow, you must be planning on doing some serious partying."

Ian quickly texted Ned back. *How long ago was that?*

About 30 minutes ago. Why?

Ian looked up at Zoey. She could tell instantly that something was wrong.

Ian again fired a text back to Ned. *I haven't seen her since we talked at the bar. I got visited by Salizzar. He knows everything. I'd get out of there now.*

Ian waited for a number of minutes, but there were no more texts from Ned. Ian even tried calling Ned, but it just went to voice mail. Ian opted not to leave a message.

Zoey couldn't take being in the dark regarding what might be happening any longer. "What's going on? And what's with this thing?" She pointed at the dispenser.

Ian took a deep breath before speaking. He no longer cared much if anyone heard him or not, so he exclaimed loud enough for Zoey to hear him without having her lean in towards him.

"It's all gone to shit! We've been made! That FBI agent's missing. And Ned, last I heard he's in the basement. But now he's not responding, which pretty much means he's either hiding or has been caught or …"

Zoey suddenly got wide-eyed. She placed her right hand over her mouth as she took a large gasp of air. Then she removed her hand from her mouth and loudly exclaimed, "Oh my God! What are we gonna do?" Nobody in the room seemed to take any notice of Ian and Zoey whatsoever. It was then that Ian spotted their waitress from the Soggy Dog Saloon, Madison. She was with two other young women. Ian nearly jumped up out of his seat. He made his way over to where they were all standing, just leaning against a wall.

Madison recognized him immediately. "Oh, hey. How're ya doing? These are my friends, Tina and Emily. Where's your friend?"

Ian couldn't help sounding desperate as he nearly shouted, "Listen,

227

Madison. You and your friends gotta get out of here. Something very bad's about to happen."

Madison frowned and took a half step away from Ian. "What …? What-a ya mean something bad's gonna …?" Madison's girlfriends were both looking around at various young men.

Ian decided that a lie might be the best way to go given the circumstances. "Okay, listen. The lady I'm with and me, we're undercover cops. We've called in for a drug raid on the place. In less than five minutes this place is going to be crawling with cops arresting pretty much anyone and everyone they can get their hands on, understand?"

"Oh my God! Yes. Yeah, I understand. I do. I totally … holy crap!" Madison grabbed the arms of her girlfriends, then quickly told them an abridged version of what Ian had just told her. They all believed the story. Madison turned to Ian and thanked him, then the three young women made a beeline for the elevator.

Zoey left the table and quickly joined up with Ian. She had seen enough to figure out that Ian had said something to warn Madison.

Ian said urgently, "All right. We've got to get the hell out of here. I'm telling you, something hugely bad is about to happen. My gut tells me just before midnight. Anyway, there's nothing more for us here. Our cover's blown, and we are in serious danger."

Zoey fired back, "What makes you think … Why are we in so much danger? I mean in such a public place?"

Ian grabbed both of Zoey's hands and looked her in the eyes. The extreme grimace in his brow and tightlipped facial expression left no doubt in Zoey's mind that Ian was deadly serious.

Ian said, "It's been my experience that when an enemy tells you that you've nothing to fear from them if you behave a certain way, you better beware. Now, let's get out of here and see if we can find Ned before …"

Ian held Zoey's left hand within his right and began nearly pushing people out of their way as they hurried for the elevator. Once inside, Ian pressed the button for level one. They were alone in the elevator. The nightclub was packed. Apparently, they weren't letting anymore people up into the club, and nobody was leaving so early.

"Zoey, you didn't drink from that dispenser at our table or suck on any of those sugar cubes or anything like that, did you?" Ian asked with noticeably elevated stress.

Ian saw the panic suddenly come over Zoey's face. "Yes! Yeah, I drank some of it. Absinthe, right? And I poured the cold water over a sugar cube in a spoon, just like I've heard you're supposed to. Oh my God. You don't think it wasn't poisoned or drugged, do you? I mean, was it?"

Ian couldn't hide his concern about that very possibility. But he knew the possibility existed with each drink they'd consumed.

"No. No. You're fine. Let's go … No wait. You go straight to the car." Ian handed Zoey the car keys. "Bring the car as close as you can to the south side of the parking lot. Try to find a spot that has a line of sight to that side door. If you can't find a parking spot, I don't care. Park the car any way you can, but again, position the car so you can see that door. This is important. Make sure the car's locked, but keep it running. We may need to make a quick run for it. That side door … That's where I'm gonna try and go inside to find Ned. My guess is the locks have already been picked open."

Zoey spoke up. "Ian, maybe we should just call the cops."

Ian smiled at Zoey and gave a perfunctory nod as he replied, "Yeah. Maybe. But I'm gonna first try and find Ned. I don't want to get bogged down answering questions all night and maybe for days if it's not absolutely necessary."

Zoey nodded her head in agreement. The elevator door opened

and they were both surprised to see no one. No line of people waiting on the huge ramp waiting to get in. No giant bouncer. No dwarf. Nobody!

Once Ian and Zoey left the elevator, hurried down the ramp and had gotten well away from the club, Zoey wrapped her arms around his neck, hugged him, and gave him a kiss. Without a word, Zoey took off running to retrieve their car. Ian walked out onto the suspended parking lot, looking in all directions as he headed towards the south side of the warehouse.

Zoey opened the car door, climbed in, and immediately started it. Scout came forward to sit tall beside her in the front passenger seat.

"Don't worry, boy. We're going to get Ian." Scout barked twice as if in reply.

Zoey drove across from the adjacent parking lot to the south side of the warehouse just as Ian had instructed. She was able to find a parking spot which afforded her the line of sight that Ian asked her to maintain, backed into the spot, and kept the car running. Lighting from a security lamp located above the warehouse side door afforded just enough light that from her vantage point she would be able to see anyone coming or going from the doorway.

"Okay. Now, Scout, we wait. And as you know, waiting's the hardest part."

Suddenly from between two parked cars Ian emerged; he rapidly approached the driver's side of the car. Ian signaled for Zoey to roll her window down.

Ian exclaimed in an excited voice, "I think I saw him in there through a broken window, but I'm not certain. The door's unlocked, but I came back for … Zoey, open the glove box and hand me the handgun inside." Zoey flashed Ian a look of extreme apprehension, but she did what he said.

"Ian, are you sure about this? I mean, we could just get the hell out of here."

He smiled at Zoey, "If I'm not back in just a few minutes, you're gonna do just that. Then make an anonymous call to the cops and have them get here as soon as they can. Tell them there are gun shots being fired and you hear screams, then hang up. That should do the trick. That'll get 'em coming from every doughnut shop around and …"

Zoey frowned and slumped down in the driver's seat. She realized that Ian was going back into the warehouse no matter what she said to try and convince him otherwise.

Ian put the heavy pistol into his jacket's front pocket then briskly headed off towards the warehouse's side door entrance.

Zoey remembered that her purse was locked in the trunk of the car. She turned off the ignition and took the keys with her as she exited, using the keyless button on the key ring to open the trunk. She quickly snatched up her purse and climbed back into the car. Zoey then inserted the key into the ignition and promptly switched the car back on and locked the doors.

She reached into her purse and retrieved her cell phone. Seconds later, near panic struck. "Damn it! Goddamnit!" she exclaimed as she noticed that her phone's battery was completely dead.

Ian was within thirty feet of the side door when he saw someone step outside. That someone then aggressively pulled another somebody by the hand, and they both exited the warehouse basement through the side doorway. Their backs were turned, but in a second, Ian recognized both of them by their clothing.

Ian drew his pistol from his jacket. "Hey!" he shouted as loud as he could.

Instantly, the man turned towards him. Then with great force, he swung the woman that he held with one hand in such a way as to wind her in close to his body. In some terrifying yet near impossibly odd way, it reminded Ian of the retraction effect of a yo-yo. The man, Salizzar, held the female FBI agent closely against him with his right hand wrapped around her throat.

What Ian witnessed next he would have deemed impossible had he not seen the impossible before. Salizzar's fingernails began rapidly growing until they were several inches long. His hands then fully transformed from those of a human into claws. His face also began rapidly changing, morphing into what Ian could only grasp in his mind as being that of a human-sized fanged vampire bat. A devil. Even in the low light, Ian could see the man-monster's horrifically demonic eyes, piercing blood-red luminescent orbs. Salizzar continued his metamorphosis, which included enormous, bat-like wings that burst through his clothing and unfurled themselves. His wings began to slowly, powerfully flap like he was going to leap into the air, catch the wind, and soar away with Special Agent Alisha Simmons clutched in his grasp.

Salizzar didn't say a word, but even at that distance, Ian could smell the rotting stench of his breath. Just then, two more men emerged from the doorway. The first man was of medium build. The second one was so large that he had to turn sideways and duck slightly just to fit through the doorway. Ian could see right away that both men held handguns as they stepped into the dim light emitted from the overhead security light.

Ian's knees almost buckled when, to his utter shock and dismay, the realization hit him that the medium-sized man was Ned. The other man was the near-giant bouncer.

Ian couldn't help himself. "Ned, you son of a bitch! You played me. You played us all! So you're the mole inside your department. You're the reason this man, this monster, stays one step ahead of the law."

Ned shook his head as he laughed. "Oh, come on, Ian. Don't sound like such a pompous ass. You're no different. We're the same, you and I. We both hire out to the highest bidder. Oh yeah, and did I mention that he's promised to make me immortal besides filthy rich? Now, Ian, face facts. You're outgunned and outclassed. Why don't you just set that Glock of yours down and, hell, join the winning team. Salizzar's like the Marines. He's always looking for a few good men."

Just then, Agent Simmons made her move. Unaware of Salizzar's full metamorphic appearance, she broke away with a quick jiu-jitsu move and in one deft motion retrieved her thigh-strapped pistol and rapid-fired three shots point blank into Salizzar's chest. It all happened too fast for Agent Simmons to even comprehend what Salizzar had become as he reeled backwards from the impact of the slugs.

The mammoth-sized bodyguard leveled his gun at Ian, but Ian turned his attention from Agent Simmons and the monster just in time to beat him to the trigger. Ian fired one round into the bodyguard's stomach. The large man let out a bellowing moan as he grabbed at his guts with both hands before dropping first to his knees then falling face down onto the pylon decking.

From the rental car, Zoey could make out only some of what was happening. She heard shots fired, and she'd seen the large man fall. But she couldn't make out any details regarding Salizzar or who he'd been holding.

Scout too heard the gunshots and, sensing that Ian was in danger, began to go wild. Nothing Zoey could say to him had any effect on calming him down. Scout began pawing feverishly, violently, at the passenger door and window.

The now devilishly, fully-transformed Salizzar was little more than a blur as he almost instantly closed the distance between himself and Agent Simmons. Then with a powerful thrust, he buried his clawed hand into the female agent's chest and ripped her still-beating heart from her body. Blood gushed and projectile-spewed in nearly every direction. Agent Simmons collapsed to the deck onto her back. She began spasming violently as blood erupted from her nose, mouth, and vacant chest cavity. Due to the cold night air, the blood that pooled all around her animated, convulsing corpse began lightly steaming.

Ian was stunned, sickened beyond rational thought at the grotesquely impossible sight.

Salizzar began laughing manically as he slurped the sticky blood from his fingered claw.

Ned too was shocked beyond comprehension. Involuntarily, he began screaming out, "OH FUCK! FUCK NO! FUCK!"

Suddenly from the doorway appeared the dwarf. Seeing his demonically diminutive cohort, Salizzar took a large bite out of the heart as he spoke in a throaty, gurgling voice, "Here, Faust. This is for you!" Then like throwing a bone to a dog, Salizzar tossed the remains of the heart to the evil elf.

Faust instantly became wide-eyed and displayed a maniacal ear-to-ear grin as he leaned against the warehouse wall and held the heart above his head, allowing the syrupy-thick evacuating blood to cascade down his face and onto his disproportionately long, V-split snake-like tongue.

Now frightened nearly out of his mind and shaking violently, Ian somehow managed to muster enough presence of mind to train his gun at Salizzar with both of his hands clenched around it.

Salizzar shouted at Ned in a sickeningly shrill demonic voice, "Shoot him! Kill him! You worthless maggot!"

All at once, in response to his master's command, Ned fired his .357 three times in rapid succession – but not at Ian. Ned utterly blew the dwarf's head apart just short of total decapitation. Brains and skull fragments hung and dripped down the side of the warehouse like a slurry of dark molasses mixed with chunky oatmeal.

Before Salizzar could close in on one or the other, both Ian and Ned began emptying the remainders of their clips into him. But when their guns were empty, Salizzar was still on his feet, and it appeared he was going to remain that way.

Ian dropped down on one knee and retrieved his ankle-holstered .32 Berretta loaded with hollow-point rounds. He then began slowly walking towards Salizzar. With each step, Ian pulled the trigger time and again, emptying his gun into Salizzar's chest. Even in his totally fright-filled altered mental state, Ian remembered one thing that Clayton had told him with empirical clarity. *The heart must be totally obliterated.*

Ned holstered his empty gun and quickly glanced back inside the warehouse to see if he could spot anything that he could use as a weapon. Salizzar, even in his weakened condition, moved quickly towards Ian, too quickly for Ian to escape. In less than a second, Salizzar had Ian in his grasp. His demonic eyes rolled back into his head like a shark when feeding as his fangs enlarged.

Scout continued to paw frantically with all his might at the passenger car door until he finally managed to activate the window's down button.

"SCOUT, NO!" Zoey screamed as loud as she could, but it was too late. Scout leaped out the car's window. He hit the pylon dock running, and in a blur, he was heading to save Ian, his master and friend.

Salizzar spotted the large dog heading directly at him like a four-legged freight train, gums fully retracted, exposing his enormous canines. He was barking and growling in a way Ian had never heard from Scout. Saliva poured from his jowls. Scout sprinted at his target at a speed that would have rivaled the fastest racehorse. Salizzar tossed Ian aside to make his escape, but in less than a second, Scout leaped into Salizzar's arms, crashing into his chest. Instantly, Scout locked onto the monster's throat with his powerful jaws in a vice grip and began ripping at Salizzar's throat with the ferocity of a wild, rabid wolf.

Try as Salizzar might to desperately dig his claws into Scout, to try and gain some upper hand, Scout was too powerful. He twisted his body violently back and forth, continuing his vicious attack. In less than a minute, Scout had nearly ripped all the way through Salizzar's throat and neck. No matter how many times Salizzar struck powerfully at Scout, the large dog was completely adrenaline-enraged and totally unyielding.

Finally, Salizzar managed to throw the large dog off of himself. He began to buckle as he let out an inhuman shriek while grabbing his neck to try and stabilize it from snapping off under the weight of his head, decapitating him. Blood gushed in every direction from his nearly-severed neck. But still relentlessly enraged, Scout backpedaled a few feet then began his charge. He leaped once again directly into Salizzar's chest and bit down on what was left of Salizzar's neck. Scout began aggressively thrashing his head, increasing the ripping effects of his bite tenfold.

Then in one last summoning of all his monstrous strength, Salizzar managed to heave Scout off of him yet again. Now barely conscious, Salizzar began staggering backwards until he fell back hard into the dock railing. His monstrous metamorphosis was beginning to wane. His features were becoming more human by the second.

The banister began to give way under Salizzar's weight as Scout started backing up even further from Salizzar than he did in his last attack. This time Ian thought he saw a fire in Scout's eyes. Ian had no doubt that Scout was going in for the final coup de grâce. In seconds, Scout hit full charging speed and leaped with everything he had into Salizzar's chest as he bit down like a bear trap on the thin remains of Salizzar's throat. Salizzar was helpless this time and was nearly finished, but then it happened. The fierce battle proved too much for the badly-damaged railing to support any further. It suddenly gave way. Both Salizzar and Scout tumbled backward as they plunged thirty feet off the deck into the icy-black, turbulent water of the Columbia River.

Ian screamed, "No!" as he ran to the edge where his best friend had gone over. He frantically called out Scout's name. Over and over, he cried out for Scout as he ran up and down the edge of the docks trying to see any sign of him. But it didn't take long for Ian to realize it was no use. Scout was gone.

Simultaneously, Ian and Ned heard the sound of a helicopter as it came rushing in from downriver. In mere moments, the helicopter had landed on the roof of the warehouse nightclub. Ian and Ned could only surmise that it had been called in to pick up Salizzar and any of his more important cronies. Not two minutes passed before the helicopter left, heading towards the ocean.

Then came a giant explosion. Fire burst out, shattering all of the warehouse's windows at once. People began pouring out of the nightclub, mainly by way of the external fire escape stairway located on the other side of the building.

Ian thought, *No loose ends. Tonight was always going to be the last night for this business. Time to open up shop elsewhere.*

Then came the welcome sound of sirens.

Ned took Ian's Glock 9mm and put it in his pocket. He then quickly pulled the body of Special Agent Alisha Simmons into the burning warehouse, and did the same with the body of the dwarf. He left the massive-sized body guard where he lay just outside the doorway to the warehouse. Ned then took a handkerchief out of his pocket, and with it, he snatched up the bloody remains of Agent Simmons' heavily chewed-on heart and tossed it into the burning building as well. He fired Ian's Glock once into the building then also tossed it into the now raging inferno. Lastly, he pulled out his cell phone and made a brief call to the Coast Guard.

Ian was too stunned to even speak as he watched Ned. Once Ned's desperate tasks appeared to have been completed, he walked briskly up to Ian. "You didn't really think I was the mole, did you?"

Ian looked at Ned suspiciously. But then smiled as he shook his head and replied, "No."

Ned spoke as best he could though he was winded from all the heavy lifting and fast moving. "Ian. What we just … I mean what I saw, it's not possible. I mean, maybe Salizzar slipped me some kind of hallucinogenic, 'cause what I saw … It's just not possible, is it?"

Ian looked Ned straight in the eyes. "Ned, in my business, I've learned that, believe it or not, monsters do exist. Most are of the human variety. Some aren't."

Ned just stared for a moment blankly at the ground while he shook his head slowly from side to side. He then took a deep breath and looked once again at Ian. "Fuck me! I just don't … I mean I can't! Well anyway, Salizzar's not the only one who knows how to tie-off loose ends. Nothing makes sorting things out more difficult than fire, especially one like this. The FBI will look into Agent Simmons' death. With her totally burnt remains, they'll note her heart was somehow extracted, but it will be impossible to determine exactly how. They'll conclude it was done by Salizzar or his people, harvesting organs. Nothing will make much sense, but nothing in cases like this ever does. It will settle itself out in time. By the way, I shot the bodyguard, but before he keeled over, he knocked the Glock from my hand, and it flew into the warehouse. You didn't fire a weapon. Fact is, you weren't here at all. Understand?"

By now, the entire lower part of the warehouse was a fiery inferno. Ned took a deep breath before continuing. "The truth is, and I wouldn't have believed it in a million years if I hadn't heard the Fed's tapes myself, it was Chief Mooney! Yeah! He was the mole all along. Just today, he tried to recruit me into the ranks. After I pretended to agree, he said for me to contact Salizzar tonight, that I'd help in shutting down their business.

"Yeah, the Feds had all the chief's phones tapped. Hell, come to find out they had all our phones tapped for some time. Ian, I'm really sorry about your dog. Scout was his name, right? An ex-cop dog. That dog was a bona fide hero in my book. As are you, Ian. Yeah, that dog of yours saved both our lives. I've been told if I put in for Chief, the job's mine. Hell of a way to get a promotion. Oh, and about what we saw or think we saw here tonight, no way that part's going into any report. Not the way it happened, anyway. Shit, they'd have my shield in a New York minute if I said anything about monsters; more than your run of the mill serial killer anyway. Ian, in the basement … in the walk-in freezer. Body parts galore! Bags of blood! A regular human meat market for real. But as far as much valuable evidence, it's all gonna go up in flames, making identification pretty much impossible. They knew what they were doing. These guys are pros at their sick business. They had this entire place rigged with remote-detonating incendiary explosives. Like I said, no loose ends. No matter who Salizzar managed to get in his pockets at the courthouse, no judge will deny us a search warrant any longer. We'll search his place and the Flavel House with a fine-tooth comb first thing in the morning as soon as I get a judge to sign the warrant. In the meantime, we'll have officers surrounding his place all night. I've already issued the order. But I'm not figuring we'll find a damn thing. I called the Coast Guard about the chopper. Maybe they'll get lucky and find 'em before …"

Ian interrupted, "No. They won't find them. That was an extremely high-speed turbo-copter, and they'll no doubt have landed on some ship out at sea by now, and the chopper's probably either been stashed in the belly of some freighter, or intentionally sunk to the bottom of the ocean. Loss of money and assets means nothing to these … No. These people, or whatever you want to call them, are massively funded. Too connected and too smart. As far as the Flavel House, you won't find a thing. Like you said, Ned, these guys leave no loose ends. And somehow, I seriously doubt if Salizzar's body is ever discovered either." Ian suddenly began worrying about that very thought.

Ned nodded his head in agreement and said, "Speaking of the Flavel House, looks like the Clatsop Historical Society's gonna get it back. I heard by Salizzar's own doing he put into some contract that if the place was ever left abandoned, it reverts back to them as owners. I figure the son-of-a-bitch was so arrogant he didn't want it ever again to be anyone's private home."

Teary-eyed, Ian exclaimed, "Yeah, you're probably right. Oh, and you're also right about a hell of a way to get promoted. But if it's any consolation, a good friend of mine, a lawman like you … He got promoted somewhat similarly. But in that case, a good man died leaving very big shoes to fill, but he will do just fine 'cause he's a good man. A credit to law enforcement like you, Ned. You're a good man who's gonna be replacing a real piece of shit, a man who covered up and even aided in the deaths of who knows how many people. Anyway, congratulations!" The two men shook hands.

Zoey came running up to Ian and threw her arms around him. She had been too stunned to even move from the car for a number of minutes. She hadn't been able to make out many details, but she'd seen

240

Scout's sacrifice. Zoey was heartbroken for Ian as well as for herself. She'd loved Scout too.

Ned walked up to Zoey. "Get him the hell out of here right now. I've got it from here. The Fire Department will be working all night. It will be their valiant efforts to save as much of the docks as possible. That will more than effectively pressure-wash away any blood evidence from around the place. Fire and water. Between that combination, there won't be much left of any viable evidence beyond the murders committed by Salizzar and his bunch for the surmised purpose of trafficking organs and body parts. You both have my word. Neither of you will be implicated in this mess in any way."

Ned walked over to Ian and shook his hand once again as he spoke. "Hell of a Halloween." Ian didn't reply. He just bowed his head and nodded silently in agreement.

Zoey put her arm around Ian and they began walking from the burning warehouse across the pylon-suspended parking lot over to Ian's rental car. When they were about ten feet away, they both noticed something dark, wet, and filthy but very much alive lying on the ground by the driver's side of the car.

"Oh, thank you, thank you, God!" Ian exclaimed as loud as he could as he started running towards his best friend.

* * *

Regardless of the best efforts made by the Astoria Fire Department, it was just as Ned had predicted. The warehouse fire rapidly become totally out of control; a blazing, three-story inferno. There was nothing the firemen could do other than protect as best they could the neighboring buildings and try and maintain the structural integrity of the surrounding docks by continuously hosing them down. It was obvious to everyone present that by morning The Morgue would exist no more, and there would be nothing left of the surrounding docks by the time the fire eventually burned itself out.

CHAPTER 22
All Saints Day - Stranger Than Fiction

Ian was awakened by his cell phone's alarm at 7:30 … morning came early, too early. The subject of Ian's impending departure, all the while they'd been together, had remained unspoken, but Ian and Zoey both knew that today was the day they'd been dreading.

Zoey rolled partially over on top of Ian and began kissing his neck. Within minutes, they retreated back into their own little world for the better part of the next half hour.

* * *

After their lovemaking concluded, Zoey was the first to sheepishly speak. "I guess you'll be heading out of town now that that nasty bit of business in Astoria's done with,"

Ian didn't answer right away. But after a couple of uncomfortably silent moments, he replied, "Yeah, I've got to go where my business leads me. Maybe you could come with me?"

Zoey replied, now teary-eyed, "We both know I can't do that. I have my shop and …"

Ian nodded his head as he spoke, "Yeah. I know, I was just wishful thinking."

Ian then tried to sound a little more upbeat. "But maybe someday, right? I'm guessing that I'll be coming back this way pretty often, especially since Clayton and I have become sort of business partners."

Zoey kissed Ian on the cheek and smiled at him, "You better."

Ian then got up and stretched his back. "Besides, I'm too old for you, Zoey. We both know that."

Zoey frowned as she fired back, "No. We both don't know that. I don't know that. You're perfect, and we're great together, and that's all I've got to say on the matter. Changing the subject. Are you going to tell me exactly what happened on the pier last night? I mean, besides the people getting shot and the fire. I couldn't really see that much from …"

Ian took a deep breath, exhaled, and replied, "One day, I will. One day soon. Suffice it to say, it's going to sound just as crazy as what I told you happened at Harmony Falls."

Zoey sighed as she wiped tears from her eyes, "Well, we've still got today. I'm definitely not working today. I'll call my shop just before it opens and have them reschedule my appointments, or … Anyway, today we relax and have some fun."

Ian smiled as he replied, "Sounds great. Hmm, check-out's not till 11:00. We don't have much to pack up. We could go hot tub till then. Hey, do you like museums and lighthouses? And does picnicking by the ocean and taking a long walk on the beach sound good?"

Scout had been cleaned up nicely, and his wounds had been well dressed as soon as they'd gotten back to the condo last night, but he was still a bit weak and worse for wear. He lay resting in front of the warm gas fireplace. But when he saw Zoey smiling and her mood lifting, Scout began wagging his tail.

Zoey bounded out of bed and into Ian's arms. "I love museums and lighthouses. And the rest, well, it all sounds perfect!"

* * *

The sun had set. Ian was racing up the peninsula as fast as he dared to drive. He had retrieved his Jeep from storage just minutes before. The manager of the storage facility, Bill, said he'd been instructed to return the rental car for Ian.

The Jeep's headlights seemed to dance a bounding jig of illumination on the roadway ahead due to its failing shocks and struts. When Ian arrived at Clayton's house, he pulled into the driveway, threw his Jeep into park, and switched his engine and headlights off. Ian got out of his vehicle, hardly noticing that Scout was acting uncharacteristically agitated.

Ian walked briskly up to the front door and rang the doorbell. After the third chiming of the bell, Clayton appeared with a smile that was nothing short of beaming.

He greeted his guest, "Ah, Ian. So glad you dropped by. Won't you please come in."

Ian followed Clayton on inside his house. But there was something about the way Clayton had invited him in that made the hairs on the back of Ian's neck stand on end. Also, he noticed that Clayton didn't have his typical cane in hand and was no longer walking with a limp.

"Ah, Ian. A joyous All Saints Day to you, my friend. A day for restoring balance to the universe after a night of giving the Devil his due, so to speak. I was so glad to hear you were unharmed during your Knight's Quest to slay the dragon and save my little princess."

Ian looked Clayton up and down. He was also glad to see that his new friend looked and seemed to be … fine? "Yeah, luckily. It seems, anyway, that everything worked out. Scout went a few rounds with Salizzar. He's gonna need some time to get back on his paws. Luckily, most of his wounds were not too deep. Mostly superficial. Zoey and I were able to patch him up. After a number of days of rest, I think he's gonna be fine. Fact is, he's healing at what I would consider to be an abnormally fast rate. Might have something to do with biting a vampire?"

Ian looked sheepishly at Clayton, hoping he would have something to say on the subject, but Clayton said nothing. He continued, "There was a terribly tragic loss of life, like that of FBI Agent Alisha Simmons. And there were people inside the club that didn't make it out and some that got pretty banged-up. But the loss of life wasn't nearly as bad as it could have been, I suppose. On the less-than-tragic but nonetheless unfortunate side is the property losses from the burning buildings, and … but you know doubt know all of that."

Clayton interrupted, "Yes, well, all that will be rebuilt. I've heard from very reliable sources that the Astoria City Council is planning as we speak for an entire newly-developed waterfront, one that will attract lots of upscale bistros and shops that will dramatically expand the attraction of tourist dollars. And that idea has my fullest support. No more nightclubs from hell."

Ian was starting to become more uncomfortable by the moment, though he wasn't certain why.

"Clayton, how about you? I mean, you look great. Now that Salizzar is no longer a threat, you must …?"

Clayton began laughing. "Yes, that bit about Salizzar. It's refreshing when a carefully-orchestrated plan reaches fruition. But as for him no longer posing any potential future threat … I wonder. It's difficult to know these things with absolute certainty, having not recovered irrefutable proof of his demise. Any corporeal remains, so to speak."

Ian was now both uncomfortable and totally confused. "Plan?" he asked, almost not wanting to know the answer.

Clayton motioned for Ian to follow him into the living room. "Please, Ian, come on in, and let's go sit down. I'll elaborate. After all that you've been through, I feel as friends, I owe you that much. And we are friends, are we not?"

Ian replied without hesitation, "Yes, Clayton. I believe … I certainly hope that we are. But I've got a question that I'm hoping you will answer. Just exactly who and perhaps better said … what … are you?

Clayton, with a very sly grin on his face, replied, "Well, I have been known by many names, some of which achieved varying levels of notoriety – and some fame continued long after they became, supposedly, dust to dust. But the roles I played, and we are all mere players, Ian, have long passed. I am a writer Ian. I've been a writer for centuries. Alas, poor Salizzar. I knew him well. A man, so to speak, of excellent fancy as you know. But also a creature of infinite jest, who I've bore on my shoulders a thousand times."

Ian's eyes widened. Even though the words had been colorfully twisted, he recognized them at once. "You were Shakespeare?" Ian nearly shouted.

Clayton began laughing though he did not answer. But after he stopped laughing, he walked over to his typical chair of choice and sat down. He then spoke. "Ian, the next thing you're going to ask me is if I was Bram Stoker or Percy Shelley, a man who had the ear of his wife regarding a story she wrote that was generations ahead of its time. Or perhaps you might even believe that I was Edgar Allen Poe? That would be a tale to tell. Not for faint of heart indeed if it were true."

Ian, speechless at the very possibilities, plopped down on the couch. Neither man said anything further as they stared intensely at each other for what was only a few uncomfortable seconds but to Ian seemed an eternity.

Just when Ian's tension had built to a point that he was nearly becoming faint, Clayton finally broke the ice. "Ian … Dear Ian. Salizzar was an ancient and a malevolent menace, that much is true. The rest … Well, that will be a good topic for another time. As far as Salizzar or Prince Vlad III of Walachia, if you're to believe much of anything I may tell you, colorfully referred to in history books as Vlad the Impaler, good riddance to him. When dealing with the supernatural, Ian, one must ask oneself, is seeing believing? Or rather, is believing seeing?" For a mere fraction of a second, Ian thought that he'd seen fangs emerge from behind the lips of his host, but he couldn't be certain.

Ian's chest began constricting, growing tighter and tighter. His pulse pounded as his stomach began to churn. He was becoming physically ill as well as frightened to near panic. But he attempted with all of his might to maintain the best poker face he could muster.

"Ian, you've probably figured out by now that I wasn't infected by Salizzar. I've been who, or some might say what, I am for nearly a millennium. You see, most of what I've conveyed to you up until now is truth but on a need-to-know basis. If it is ultimate truths that you seek, I urge you to take great caution, for with such wisdom comes much danger."

Clayton gave such a look of intensity after speaking his last words, Ian couldn't help the cold shivers that ran between his shoulder blades.

"Ian, know this. Many of we elders of our community live like kings. But I've chosen another path this last century. A change of pace, if you will. So here I sit beside you a modest author of horror fiction living a somewhat humble life, though I'll admit I do appreciate the adoration I occasionally receive from fans of my writing, and suffer bouts of damaged ego from critics that find my work, shall I say, unappealing. Not unlike any mortal, vampires have feelings, likes and dislikes. But such feelings, even that of deep affection, can at times be dwarfed by primordial urges."

Ian mused silently as Clayton paused for a moment, *Dwarf. I hope I never hear that word again.*

Clayton continued, "Anyway, in this life and many others before, I am an author of the macabre. Befitting, wouldn't you agree? You see, I too in my own way, like Salizzar, have been hiding or existing, as it were, in plain sight. Just how would the youth of this decade put it? Ah, yes. On the down-low."

Ian sat staring at Clayton. He was momentarily scared speechless.

Clayton continued, "Ian, as a ranking ancient, an elder, I am what you might call a councilman for our community, and as such was charged with orchestrating the demise of Salizzar, who was always a bit of a rebellious renegade. One whose flamboyance and insatiable appetites, but more to the point, choice of vocation, was drawing much too much attention. You see, we've existed since the dawn of creation primarily under the auspices of the assumption that we can't possibly exist. But alas, one of our unspoken cardinal laws is no vampire can dispatch another. Hence, even we vampires, not just you humans as I've mentioned before, need the occasional Van Helsing."

Ian, still in shock, finally managed to speak. "Um … I suppose you're going to kill me now. No loose ends."

Clayton smiled. "That is what the majority of the council wanted. But fortunately for you, Ian, there was one councilman who spoke up on your behalf. He assured the rest that you would pose no further direct threat regarding our exposure."

Ian cleared his throat. "That councilman with your community that spoke on my behalf … Am I correct in assuming that was you?"

"Of course, Ian. What are friends for? Besides, it wasn't that difficult for me to convince the council on your behalf. After all, though unknowingly, you did us a great service. I'm sure you can understand how difficult it is to find a good monster slayer these days. Yes, Ian, if you haven't figured it out yet, the council has known all about your recent endeavor ever since your nasty soiree with that loathsome lycanthrope Gevaudan. It was mutually fortuitous that you decided to investigate the problems across the river here in my little coastal neck of the woods."

Ian's elevated pulse began to slacken just a little. He was coming to the realization that he wasn't about to die. But with that realization came a sudden embarrassment regarding his naiveté to the bigger picture, and with his newly acquired knowledge also came the cold epiphany regarding how he'd been so dispassionately manipulated by his friend. He was disgruntled at the idea that he'd been so used as an expendable pawn in such a deadly game. And by such supernaturally masterful players, whose vast knowledge and power positioned them far beyond the reach of any one mere man such as himself or any law enforcement agency or even government. For all Ian knew, *Theirs may be the hands that pull all the strings.*

Clayton picked up and took a sip from his wine glass, which had been sitting on the end table next to his chair.

Before Ian had even thought through what he was about to ask, he blurted it out. "Clayton, you spoke to me the other day about the power of three. If I understood any of it correctly, that is the somewhat vampiric law of physics."

Clayton smiled, "Yes, aptly put. That is essentially correct. Tell me, Ian, what's on your mind regarding that particular aspect that rules our community?"

Ian, with little hesitation, said, "Okay, Clayton. I think I get some of ... that is to say ... Ah, hell. I'm just going to ask and see if I understood any of it or not. Exactly how is a human transformed into a vampire? And is there a power of three involved in the transformation?"

Clayton once again smiled at Ian. He truly enjoyed Ian's company and his inquisitive mind.

"Yes, Ian. The law, or power of three, does have its governing over transforming a human into a vampire. One: If a human is bitten three times by a vampire over the course of not more than three days, that is sufficient enough introduction of infection, for lack of a better word, to kill a human and give such a human rebirth into a new life as a vampire. That is enough infection to overcome a human's natural antibodies devised to fight off infection. Two: Should a vampire bite you and suck your life's essence, your blood, from you to the point of killing your mortal body, you will resurrect in three days fully infected, or possessed if you're so inclined, into my world. Three: Should you ever drink the blood of a vampire, the concentration of infection is so great that it would nearly instantly kill your mortal self, and again in three days, you'd arise as one of us. I hope that sufficiently answered your questions?"

Ian nodded but then quickly spoke up once again. "Okay. All right, I've got that. But what is the lasting result, if any, of biting someone, a human, once or twice?"

Clayton frowned slightly. "Alas, that is a bit of a mystery in the sense that the results never seem to be exactly the same. As an example, let us say for the sake of this conversation that I chose to bite you once or twice over the next few days. You might become my wanton follower, obsequious to my wants and needs in every way. Or you might develop nearly superhuman strength as well as enjoy unnaturally good health for the duration of your perhaps somewhat extended lifetime. Or of course, much worse could occur. You might become horribly disfigured from the infection and quite possibly go completely insane.

Insane, for instance, with a bloodlust primarily for lesser carnivora like, say, that of the character Renfield in my … in one of my favorite novels, Dracula, who desired to eat spiders and flies or any small animal if given the opportunity. The effects are largely unpredictable. You could even wind up with a combination of the aforementioned symptoms, or experience different symptoms altogether. I know this from personal experience. Though rare, a human initially bitten, even twice, can end up neither having nor suffering any symptoms at all. They have some kind of genetic immunity. But even they can be changed if sucked dry or bitten three times. No one is completely immune."

All at once, Clayton cocked his head sideways. His ears to Ian looked as though they suddenly perked up, much like a dog's does, when hearing something.

"Ah, finally. Here he is." Clayton got up from his chair and went to his front door. A couple seconds later, the doorbell rang. Clayton let the bell ring three times before he opened his door. A delivery man handed Clayton a small box, then returned to his van and promptly sped away.

Clayton, box in hand, went directly to his kitchen. He grabbed a knife from his kitchen silverware drawer, then sliced opened the box and removed its plastic-bagged contents. He opened his refrigerator door and placed the bags onto the top shelf and closed its door. Clayton sat the box, empty except a sleeve of dry ice, on the kitchen counter He then left his kitchen, returning to his favorite chair.

"Ah, FedEx. When it absolutely, positively, has to be there overnight." Clayton laughed at his recitation of their catch-phrase slogan. Ian smiled slightly at the irony of it all.

Ian decided to speak. "But I don't understand. I saw you eat pizza!" Clayton laughed while he responded.

"Yes, well, we ancients have evolved, Ian. We require a certain amount of human blood to sustain us, that is true. Blood that is typically harvested and re-sold through black market channels that the council controls. Harvested by our farmer-dealers from society's dregs. The homeless, prostitutes, runaways, and the like. Already lost souls. Persons that when they go missing, nobody much cares. But we, unlike those who have been turned in a time span of less than three centuries, have learned to tolerate, even enjoy on occasion, other foods. I'm especially fond of, as you know, a good pizza pie. But my favorites are steak tartare, and I do enjoy a properly prepared very rare prime rib."

"Well, Clayton, since you're not going to kill me or have me killed, where do we go from here?"

"As with this story, Ian, I'm confident in time, you will trust me enough to give me the details of your experience around the township of Harmony Falls. I smell a best-seller in that. I've already come up with a title for our little story here as well as a new pseudonym that I plan on using when writing supposed fictional accounts of your adventures."

Ian's curiosity overcame his residual fright and nausea. "Oh, yeah? Well, Clayton, what's the title you've come up with?"

Clayton paused for a couple seconds as if to build drama. "I thought I'd already told you ... but perhaps not. Anyway, the title I've come up with is, 'Red Tide.'"

Ian thought about the title and all of its intended metaphorical references before he responded. "Clayton, though in more ways than one, I hate to admit it. You're right. You may have a best seller on your hands. I'm not sure, beyond blood, what's on mine. By the way, what made you decide on ... your present name, Clayton Collins?"

Clayton smiled as he replied, "I've taken or given myself so many names. I came up with Collins from occasionally watching a very entertaining daytime television show back in the 1960's called Dark Shadows."

Ian immediately silently made the connection. *Of course. Barnabas Collins, the vampire.* With confusion resonating in his voice, Ian asked, "But how is it that Zoey's your niece? And aren't you supposed to be a cold-blooded killer? You know, demon possessed and all. You don't seem to fit that description. But somehow, I don't think you ever gave me all the facts regarding your kind."

"Ah yes." Clayton said. "Well, when you first asked me of my kind, I was to you just a man. Just a writer of horror fiction. It's true, I haven't told you all of our trade secrets, but I've told you more about us than most humans will ever know or certainly would ever believe." Clayton smiled and laughed a small laugh. "I had to tell you only that which you could, how should I say, swallow. But those are good questions now that you know what you know. She's my adopted niece, so to speak. But understand this with empirical clarity. That fact must never be revealed to her or to anyone, for that matter. Believe me when I tell you this. No good would come from such an enlightenment. I have made arrangements that when I decide it's time for the demise of Clayton Collins, Zoey will become the beneficiary of a sizeable inheritance. I have looked after her for nearly her entire life. Her parents fell victim to one of Salizzar's many serial sprees of Machiavellian malevolence. That one was principally focused around the Haight-Ashbury district of San Francisco. I was directed by the council at that time to curtail as best as possible the perpetuation of his predatory proclivities. And clean up ... tie off ... all loose ends. While doing so, I came upon a baby girl who had been discarded, left to die in a dumpster behind her dead parents' apartment. For some reason that I may never completely understand, I simply could not bring myself to tie off that particular loose end. The council knows nothing of her, nor can they ever."

Ian spoke up. "I understand and agree. There's no reason for Zoey to ever know anything different. You're her uncle." Clayton nodded, taking Ian at his word.

"As for being a cold-blooded killer, as you put it, more correctly phrased would be a warm-blooded killer. Only we ancients have the ability to somewhat control our urges. Over many centuries, we have learned with varying success to keep bottled up the devil inside. But Ian, imagine if you would, a lion. One who has recently feasted to the point of satisfaction. It stands to natural reason that it would not pose near the imminent danger as one that hungers. Yet one would be foolish to take lightly or to ignore its potential to follow its most basic instinct."

Hearing that triggered Ian's memory. Ian vaguely remembered something that at the time, he'd paid little attention to. He thought that he'd very briefly heard what sounded like a microwave running each time just before Clayton would return to the living room with wine-glass in hand. Ian mused to himself, *Missed that one. The devil is in the details.* Ian blurted out, "You reheat the blood you consume in your microwave."

"Yes, Ian, that's how I do it. Others have their own methods. Regardless of what method of heating a somewhat civilized vampire uses to warm his fix of sustenance, one must take great care to not actually cook it, especially when using a microwave."

Ian interjected, "To not break down the food value or, in cases like yours, its life-giving qualities as well as its addiction-satisfying, euphoric effects."

Clayton smiled, "Very good!"

Ian suddenly looked confused. "Clayton, a few things still remain unanswered."

Clayton grinned, "Perhaps it's best that you not know all my little secrets. But ask away."

Ian rapid-fired his questions, "What about the bite marks on your neck? And the razor-blade wounds on your wrist? How many of your kind make up the council? And how many of your kind would you guess there are worldwide?"

Clayton smiled as he spoke, "Yes, those are good questions. The bite marks on my neck. Theatrics, Ian. All smoke and mirrors devised to deceive and convince you that I had fallen victim to Salizzar. The neck bite was performed at my request by another of my kind. The leader of the council. She shall remain nameless. The wounds on my wrists I inflicted myself just as you assumed. The number of councilmen? There is the leader plus her twelve." Ian instantly thought, *Of course. The antithesis to Jesus and his apostles.*

"As to your question of our numbers. By comparison to the human race, we are few. But if one was to count my kind and our closely-related lycanthropic cousins and others which even I will not speak of, suffice it to say that it has been written in the Gospel of Mark in your Christian Bible that my name is legion, for we are many."

Ian's curiosity was piqued regarding Clayton's mention of other entities. But the way he'd said that not even he would speak of them was unnerving enough to keep Ian's mouth shut on the subject.

Clayton then showed Ian his neck and wrists. There was no sign of any injury. Clayton shifted in his chair then continued, "I have learned, besides exercising to the fullest my own personal will, to control such, shall I say, socially unacceptable impulses. It helps to consume blood in small quantities as frequently as practically possible. As you probably noticed, I do so enjoy mixing it with a fine Chianti.

"Ian, what I am is an apex predator. I make no excuses for it nor do I ask for your pity. I will be walking this planet long after you are dust."

Ian suddenly became fascinated by the sheer amount of knowledge that a person could accumulate in a life that nearly transcended time. He was still confused regarding whether vampires were alive or the living dead. Even though Clayton had touched on the subject when they'd first met and discussed such matters, Ian felt compelled to know more. He couldn't help himself from asking, "Clayton, help me better understand. Are you … Are vampires … I don't know, the living dead?"

Clayton was surprised by the question. He'd felt that he'd adequately answered that for Ian days ago. But he maintained his calm, collected composure and decided to answer the question yet once again.

"Ian, all things are either dead or in some way or another alive. If we were dead, we could not be killed. And though difficult, we, as perhaps you have seen for yourself, can be dispatched. If our heart or our brain were instantly and utterly destroyed before any effectual regeneration could occur, or should we find ourselves in daylight for an extended period of time non-protected, we are finished. And fire in sufficient quantity and intensity will also do away with any vampire. So you wonder, what are we then besides the predators of man? I, and those like me, would best be described as the byproduct of an unholy resurrection. We have died and have been reborn as a parasitic predator, hence, we are living vampires. I told you the truth the other day when I said that vampires, our metabolisms, are much, much slower than that of humans. By comparison, a year in the lifespan of a human represents no more than minutes of mine. I have nothing if not time on my hands, which I assure you can be more curse than blessing when you have lived as long as I. Anything less than modern medical tests would reveal no detectable heartbeat, no breath, and would measure a body temperature far below that of a living human being. If poked or prodded, if need be, we can endure much more pain than you could possibly imagine. All that is truth, yet I assure you that our hearts do beat, and we breathe the air, just at a pace so slow as not to be readily detected. It is this slowness of heartbeat and breathing that accounts, at least in part, for our extremely prolonged lifespans by comparison to humans. You must accept that my kind are humanoid but are absolutely not human. Are we demons in part or whole? Perhaps. This much is understood by all who share my … shall we say … affliction. We are, above all, damned. Cursed to lurk in the shadows. Forever barred from crossing over into the light. That is, as your kind is so fond of saying, the down side. But on the up side … Membership has its privileges."

Ian thought about what Clayton had just said as he fired another question. "But Clayton, you say you breathe so slowly it can't be readily detected. But I've seen you breathe. I've even seen you take deep breaths and look ... I don't know ... out of breath even. Can you explain?"

Clayton smiled. "We have learned well how to mimic such trivial human characteristics, especially when in the presence of mortals, to not draw attention to ourselves. Over time we habitually learn to do these things and more, without even conscious thought."

Clayton suddenly stopped talking as if all at once he felt that he might have crossed some undefined line. That he'd breached his oath of secrecy vowed to his ultra-secret vampiric brotherhood. But after looking into Ian's eyes, for some reason unknown even to himself, Clayton felt compelled to continue.

Ian interjected, "Are all who are bitten, I mean transformed, are they damned also, as it were?"

Clayton frowned slightly before he replied to that question. "Not without exception. Though it is extremely rare if one who is bitten less than three times … if their will or faith is strong enough to allow themselves to starve to death before ever tasting human blood other than their own … and their own will not sustain them … damnation can be staved. But few can endure that kind of pain of starvation, which is beyond yours or even my comprehension. Suffice it to say I was weak in that regard."

Clayton continued, "Make no mistake. That is, understand with crystal clarity. There are many of my kind that would kill beyond merely for food if they suspected that you know even this much. There are many that would attempt to dispatch me as well for telling you what I have. There are only two ways that can be avoided. One, you keep this knowledge that I have shared with you as absolutely privileged information between us. Or, and possibly even simpler, perhaps one day you will be able to take no more of the misery of living as you understand it, as you grow old and your body and mind begin the process of rotting even before death. Perhaps you'll unfortunately become untimely, terminally ill. Maybe one day, when one of those inevitable scenarios arise, you will consider the gift that I could bestow on you. What I could do for you now. As a matter and consequence of your own choice, a privilege that I never had. But I tell you this again, immortality, or near immortality anyway, comes with a very high price. I realize that I have deceived and taken great advantage of you and it will be very difficult for you to ever trust me again. But please understand I have the greatest admiration for you. You are one of the most clever, most honest humans I have had the honor to know in hundreds of years." Ian couldn't help but be moved somewhat by the compliment.

"In fact, I believe if anyone could in the course of investigations into the supposed supernatural world come across a person or object that could be utilized in exorcising my demon … Well, Ian, I have lived too long beyond the grace of God. If it is possible for the damned to be forgiven our sins, whereby gaining regeneration or reclamation of our souls, I would do whatever was asked of me to forever dispel my slavery to eternal lust for human blood. Ian, it also grieves me to say that it is likely that Salizzar was not dispatched. And if my suspicions prove correct, I'm afraid you've made a mortal enemy of the worst sort. Ian, I consider you a friend as well as a partner. So I tell you this: Many ancient immortals of my kind are polymorphic – capable of taking on many different forms – and none of our kind possess that gift more prolifically than Salizzar. But I and my followers will stay in the shadows and follow you as your protectors as best we can."

Ian paused for a second, then replied, "Clayton, I refuse to live my life in fear. When it's my time … Well anyway, I thank you for all you have done and can do for me. Changing the subject …" The truth was Ian was way too frightened about what Salizzar, if he was still alive, might someday have in store for him to discuss it any further.

Ian continued, "Anyway, someday, perhaps you'll let me have a sample of your blood to analyze. Who knows? And hey, I know a couple guys who have a DNA lab up in Vancouver, Canada. Tops in their field. Matt Larsen and Luke Nguyen. They can be trusted to keep things discreet, confidential. Good guys. Well … Matt, he takes a bit of getting used to, but anyway, they might be able to isolate the infection. Maybe it's possible to invent some kind of antiviral or something …?"

Clayton glanced over at Ian for a second, then began staring out his window towards the ocean. "Perhaps, Ian. Perhaps one day."

Clayton then changed the subject. "Regardless, Ian, would you not agree that human, vampire, or otherwise, we all have our inner demons of sorts that we must learn to deal with? Ian, should we never, due to our obvious differences, become the very best of friends, we shall I'm certain, at the very least, peacefully coexist as mutually beneficial collaborators. I shall of course market our collaborations through my publisher as works of fiction. Loosely inspired by your adventurous investigations. Think about it, Ian. With me as your benefactor, though admittedly not entirely without selfish motives, you will have the financing necessary to further your investigations of the supposed paranormal."

Ian paused for a moment as he stared intensely into Clayton's eyes, looking for any sign that he wasn't being one hundred percent serious before he replied, "The truth is, Clayton, on so many levels, I don't know how I could refuse your generous offer. I don't want any further situations where I have to rely on funding from any police or community. It's too complicated and carries potentially too many strings. If I must have any sort of puppet master, at least I'll know in advance who it is."

Clayton smiled. "Yes. Yes, I suppose you will."

Ian then continued, "I think I'm gonna take some time off to regroup and ... But after that, I'll be heading south down to New Orleans. I've always wanted to investigate Haitian voodoo practiced here in America and, well, see for myself if there's any truth to the supposed myth of zombiism. Which in essence was the subject of my doctoral dissertation titled Schizomega Syndrome, the name I gave to a theoretical mental as well as physical disorder that I perceived could, under the right circumstances, theoretically be induced in higher primates, in particular humans. My theory, which I named Schizomega Syndrome or the Schizomega Effect, was intent on eclipsing all pre-existing scientific assumptions that zombiism is no more than pure myth. I believe that it is plausible that under the correct administration of a regimen of very specific drugs and/or neurotoxins in conjunction with cellularly-manipulated virus or bacteria – all of which of course are performed by someone highly skilled in the art, perhaps enhanced by a person's strong belief in the powers of voodoo – it could result in a mental and physical condition that closely reassembles zombiism."

Clayton smiled. "Schizomega … Very nice! Which you must of course in part have derived from the novel by Richard Matheson, *I am Legend*. More specifically, from one of its film adaptations starring Charlton Heston, *The Omega Man*." Ian nearly blushed at how fast Clayton had surmised all of that.

"By the way, Ian, I'm giving you my car. I've grown tired of it. Time for something a bit more sporty, in say …blood red." Clayton tossed his keys to Ian, who reached out with his right hand and fielded them.

"Wow! Uh. I mean … your Mercedes? I'm overwhelmed. I don't know what to say other than a profound thank you." Ian knew better than to ask if Clayton was sure. If Ian knew one thing for certain about Clayton, it was that he was always sure.

Clayton smiled. "Also, in an envelope in the glove box, you will find a little traveling money. Not all that much. You deserve much more and will continue to receive much more as long as you simply abide by our little arrangement that you will provide me, when possible, news of your adventures that I might translate to fiction. An amicable agreement, I am certain. As an example, your adventures at Harmony Falls. I believe I've come up with a good title for that story as well. *The Beast of Harmony Falls*. Well, that's a start anyway."

Ian nervously shrugged his shoulders as he cleared his throat. "Sure, I mean fine, I'll do what I can. I just can't promise I'll be that much help. I mean, who knows what I might turn up or not, investigating this and that."

Clayton continued, "I'm certain you'll do fine. And I may, from time to time, steer you myself towards potentially interesting topics to investigate. Anyway, Ian, you're going to New Orleans to chase after necromancers and fire dancers. Well, I suppose that's as good a place as any for researching that sort of thing."

Clayton smiled and laughed as he continued, "You'll no doubt be driving there. Make certain you see many sights along your journey and stay in nice, pet-friendly motels. It is of the utmost importance to me that you keep out of harm's way. Oh, and once in New Orleans, I insist that you and that handsome dog of yours consider staying at the Château LaRivière, a quaint place in the French Quarter. If you mention my name, that we are friends, Madame LaRivière will undoubtedly accept your four-legged friend. She and I go way back. Ian, you keep poking around for the truth as you put it. You never know what you might dig up. Once again, for my favors, you will of course do me the honor of supplying me with a journal, or at least summary, of your various exploits so I may commit them to pen and paper. Well, these days I use a computer like everyone else. I'm certainly ancient but not THAT archaic. Anyway, Ian, I anticipate many adventures await us both. After all, as you've come to understand, the truth can be ... stranger than fiction."

~Fini~

AUTHOR'S NOTE

This book takes place at locations both real and fictitious in and around Astoria, Oregon, located at the mouth of the mighty Columbia River, around Long Beach, Washington, as well as along the Long Beach Peninsula, an arm of land bound on the west by the Pacific Ocean, and on the east by Willipa Bay. At the northern tip of the peninsula are Leadbetter Point State Park and the Willipa National Wildlife Refuge. To its south is Cape Disappointment State Park and the Columbia River.

Several of the places written about within this book are actual locales, and some persons mentioned as characters in this book are real as well (consensually). Example: The Flavel House, also known as The Captain George Flavel House Museum, is located at 441 8th Street in downtown Astoria, Oregon. This location is used fictitiously in the story *Red Tide: Vampires of the Morgue* as the private home of a character of this author's own invention/imagination. The Flavel House, along with its carriage house, was listed on the National Register of Historic Places in 1980. The Flavel House is a fabulous Victorian mansion turned historic museum, and is owned and operated by the Clatsop County Historical Society. Another locale/business of distinction is Banana Books, located at 114 SW 3rd Street, Long Beach, WA. This magnificent bookstore is owned and operated by Ed Grey and Mary Johnson, who are characters in *Red Tide,* with their permission. Also mentioned and referenced in this book is Marsh's Free Museum, a Long Beach, WA landmark business that in this author's opinion is the most unique, fantastically-intriguing store/museum to be found anywhere. It features *Jake the Alligator Man.* Additionally mentioned in this book are some specific cities, towns, townships, buildings, businesses, state parks, wildlife refuges, and various other places.

ACKNOWLEDGMENTS

Special thanks to the following people:

Ed Grey, Mary Johnson, Nancy Crow, Crystal Cooper,
Angie McCain, Pam Wilson Portwood
Mark Taylor, Author
Amanda Shore

And a very special thanks to my editor,
Monique Lewis Happy